The Promise Tree

The Promise Tree

By

Janalyn Voigt

MBI

The Promise Tree
Published by Mountain Brook Ink
White Salmon, WA U.S.A.

The website addresses shown in this book are not intended in any way to be or imply an endorsement on the part of Mountain Brook Ink, nor do we vouch for their content.

This story is a work of fiction. All characters and events are the product of the author's imagination other than those stated in the author notes as based on historical characters. Any other resemblance to any person, living or dead, is coincidental.

Scripture quotations are taken from the King James Version of the Bible. Public domain.

ISBN 978-1-953957-10-8

The Team: Miralee Ferrell, Alyssa Roat, Kristen Johnson, Cindy Jackson
Cover Design: Indie Cover Design, Lynnette Bonner Designer

Mountain Brook Ink is an inspirational publisher offering fiction you can believe in.
Printed in the United States of America

Dedication

To my brother, Leonard,
who reminds me of the hero of this story.

Acknowledgments

Beginning a new series is a challenging venture, and never more so than in the midst of a pandemic. When it came down to the wire, my publisher, Miralee Ferrell, gave a beautiful example of grace under fire. This book and its author are both better for her guidance.

WordServe Literary offered practical help for which I am grateful.

My family members supported me in too many ways to number, including washing dishes more often than was fair. Thanks so much.

There must be a special place in heaven for proofreaders. Thanks, once again, for saving me from myself. My thanks to all those who read this book for review.

Most of all, I appreciate you, dear reader, for traveling with me into the pages of this book.

CHAPTER ONE

Liberty Township, Montana Territory, June 1884

LIBERTY PICKED UP HER PACE AND hurried toward Jake. He was leaning against the cottonwood tree that had a low bough they used as a bench. She hoped he hadn't waited long. She'd met him in the cottonwood grove on Saturdays since they were children, but today Ma needed her to help prepare supper for company. Slipping out for a few minutes was all she could do. With that in mind, Liberty ran the rest of the way through the grove.

Jake straightened, and she landed against him. He stepped backward. "Whoa there! You almost knocked me down." Jake steadied her in his arms.

The thought of her slender weight budging Jake's solid frame made her giggle. They swayed together, his laughter joining hers—as well it should. A lifetime of working livestock had developed Jake's muscles. He'd shot up over the years, forcing her to look up to him. Her two brothers had done the same, despite being younger. That men should grow both stronger *and* taller hardly seemed fair.

Jake lifted her without invitation and deposited her on the low branch. Liberty frowned. "I don't need your assistance, thanks all the same." What had gotten into him? She'd been scrambling onto that limb by herself since she was six.

"Take your nose out of the air, Liberty." He grinned. "You

can blame it on Ma. She's renewed her efforts to teach me proper manners."

Liberty could understand Felicity Buckthorn wanting to impress social graces on her son. Jake's mischievous streak often landed him in trouble. Liberty usually couldn't fault Jake's behavior toward her, but today she didn't mind helping his ma out. "Then maybe you should ask permission before you hoist a person like a sack of potatoes."

"Sorry to offend you." Jake levered upward and sat beside her. "I thought we were on different terms, or I'd have asked."

Liberty didn't know how to respond. Their friendship was shifting in ways she didn't entirely understand. She tilted her head and squinted into the tree's leafy crown. From that high, a person could see all the way to the Bitterroot Mountains. She'd climbed the laddered branches many times with Jake, but not lately. When had they stopped? She brought her attention back to him. "I wish we could act the way we did before."

His gaze softened. "Things can't stay the same."

"Why not?" A wistful note crept into her voice.

"I'm twenty now, and you will be too before the year's out."

What emotion tinged his voice? Regret? Anticipation? Liberty couldn't tell. "That doesn't have to matter."

He cocked an eyebrow. "Do you really think so?"

The question silenced her. Liberty sighed. She was so very tired of being confused about Jake.

He turned toward her. Liberty held on while the branch creaked like an old door on rusty hinges. Jake gripped the bough as if ready to set it swaying again. It was an old game they'd played since childhood, only now the tree protested louder. She shook her head at him. The bough never broke, but she didn't like putting it to the test.

Jake grinned mischievously but stopped moving. "If you could have anything in the wide world, what would you name?"

Liberty shrugged. "I don't know."

He nodded. "There's your problem."

"*I* have a problem?" That was rich, coming from Jake. Trouble seemed to find him without assistance.

He studied her face. "Have you considered what you want from life at all?"

"That's easy. Rise early, help Ma bake bread, tend the garden, feed the chickens, don't call attention to myself during Sunday service—"

He whistled, low. "Those don't sound like your own plans, but more the expectations of others."

A gust rustled the leaves and scattered dappled light over Liberty. She breathed in air scented of grass and cottonwood flowers. Was Jake right? As a preacher's daughter, she'd grown up under the scrutiny of an entire congregation. That didn't allow much room for error, but an easier childhood might not have served her better. She'd learned that appearances mattered but so did honesty. Her parents had taught her by word and deed to put others first, even when that was hard. No, she couldn't complain about her upbringing. "It's not wrong to please others."

"Fair enough, but don't forget to look after yourself."

She laughed. "I doubt you'll let me."

His lips curved in a slow smile. "It's your cross to bear for living next door to an interfering man like me."

"I endure it." She lilted the words, brushing them with a hint of her father's Irish accent.

He gave her an intent look that made the tree limb feel too narrow. She shifted a little away from him. "How would you answer your own question?"

"Me?" He leaned closer. "*I* know what I want."

Something told Liberty not to pursue the matter, but she couldn't resist. "Oh really?"

His arm slid around her. "I'd have a home, a family—and you at the heart of it."

Liberty heard her own indrawn breath. "Jake—" Whatever she'd been about to say vanished beneath his kiss. The yearning she'd long denied broke over her like a wave, washing away every defense. Swept along by giddy sensation, she clung to him. Emotion threatened to submerge her, and he was the raft to which she clung.

A preacher's daughter does not behave in such an outlandish manner.

Liberty jerked away and pulled in air. How had she forgotten herself so far? Jake released her, and she put a small distance between them on the branch. "It's not fair to kiss a person without warning."

He ran a hand over his face. "I shouldn't have done that."

"No." She touched her own face, which felt heated. Her heart was racing faster than when she'd run to him.

Jake jumped down into a patch of sunlight. He looked up at her, his green eyes gleaming. Liberty gripped the smooth wood beneath her skirt, clinging to the branch while it dipped and rose. "I meant every word of the promise I made you."

"Don't remind me about that." She lowered herself to stand beside him.

He peered into her face. "Why not?"

"We were twelve. That's too young for a betrothal." Feeling altogether too close for comfort, Liberty stumbled backward.

Jake caught her arm, saving her from a fall. "Maybe for you, but not for me."

She couldn't look at him. "I've come to think of you as a

friend."

He smirked. "That's not how you kissed me."

"You took me by surprise."

"And received an honest reaction." He crossed his arms and planted his feet apart, solid as the cottonwood beside him. "When are you going to admit the truth?"

"It's not that simple." Liberty bit her lip, recognizing how illogical she sounded.

"Sure it is." His tone smoothed to the consistency of warm honey. "Just stop fighting yourself."

Liberty felt herself yielding. "This is getting—"

"Promising?"

"Confusing." She wrapped her arms around herself. "I have to go. Ma will be needing me. We're having company tonight."

He stroked her arm. "Stay a little longer—"

"Stop looking at me like that."

"Like what? If I appear baffled, it's because I am. I care about you, Liberty, and I think you feel the same about me."

"*Please.*" She hauled in air. "I think we should stay away from one another for a while."

A pained expression settled over his face. "All right. If that's what you want."

"It's best." The urge to turn into his arms shook her, but she needed to distance herself for both their sakes.

"I doubt that, but you believe it." He stepped away from her. "Go on then."

She didn't want to leave him, but that was all the more reason she should. Liberty forced her feet into motion. Before taking the turn that would hide them from one another, she glanced back.

Jake stood watching her from beneath the tree that had witnessed every one of their rash promises. Liberty blinked back tears. She had no idea how to proceed. If only he'd had the sense not to kiss her. She dashed away tears. Jake had ruined the delicate balance between them, and nothing would ever be the same again.

Tears rolled down Liberty's cheeks, not all of them from chopping onions. *Why was I so idiotic as to entertain that kiss for one second?* She shook her head at her own foolishness. Joining lips, breath, and soul with Jake was a dangerous business. She couldn't let it happen again. Never mind what she wanted. She couldn't forget her duty to marry someone suitable to become the son-in-law of a preacher. Jake was too much of a rascal, and she doubted he would ever change.

Boots thumped the porch. Liberty swiped the back of her hand over her eyes. The screen door screeched open and slammed shut. She glanced over her shoulder in time to see her brother, Seth, take off his derby hat. He slung it onto a hook beside the door, then shoved a hand through his burnished blond curls. At seventeen, Seth had lost the softness of youth. He had the same shade of hair as their mother, but his resemblance to Pa grew more marked every day.

Sniffling, Liberty lifted her knife for another cut.

Seth leaned on the counter beside her. "Are you all right?"

"Onions always make me cry."

A teasing light dawned in his blue eyes. "Be glad you don't have to help Pa tame Chief along with me."

"I'd rather do that than this." Tears ran down her face.

He chuckled. "You don't know what you're saying. Why Pa wants to turn a stallion into a saddlehorse, I'll never know."

She shrugged. "People do it."

"Well yes, but not riders pampered by the likes of Archibald."

"You won't find any such riders. No other horse compares

to Pa's for gentleness."

Seth smiled. "That's a fact. The old boy deserves his time out to pasture."

She sliced into another onion, and tears crowded her eyes. "You won't suffer long. Uncle Nick is on his way."

"If anyone can tame that beast, he will." He peeked into a steaming pot on the stove. "What are we having for supper?"

"Stewed chicken with rolled dumplings." Liberty blinked away her tears. "Provided I can chop these onions in time."

"Put a spoon in your mouth."

Liberty squeezed her eyes tight shut. "That's an old wives' tale."

"It might work."

"I doubt it."

"You won't know unless you try."

Liberty could no longer see Seth through her tears, but she heard his footsteps cross the kitchen and thump down the hallway.

The door opened and closed, this time more lightly. "Goodness," Ma exclaimed. "Let me do that. Go bathe your eyes."

Liberty relinquished the knife to Ma's gentle fingers, then felt her way outside to the pump. The cool water soothed her eyes, but nothing could ease the ache that came when she thought of Jake. Hopefully Phoebe's arrival would distract her. Liberty returned to the kitchen, feeling a little better at the idea of seeing her best friend and adopted cousin. She'd grieved when Phoebe moved a day's travel away. Seeing one another once a month at Sunday Meeting and the potluck afterward wasn't the same.

Maybe she should ask if Phoebe wanted her to come visit. Leaving town for a little while seemed a good idea at the moment.

Liberty returned to the kitchen, where her mother was still chopping onions. Ma's blue calico dress brought out her amber eyes and complimented the auburn curls she'd piled loosely on her head. The few silver strands gleaming in the light from the window only ornamented her beauty. Ma waved a hand toward the wicker basket on the table. "Fold the laundry, please, while I finish the onions."

Liberty gave her mother a grateful smile and reached into the basket. She selected a cotton flour-sack towel and smoothed it on the table, content to perform the simple task in silence. With her younger sisters, Shannon and Aisling, preparing the cabin Phoebe and her family would share, the house felt unusually tranquil. The girls, aged twelve and ten, were regular chatterboxes. Ma didn't speak much as she tipped the chopped onions into a bowl and peeled several cloves of garlic. Maybe she was enjoying the quiet too.

Liberty finished the laundry and lent a hand mixing the dumpling dough. All her kin made a lot of mouths to feed. Besides her large family, others who traveled for Sunday Meeting would need a place to stay and a warm supper. Liberty could remember a time when cots crammed the schoolhouse and tents dotted the lawn in fair weather. They congregation had met in the schoolhouse until the church and meeting hall went up, freeing more space in the schoolhouse for temporary lodging. Ironically, it wasn't needed so much anymore. With more churches erected in outlying areas, fewer people needed to drive long distances to attend services.

Hooves clomped on the road that ran past the house on the way to Liberty township. The barking of Pa's sheepdog and excited voices from the barn announced the advent of callers.

"They're early." Ma reached to untie her apron. "What on earth? I can't seem—"

"Here, let me." Liberty loosened the knot her mother must have accidentally tightened. Ma seemed flustered, which wasn't usual. The perfect preacher's wife, she took interruptions, changed plans, early arrivals, and unexpected company in stride. Come to think of it, Ma had seemed distracted of late.

There was no time to puzzle over the mystery as Ma hurried from the kitchen. Liberty followed her through the entrance hallway and outside to the trellised gateway on the front path. Ma swung the gate open and stood poised beside it. Liberty stationed herself on the other side of the opening. Phoebe's bright voice rising above the quieter tones of Liberty's brother, Liam, reached her first. Aunt Maisey, Phoebe's mother said something, after which Aisling and Shannon chimed in to answer her. The deeper rumbles in the barn belonged to Pa and Uncle Rob.

The front screen door banged. A moment later Seth rushed through the gateway and barreled around the corner of the house on the path to the barn. Liberty picked out snippets of conversation between Phoebe's brothers and Seth.

"Have you tried…" Thirteen-year-old Quinn murmured.

"That's not going to…" Seth's protest dropped to a murmur.

"Let me ride him, and I'll…" Murphy, the youngest, spoke with all the confidence of an eleven-year-old.

It sounded like the boys were discussing how best to break Chief, a topic much on Seth's mind at the moment.

"Why not use a hackamore?" Phoebe's light tones rose above the rumble of masculine voices.

"I thought of that, but…" Liam's voice blended into the general chatter. Liberty wasn't surprised at their choice of topic. Anytime Phoebe and her brothers got together, horses came up. Mention of cooking between Aunt Maisey and Shannon was likewise expected. What had Seth just said? Liberty perked up, but she couldn't make out any details. She'd have to ask him later, but she could swear he'd mentioned a medicine show.

Phoebe and Liam rounded the corner first. Even after the long trip, Phoebe looked rested. How she managed it, Liberty never knew. Blessed with abundant energy, Phoebe walked with a spring in her step. Her golden hair, piled neatly on top of her head, cascaded in ringlets down her back.

Phoebe broke into a grin. "Liberty!"

Forgetting to wait politely to greet their guests, Liberty rushed to hug her friend. They broke apart and stood grinning at one another.

Most of the others passed them and stopped to embrace Ma. Aisling and Shannon waved and turned back. They must not have finished readying the cabin. Aisling's hair gleamed rose-gold in the sun, like Ma's. Shannon, the oldest of the two, had Pa's black hair. Plaited down her back, it swayed as she walked.

Phoebe swept a glance over Liberty. "You look a little frazzled. How are you?"

Liberty shrugged. "All right, I guess." She didn't sound convincing, even to her own ears.

Phoebe drew her brows together but didn't challenge the remark. "I've missed you."

"I feel the same about you." Liberty threw her arm around Phoebe's shoulders, and they started for the house. Although tempted, Liberty refrained from asking about Drew Addison. Phoebe's latest admirer wasn't the first to try wooing her. Phoebe collected her share of hearts. Liberty found the antics of the thwarted suitors hilarious, but Aunt Maisey was less amused. She despaired of Phoebe allowing anyone to court her. At twenty-two, Phoebe was one year away from becoming a spinster.

A sweet fragrance wafted from the trellis covered in climbing roses that had leafed out and formed buds. Liberty glanced over her shoulder, but no one else rounded the corner of the house. "Where's the rest of the family?"

"Uncle Con won't arrive until tomorrow. He stayed behind to interview a new ranch manager."

Liberty blinked. "That's Uncle Nick's job!"

"He and Aunt Bry bought a ranch. They don't plan to move far, I'm glad to say. We'd miss them too much if they did."

"I can't imagine Uncle Con's ranch without Uncle Nick and Aunt Bry."

Phoebe nodded. "I know. It's strange to think about. They didn't say anything until they'd saved up enough to buy a place of their own. They must feel a bit crowded with Aunt Elsa's German kin living within a stone's throw of them."

Liberty held the front screen door open for Phoebe. "I can guess that Uncle Con doesn't like the idea of their moving."

"Well no, but he's accepted it. I can't blame him for wanting to keep everyone together. I hate it that you and I live so far apart."

"I was thinking that very thing not an hour ago. I'd love to come over for a week or so." Liberty led the way into the kitchen, where Ma had started cooking again and Aunt Maisey was choosing an apron from the selection on pegs along the wall.

Phoebe brightened. "That would be wonderful, wouldn't it, Ma?"

"You girls are due a visit—that is, if Liberty's family can spare her." Aunt Maisey angled a questioning glance at Ma.

Ma looked up from slicing beets. "Of course, we can."

"I'll discuss it with Rob then." Aunt Maisey lifted a plain white apron from its peg.

Liberty could guess what the answer would be. Aunt

Maisey always tried to sound stern when she was going to say yes, plus Uncle Rob gave Phoebe most everything she asked. From the excited glance Phoebe sent Liberty, she shared the same opinion.

Liberty reclaimed her apron from the chairback she'd tossed it over before going outside. Embellished not with ruffles or frills, but by a patch of embroidered bluebells in the center, it had faded over the years. The stitches looked clumsy compared to what she could accomplish now. Liberty wore it anyway.

Phoebe tied on a ruffled blue concoction splashed with damask roses. She always wore that apron, even though it was washed-out like Liberty's. "What can I do to help, Aunt America?"

"Would you see if Aisling and Shannon need anything? They should be finishing up in your old cabin. I don't want them out after nightfall."

Phoebe nodded. "I'll check on them."

Liberty went to the pump and washed her hands with Aunt Maisey. Ma was a stickler for clean hands in the kitchen. The presence of company made kneading, rolling, and cutting the dumpling dough seem less like work. Better yet, it almost succeeded in driving thoughts of Jake Buckthorn out of her mind.

CHAPTER TWO

PHOEBE CREPT PAST THE OPEN BARN doorway to avoid disturbing her father and Uncle Shane, who were deep in conversation. Rays from the lowering sun slanted sideways across the path at her feet. The shadows were lengthening, but she didn't need light to find her way. Strange to think that it had been more than a decade since she'd lived in the old cabin. The future had felt uncertain then—much as it did now, but for different reasons.

She'd counted herself fully grown after her eighteenth birthday, but she hadn't met anyone she wanted to marry. Four years later, the idea of marriage still didn't appeal.

Phoebe reached the divide where she could continue through the schoolyard or turn toward her old cabin. She paused to gaze at the building where she'd spent countless hours learning alongside the Bitterroot Salish children taught by her mother. Never once had she noticed that the color of her skin differed from theirs, until Spukani pointed it out. She shuddered at the thought of the man who had kidnapped her, and then returned years later to abduct her ma.

Beyond the schoolhouse, the steeple of the church pointed heavenward, dark against the pewter sky. The whole town had turned out to build the sanctuary in record time. She could recall Pa swinging a hammer while she and Ma helped with the cooking. Her young brothers had swept and picked up nails at the end of the day. She sighed at the memory of happier times.

Phoebe turned toward the cabin, but hoofbeats thudded at the edge of her hearing. She looked over her shoulder. Who would travel the road to Liberty township so late and at such a clip? Someone riding on an important errand, no doubt. Whatever the urgency, it could have nothing to do with her. She ought to seek the safety of the cabin and leave the small mystery behind.

Curiosity held her fast. All sorts of scenarios played in her mind. A desperate husband rode to fetch the doctor for his wife, lying on her death bed. Or maybe a soldier from one of the eastward forts bore news of a cholera outbreak. What if a renegade Indian was on the way to raid the town?

Phoebe shivered. She shouldn't let her imagination get the better of her. Rather than gape like an idiot at the empty road, she should attend to her own errand. Her two young cousins needed to be delivered to the safety of their home.

Phoebe gave up telling herself what she *should* do. She could argue with herself until the cows came home. It wouldn't change her inquisitive nature. Rooted to the spot by curiosity, she waited to discover the truth.

The hoofbeats grew louder, punctuating the silence in a staccato rhythm. Phoebe was certain she heard the horse's huffing breaths. The next instant erased any doubt, for the steed burst into view. Even in idleness her mind registered the expert posture of the rider outlined against the sky. Exhibiting a mastery few possessed, the horseman guided his mount onto the path that would carry him past the school towards where she stood.

Phoebe's heart pounded, and her mouth went dry. She backed into shadow. Pa and Uncle Shane, who had seemed close before, felt a long way away.

Phoebe reined in her imagination and drew a steadying breath. If she should scream, rescue would surely come. She stood poised in indecision, not certain whether to run toward Pa in the barn or bolt for the cabin, which was nearer.

"Wait, miss!" The rider reined in before reaching her.

Phoebe hesitated. He didn't sound like someone she should fear. Still, his willingness to hail a lone female at dusk didn't recommend him. Ignoring his call, she ran for the barn. Should the stranger pursue, facing him on the tree-shrouded path to the cabin was out of the question.

He rode forward and reined in between her and the barn. "I mean you no harm."

"What do you want?" Her voice sounded harried. *Oh, why couldn't I have heeded common sense and escaped before he arrived?*

"Only your guidance." He tilted his head, casting his face even more into shadow. "I'm looking for Reverend Shane Hayes."

His words did not relieve her feverish imaginings. What did he want with Uncle Shane? Could he be an outlaw, hoping the local preacher would hide him from the sheriff? He might be a hired gun looking to make a bounty.

Phoebe tamped down her wayward thoughts, the product of reading too many dime novels. This is what came from indulging in the cheap fiction her brother Murphy brought home from the general store. "Who are you?" she managed to croak.

"I'm William Canfield, but folks call me Will." He doffed his hat, belatedly. "Pleased to meet you, miss. I wonder if you would direct me to the house of Reverend Hayes." With the shadow cast by his hat brim removed, the fading light picked out his lean jaw and handsome face. He sounded young, but it was hard to tell his age in the poor light.

"On what errand?" Phoebe knew she was being nosy, but how else could she decide whether to reveal his proximity to Uncle Shane?

"I'm to deliver a message to Reverend Hayes from his cousin, Connor Walsh. Mr. Walsh invited me to come for Sunday Meeting. He asked me to ride ahead. I'm his new ranch manager—or I will be once he teaches me the ropes."

The tension went out of her. "Give it to me, and I'll make sure Reverend Hayes receives it."

He returned his hat to his head. "Begging your pardon, but who are you?"

Her face heated. She hadn't anticipated his cautious response. "I'm Phoebe Walsh, Reverend Hayes's niece."

He swerved his head toward the lighted barn. "Is he about?"

"I'll take you to him."

"Thank you." The deep gratitude in his voice shamed her. He'd obviously ridden a long way but needed to discharge his duty before he could rest. Delaying no further, she led him to the barn.

Pa and Shane had finished grooming the horses and were talking in low tones. Uncle Shane saw them first, she could tell by the lift of his head. He pushed away from the stall gate and started forward. Pa caught up to him.

Phoebe bestirred herself to speak. "This is Will Canfield, Uncle Con's new manager."

Will divided a glance between the two men. "Which of you is Reverend Hayes?"

"Me." Uncle Shane looked past them. "Where is Con?"

"He's on the way." Will dismounted. "I'm supposed to let you know that he expects to arrive tonight after all. He didn't want to surprise Mrs. Hayes with so many extra supper guests. Mind if I water my horse?"

"Not at all. This is Rob Walsh, my cousin and brother to your new employer."

"Pleased to meet you." Will extended his hand.

"Likewise." Pa offered his own, and they shook.

"Come in." Uncle Shane stepped out of the doorway. "You'll find hay and a warm stall for your horse. You're welcome to a meal and bed also."

"I'm obliged." Will led his horse into the barn.

Pa stepped closer to Phoebe. "Why are you outside so late?"

Will glanced away, as if he didn't want them to think he was eavesdropping.

"Aunt America sent me to check on Aisling and Shannon at the cabin. It seemed a lot earlier when she asked me."

"I suppose you dallied." Pa shook his head but smiled.

"No, I didn't—at least not much."

"I'll come along and help you walk the girls home. I need to carry our trunk to the cabin anyway." Pa turned into the barn.

Phoebe was glad of her father's company when they reached the wild stretch before the cabin came into view. The trees crowded in thickly, casting them into darkness. Rustlings in the undergrowth alerted her to the presence of hidden creatures. Phoebe pressed closer to Pa. They emerged into the small clearing where the cabin drowsed, and she let out her breath. The smoldering sun caught the clouds on fire, and a pale sliver of moon already hovered overhead.

Through the cabin windows, the lantern suspended above the table sent out warm light. The faint breeze ruffled the treetops and caressed her cheeks. Shouldering the trunk he'd brought, Pa went up the steps first. Phoebe climbed the stairs behind him, and the excited chattering of the two girls moving about inside reached her. She could guess why it took them so long to clean the cabin.

She crossed the porch with a lighter step. Her love for the large ranch house she and her family lived in didn't change the feeling of homecoming that came over her. Everything that had happened in this cabin came rushing back, good and bad. Ma's sadness over the loss of Phoebe's father stood out. Sometimes Phoebe wished she could remember him, but she'd been too young when he died. She loved the father she had now, although Ma had cried over him too. After Ma married Rob, the tears stopped coming.

They'd given the old cabin better memories during return visits. It had shrunk since Phoebe's brothers came along, but they made do. The boys liked to camp out on the porch on a summer night, which helped. Phoebe would share their fascination, but she didn't like wondering if some bear or other fierce nocturnal creature would chance upon her sleeping self.

Running afoul of an angry Indian was another unsettling possibility. She would rather not repeat the experience of being captured by a renegade. Although that had happened many years ago, it affected her still. She'd never seen Spukani again after Uncle Con talked him into releasing her, but his rage-filled face sometimes haunted her dreams. He'd returned years later and captured Ma. Phoebe clenched her fists. The death of Spukani's daughter from measles hadn't been Ma's fault, and he shouldn't have held it against her. Phoebe didn't understand how Ma could forgive Spukani for his crimes.

Shannon, the oldest of Liberty's sisters, gave Phoebe a sheepish smile. "We're almost done."

Phoebe glanced about. "What's left to do?"

Aisling, wielding the feather duster, blew a straying lock of red-gold hair off her forehead. "We need to make the beds and carry in firewood."

"I'll take care of the last chore." Pa started for the door.

"Come on, Shannon." Phoebe led the way into the short hallway. "Let's take care of the beds while Aisling finishes dusting."

Within a short while, Pa shut the door on the cabin while the girls skipped ahead on the path. "Hold up!" Pa held up the lantern he'd lit. "I know you're close to home, but let's keep together in the dark. Your Ma would want you to."

After her earlier fright, Phoebe didn't need prompting. She would have once been as heedless as the girls, but she understood the dangers of the wilderness skirted by the path better now that she was grown.

CHAPTER THREE

"WHY DO YOU SUPPOSE PEOPLE ACT so strangely when they're in love?" Liberty whispered to Phoebe in the darkness of her bedroom. They should be sleeping, but they'd found precious little time to catch up earlier. As Will had warned, Uncle Con and Aunt Bry had arrived with their families in time for supper. Even with extra hands to help, kitchen duties had claimed their attention most of the evening.

"I don't know," Phoebe whispered in a sleepy voice. "It must be pretty overwhelming."

"Jake kissed me today."

"Oh really?" Phoebe's mattress rustled. Moonlight filtering through the curtains outlined her as she sat up on the cot. "I'm not surprised. Anyone can see what's going on between you two."

"Perhaps you would tell me what that might be, because I have no idea." Liberty scolded herself for snapping and resolved to speak with more charity. Phoebe didn't deserve her annoyance. No, that belonged to Jake.

"Maybe you don't want to know."

Liberty sucked in a breath. Phoebe couldn't have heard Jake say something similar this morning. "Whatever you imagine, Jake and I are only friends."

"Of course." Phoebe yawned. "That's why he kissed you."

Liberty sighed. "I hate feeling confused."

Phoebe laid back down, making the mattress crunch. "Give it time."

Liberty smiled at Phoebe's usual response to complicated situations. Come to think of it, that's what she planned to do. Putting Jake off gave her a chance to decide what to do about him. "Have you seen Drew Addison lately?"

"Nope. Our romance failed, I'm glad to say."

Liberty smiled. "Did Uncle Rob chase him off? That happened to one of your other suitors, as I recall."

"Pa didn't have to. Drew developed an attachment to someone else."

"My condolences. I can tell how heartbroken you are."

"Thank you." Phoebe laughed. "I'm coping the best I can. Did Seth tell you? He saw a poster in town. Doc Woburn's Medicine Show is coming to Corvallis next week."

"Corvallis? Isn't that a town at the end of the Oregon trail?"

Phoebe laughed. "Not that Corvallis. A settlement sprang up northeast of our ranch a couple of years ago. They named it after the town in Oregon Territory. Pa is thinking about taking us to the medicine show. Do you want to go?"

"I've never been to one." A yawn caught Liberty by surprise.

"Nor have I, but it sounds spectacular. There'll be a magic show, acrobats, jugglers, and I can't remember what else. Maybe your family will want to go too."

"That would be fun." Liberty stifled another yawn and nestled into her pillow. "Good night."

"Sweet dreams. I hope you and Jake sort yourselves out soon."

Liberty had almost forgotten Jake until Phoebe reminded her of him. Truth to tell, she would rather not resolve anything with Jake when she could avoid him instead. She frowned. Giving Jake a wide berth during church shouldn't prove difficult, but how was she going to manage during the potluck afterward?

Liberty ladled a portion of her ma's smoky beans onto her plate. She stole a glance at Jake, seated at one of the trestle tables in the church meeting hall. Although avoiding him seemed awkward, Liberty wasn't sorry he had stayed. She wouldn't want him to miss out on her account. The few times their eyes met, he immediately looked elsewhere. How ridiculous to feel slighted when he was only giving her the distance she'd asked for.

Pleading a headache in order to escape would be telling a falsehood. A preacher's daughter of all people should never lie, and certainly not in church. She felt fine, apart from a certain weariness caused by staying up late talking with Phoebe.

"May I carry your plate?" An attractive male voice asked.

Liberty turned and found herself gazing into pale hazel eyes that reminded her vaguely of a lion's. Beau Hensley's red-tinged hair furthered the impression. He'd created a stir among the town's female population within a few months of moving to Liberty, the township her parents had founded and named after her. It felt like Beau had lived here much longer, he fit in so well. His smooth manners and charming smile ingratiated him to almost everyone.

"No thank you." Liberty held onto her plate. "But it's kind of you to offer." She sounded stilted despite her wish to appear neutral. The last thing she wanted was to encourage Beau. Neither did she wish- to hurt another person—especially not someone who looked at her with such admiration.

Beau's eyebrows shot upward, and the corners of his mouth angled downward. "As you wish." He picked up a plate from the stack at the end of the table and inserted himself beside her. "Should you change your mind, I'll be right here at your elbow."

Liberty didn't miss the way he eased into her company

despite her refusal. She bit her lip to avoid saying anything less than graceful. He might only be dense, not arrogant. Not wanting to convey the wrong impression, she studiously ignored Beau while they filled their plates. This was not easy, since he insisted on continuing the conversation he'd started.

"Now tell me—" Beau lifted a ladle from a blue willow tureen. "Which of these bean dishes do you recommend?"

The sensation of someone watching prickled Liberty's skin. She raised her head. From across the room, Jake's green gaze pinpointed hers. He looked fair to bursting. It wasn't hard to guess that he disliked seeing her with Beau. Heat washed into Liberty's cheeks, and she jerked her attention back to Beau "You won't go wrong with my mother's smoky beans." She waved a hand toward the tureen beneath his ladle.

"Thank you." Beau smiled as if she'd awarded him a prize. "I'll trust your recommendation." He scooped a healthy portion onto his plate, which was becoming more crowded by the minute. Liberty took more modest portions, and not of everything. She'd learned long ago that overeating at a potluck brought on a stomachache. After Pa moved Sunday meeting from afternoon to morning, a person who overindulged at the potluck had time to recover before bedtime. Pa hadn't made the change for that reason, however. He'd set it to accommodate folks who lived closer but still traveled to service. The new time allowed them to rise early and start home before nightfall. Safe travel had become more important in these days of tension with the Bitterroot Salish.

Twenty-nine years ago, the Hellgate Treaty removed ownership of the Bitterroot Valley from the Salish, making clashes inevitable. The tribe retained the right to hunt and fish, but increased settlement stirred conflicts.

Late travelers might find themselves at the mercy of

outlaws. A rash of hangings by vigilance committees in earlier days had reduced this threat, but it persisted, nonetheless.

Despite Pa's effort to protect them, many churchgoers lingered in the meeting hall. Basking in the glow of long friendships must make it hard to remember the dangers of the road. Later, the night would fill with the creak of leather and the glow from lanterns as wagons ambled homeward.

"May I join you at your table?" Beau's question cut into her thoughts. "I'd be honored."

Liberty hid her shock at his forthrightness when she'd already turned him down. "There's no room." She responded with the simple truth. Uncle Con and Aunt Elsa had brought their brood and also some of Elsa's German kin. Uncle Rob and Aunt Maisey were surrounded by their three children. Uncle Nick, Aunt Bry, and their children had found places at the preacher's table. Liberty's family occupied four large tables, and there wasn't a vacant seat at any of them. "I'm not sure where to sit myself."

"Wherever you choose is fine by me." He gave her a beatific smile.

Good manners were one thing. Letting yourself be pushed around was another. Liberty opened her mouth to refuse his company, yet again. Jake's scowling face intruded into her side vision. Her hesitation was all the advantage Beau needed. He pulled out a chair at the nearest unclaimed table. "Will this do?"

Liberty sank into the seat, annoyed at herself for surrendering. She pushed away the unworthy thought that encouraging Beau's interest might put Jake off. That had nothing to do with her decision to sit with Beau. Of course, it didn't.

Beau plunked down his plate across the table but remained standing. "Which drink would you like?"

Liberty swallowed the retort that she could fetch her own

drink and considered her options. She could choose lemonade, a rare treat for a warm day in early summer. The crisp taste of ginger and vinegar in switchel beckoned to her. But then again, a glass of sweet tea chilled in Mrs. Buckthorn's icehouse wouldn't go amiss.

Beau awaited her decision with a lifted eyebrow.

Liberty summoned a smile. "I'll have the lemonade, please."

"My pleasure." Beau set off with the air of a man on a cavalry mission.

Liberty unfolded her napkin and spread it across her lap but refrained from picking up her fork before he returned. Phoebe waved from across the room and gave her a questioning look. Liberty shook her head faintly. Heat rushed into her face, and she pressed her palms to her cheeks. *What am I doing?*

Jake slid into the chair beside her. "Did you fob me off because you planned to keep time with Beau?" He murmured, so close that his breath stirred her hair.

She didn't turn her head. "I'm not going to dignify that with an answer."

"He's a trouble maker."

"You can't possibly know that." Liberty didn't point out her own reservations about Beau.

"I have a bad feeling about him. I don't want you to get hurt."

She shook her head. "I can look after myself."

"I'm not so sure about that."

She turned her head, and their gazes clashed. "Do you realize how insulting that sounds?"

"I'm sorry, Liberty. I don't mean it that way."

She nodded her forgiveness. "Even so, who I spend time with is not your concern."

"You made it mine." He ground out the words.

"I asked you not to remind me about that."

"Is this gentleman troubling you?" Beau asked in a steel-edged voice.

Liberty started. She'd been too involved with arguing to notice Beau's approach. She cast back over the last things she'd said and felt her face flame all over again. "Jake was just going."

"Do you hear that?" Beau gritted. "The lady wants you to leave."

"Well now—" Jake stood, never shifting his glare from the other man. "That makes two of us."

"I hope you don't mind if I join you." Phoebe inserted in a breathy voice. She slipped into the seat across from Liberty and Jake, next to where Beau stood with clenched fists. Phoebe's bright smile gave away that she was aware of intruding.

"You're always welcome." Liberty wasn't sure whether Phoebe's presence would help or hurt the situation, but she wouldn't reject her help.

Jake turned on his heel and strode from the room so abruptly that heads turned. His brother, Gideon, rose and followed him.

Liberty stared at the table, wishing she could vanish.

Beau thumped a tall glass in front of her. "Here's your drink." He dropped into his chair and sipped his own drink. "My, the lemonade's good. You have excellent taste, Liberty—if I may call you that."

"What?" Liberty pulled her thoughts from Jake long enough to answer. "Thank you." She ought to respond to his use of her first name. She would correct him after she regained the ability to think clearly. Her presence of mind seemed to have walked out with Jake.

Jake didn't slow down until he reached his front porch, and even then he fell to pacing. He needed a moment before he went inside. He'd been through a lot with Liberty, but this took the cake. He didn't like thinking she had so little judgment as to involve herself with Beau. Liberty was a rose others would want to pluck. Jake was keenly aware that he might lose her, but he'd never expected to face so disreputable a rival.

He halted at the sudden realization that his own reputation was no better than Beau's and would probably worsen after today.

Jake slumped onto the top porch step. *What an idiot I've been.*

Picking a fight at the church potluck had not been his finest moment. He must have embarrassed his mother, yet again. Not only had he given those who talked about him more to say, he'd reinforced Liberty's reservations.

Jake shook his head. He didn't need his enemies to bring him down. He was capable of doing that all by himself.

Movement in his side vision alerted him. Immersed in misery, he hadn't noticed his brother behind him on the footpath. Jake sprang to his feet and bounded down the steps. He met Gideon beneath the cottonwoods.

Gideon's starched shirt and string tie beneath a tan vest and his pinstripe trousers announced him as the respectable citizen he was. After marrying the schoolteacher, he'd settled into domestic bliss on a nearby farm.

Jake met his brother in a patch of sunlight, which gleamed in Gideon's blond curls, giving him an angelic appearance.

Gideon crossed his arms. "Care to tell me what you were doing back there?"

Surely that was obvious, but his brother must want him to say it. "Making a fool of myself."

Gideon nodded. "I'm glad to see you own up to it."

"The truth isn't hard to miss, even for someone so thick as I am."

Gideon smiled. "Don't be too hard on yourself. I'm sure you had help."

"I don't trust Beau." Jake jerked out the words.

"You've mentioned that before but not the reason."

"Maybe it's a hunch." Jake went back to pacing.

"That's not good enough. You can't impugn a man's character without cause." Gideon leaned against a tree. "I hate to mention it, but you sound like a jealous suitor."

Jake halted in front of his brother. "Why couldn't Liberty have taken up with someone I could stomach better?"

Gideon chuckled. "Seems to me you'd find fault with anyone but yourself."

"You're wrong there." Jake shook his head. "I'm not good enough for her, either."

"Don't count yourself out." Gideon lifted himself onto the low branch. "You may have made a few mistakes after Pa died, but that's in the past."

"I wish that was true." Jake sat beside his brother, although he'd rather Gideon hadn't chosen that particular spot for a conversation. It brought back yesterday's rejection all too vividly. "Certain folks won't let me forget it."

"Let me guess—Jimmy Jackson is still mad about you posing as a scarecrow."

"I'd never have moved when he went by if I'd realized he would hold a grudge all these years."

"He's never liked being bested." Gideon's chuckle mingled with the voices drifting from the meeting hall. "You were all of thirteen, not that youth excuses bad behavior."

"It isn't only that."

"If you're talking about Granny Butler's vanishing and

reappearing weathervane—"

"She's forgiven me. No, I was referring to the Baileys."

"Ah." Gideon winced.

"They hold me liable for their mule running off and getting killed."

"There were six pranksters, and you weren't the one who tried to ride the mule. Why blame you in particular?"

"I'm the one with the reputation. My accomplices took full advantage of that fact. They swore that I lead them into mischief."

"I can't recall you objecting at the time."

"I didn't want to accuse my friends of lying."

"Your forbearance was noble but misguided. Taking responsibility that belongs to others is not good for you or them."

Jake blew out a breath. "You're right, but it's doubtful I can change anything at this late date. The Baileys wouldn't believe me if I tried."

"It's probably best to leave it alone. You've apologized and made restitution. Don't let their opinions affect you."

"Liberty takes them to heart."

"I see." Gideon brought his knees up and rested his back against the tree trunk. "I know a certain person who at age eight told me something very wise. Do you remember saying that you could try really hard to make Liberty like you, but she either did or didn't?"

"I'm surprised you do."

Gideon shrugged. "It applied to my own situation at the time."

"I'm glad it worked out between you and Emma."

"I am too, although we both had to grow up more before it could. You and Liberty might need to do the same. There's also the possibility that you shouldn't be together. Time will tell. Meanwhile, stop trying so hard to make her like you."

Jake sighed. "Thanks for the advice. I'd better take it for my own peace of mind. I suppose I came across as an unreasonable hot-head today."

"You did." Gideon jumped down from his perch, making the branch groan. "I'll leave you to consider whether to apologize."

Jake nodded. He already knew the answer, but he needed a moment to calm down and reflect before he spoke to Liberty. He had nothing to say to Beau.

After Gideon left him, Jake took the position his brother had vacated—knees up and back to the tree. Warmth from the trunk seeped into him, and a slight breeze stirred the leaves. The weather had been as balmy that long-ago day when Liberty promised to marry him. He felt again the passion and reverence of holding her in his arms. She lifted her sweet lips for his kiss, and he caressed them with his own. Her mouth yielded beneath his—soft like the petals of a rose. He'd known enough not to take matters beyond that point. Later, when they exchanged formal vows in a church, he would gain that right. He'd held her with the protectiveness of a husband and restrained their embraces during the brief period before she withdrew from him.

Liberty thought he wanted to own her, but that was never a possibility. She possessed a mind of her own, which was the whole trouble. He'd been selfishly trying to ease the pain of losing her. For that, he owed her an apology.

His own words, repeated by Gideon, returned to him. *You could try really hard to make Liberty like you, but she either did or didn't.*

With a flash of brindled wings and pleated tails, a flock of flickers landed higher in the tree. The crestless woodpeckers' chuckling cries rippled through him, reflecting the joy of their Creator. Jake closed his eyes and breathed the words he'd held back.

God, help me let go of Liberty.

CHAPTER FOUR

PHOEBE MANAGED NOT TO ROLL HER eyes, but she couldn't understand why Liberty seemed determined to do everything wrong. It was tough watching Liberty turn her childhood sweetheart away for a man she barely knew and didn't seem to like. Beau had ridden into town one day and talked the owner of the mercantile into employing him. He could be an outlaw for all anyone knew.

Outlaws usually don't hire on for honest work.

Phoebe sighed. Employing her powers of observation would be more useful than allowing her imagination to run amok.

Liberty's hangdog expression did not escape Phoebe's notice. Small wonder with Beau ranting endlessly about the lack of conveniences in town. "Really, there should be some form of entertainment," he concluded at last, or at least he stopped for breath.

"The congregation of my father's church built Liberty township." Liberty put down her fork, which she hadn't been using much anyway. "Our amusements might seem paltry to you, but we enjoy them. No one I know has expressed boredom at visiting neighbors, taking walks, or attending gatherings like this one."

Phoebe lifted her chin. "If you want a saloon or dancehall, Mr. Hensley, you'd better look elsewhere—maybe even relocate." *That would solve a few problems.* She ignored Liberty's scandalized look. A lady did not speak of such places, nor did she make a guest feel less than welcome. Phoebe didn't care about fuddy-duddy rules, not when her dearest friend needed help. Liberty's politeness sometimes robbed her of the ability to protect herself, in Phoebe's opinion. Smiling at her mischievous thoughts, she glanced toward her family's tables. Will looked up, and their eyes met. Phoebe averted her gaze, not wanting him to think she'd been staring.

"I don't expect to move, Miss Walsh. Thanks all the same for the suggestion." Although Beau's lips curved, his eyes did not warm. He turned his smile on Liberty. "I'm finding enough to interest me here, after all."

Phoebe wanted to groan. She hoped Liberty would see through his flattery, come to her senses, and make up with Jake.

"Liberty township is small, as I'm sure you've noticed." Liberty sipped her lemonade. "You must be used to a larger location. Where are you from, Mr. Hensley?"

"Call me Beau." His lips tilted in a smile, but he sounded miffed. "I left my home in Cheyenne when I crossed the Continental Divide into Montana Territory. I was headed for Helena but fell in love with the Bitterroot Valley."

"What business had you in Helena—if I may ask?" Phoebe tacked on the last few words after noticing Liberty's shocked expression.

"A private family matter called me there, but a telegram from my brother in Helena assures me my presence is not needed." He lifted his own glass in a salute to Liberty. "I'm more than happy to remain in Liberty township, where I may enjoy delicious lemonade, the best beans I've ever tasted, and your most excellent company."

"I see." Liberty's smile couldn't have appeared more strained.

Phoebe wanted to shake her but decided on a different

tactic. "Katie and Fiona were disappointed to spend so little time with you." Surely Liberty would want to get away from Beau to talk with her two oldest female cousins. Phoebe treasured her family, and she knew Liberty did too. Their cousin Katie had made her parents, Uncle Nick and Aunt Bry, proud with high marks in school. Fiona possessed the beauty of her mother, Uncle Con's wife Elsa, and she sang with the voice of an angel.

Liberty brightened, but then a helpless expression crossed her face. "I'm sorry to miss them. Maybe we can catch up later."

Phoebe should have realized her friend's difficulty. Having accepted Beau's invitation to dine with him, Liberty wouldn't display the bad manners to desert him in the middle of the meal. Fair enough. At some point, Phoebe intended to wrest her away from Beau. If the man had any empathy, he would free Liberty from her sense of obligation to him. Beau remained silent however.

Beau largely ignored Phoebe but regaled Liberty with tales of life in Cheyenne. He'd lived on a cattle ranch, although whether or not he'd owned it remained obscure. He'd probably served as a ranch hand. In Phoebe's experience, ranchers were too busy working to boast about their holdings. Even so, Beau's stories about attending Cheyenne's elegant theater intrigued her. Accounts of his life in the city were less interesting. She suspected Beau of editing the sparse information he gave. He was hiding something. Why else would he skirt issues and leave so much unexplained?

Liberty sighed. "It sounds like a grand life compared to my quiet existence."

Beau captured Liberty's hand. "I would love to show you Cheyenne someday."

Liberty's eyes widened. "That's too far away."

Beau shrugged. "The railways make distances easier to travel these days. The tracks will reach the Bitterroot Valley soon, but we don't have to wait that long."

"It wouldn't be proper for me to accompany you." Liberty shook her head. "It's fun to dream of travel, but I must find contentment in a simpler life. Elaborate parties and theater galas are not for me."

"I remain unconvinced." His smile broadened. "You would be a vision in fancy dress."

Phoebe jumped up, unable to take any more. "Are you finished, Liberty?" She plucked her friend's half-full plate off the table before Liberty had a chance to answer. Sustenance was less important than freedom, in Phoebe's opinion.

Liberty might agree, for she relinquished her plate without protest. "Thank you."

"Give it back." Beau frowned at Phoebe but smiled at Liberty. "You've barely touched your food."

"I seem to have lost my appetite." Liberty proffered a faint smile. "I'm sorry, but I'm not feeling well. I should go." She shifted as if to rise.

Beau's hand covered hers. "I'll see you home."

"Let me." Phoebe plunked the dishes she held onto the table, making them clatter.

"It's no trouble." Beau jumped up.

Liberty rose from her chair. "Thank you, but I don't think—"

"I must insist. You are unwell." Beau's voice grew steadily louder, and several people turned their heads.

Liberty wilted in her chair, red staining her cheeks. "All right."

Phoebe suspected that she had only agreed to avoid embarrassment. "I'll go with you." Ignoring Beau's frown, she skirted the table to reach Liberty.

"I'd rather not keep you from the potluck." Liberty's protest sounded weak.

"Never mind about that." Phoebe spoke bracingly. "I can go back after you're settled, if I want."

There was no way Phoebe wanted Beau walking Liberty home alone. He seemed entirely too besotted on short acquaintance. The man had taken advantage of Liberty's everlasting politeness, but Phoebe did not suffer from the same constraints. If Beau overstepped, she fully intended to interfere.

Liberty stopped herself from asking after Jake as she passed Gideon outside the meeting hall. It would be too awkward with Beau present. Gideon might not hold her in his best graces at the moment. Was that frown on his face for her? It could also signify that he didn't care for Beau. She hoped it didn't mean that Jake wasn't doing well. She frowned at the possibility.

Liberty felt a little stifled with Phoebe on one side and Beau too near on the other. Her relief at Phoebe's presence felt a little craven. Liberty wished she possessed Phoebe's strength of mind. Then she would know how to stand up to a domineering person like Beau. While reeling from Jake's outburst wasn't the best time to do so, however. The urge to flee pressed her, but she tamped it down.

Beau offered Liberty his arm, a gesture she discreetly ignored. She wasn't about to encourage him. She'd only allowed him to walk her home to avoid an embarrassing scene. Implying she suffered from an illness was less than honest. She hadn't lied, exactly. Her churning stomach, headache, and general heaviness were indeed physical symptoms—but of an emotional malady.

She was heartsick. Letting go of Jake hurt more than she'd realized. Liberty could think of no other course to spare him pain. She might have known what to do sooner if her long-ago promise hadn't confused matters. The thought of breaking her word made her stomach ache. If only she had kept quiet that fateful day, she and Jake might preserve their friendship. That was no longer possible.

She'd tried so hard to convince herself, if not Jake, that nothing had changed between them. Liberty sighed. She'd only postponed the pain of losing his friendship. She could admit to other mistakes. Feigning an interest in Beau had been foolish. Her pretense had sparked confrontation between the men and created her present predicament. It served her right, Liberty supposed.

She couldn't think of a single way to let Beau down gently. He might not stop pursuing her unless she demanded it, and maybe not even then. Asking Pa to explain matters to her unwelcome admirer would be embarrassing, but that might be the only way to stop Beau's advances.

They left the church grounds and crossed the schoolyard. The sun scorched the top of Liberty's head and heated her face. She was glad when the path plunged into the tree tunnel that would open onto the clearing where the cabin stood. Dappled light danced along the path at Liberty's feet. Birdsong swelled the air, and the sweet scent of cottonwoods in bloom embraced her. Even with Beau beside her, it was hard to remain gloomy.

"You're sunk in thought." Beau grabbed her arm, jealousy coloring his voice.

Liberty resisted the impulse to jerk away from his touch. Gently, but firmly, she pulled her arm free. "I'm enjoying our surroundings."

"It's always beautiful here," Phoebe murmured.

Liberty smiled. "Your ranch sits in a lovely spot too."

"The Bitterroot Valley is impressive." Beau spoke in a reverent voice.

Liberty would never expect someone so overbearing to nurture finer feelings. Had she mistaken Beau's character? "I can't imagine living anywhere else."

"Where do you call home, Mr. Hensley?" Phoebe chimed in with another personal question.

Liberty didn't bother to send Phoebe censoring glances. She only ignored them.

"Why, Liberty township, Miss Walsh." Beau gripped Liberty's elbow. "Watch your step, ladies. There's a tree root across the way."

"Thank you." Liberty didn't point out that she could walk the path blindfolded, and so could Phoebe.

"I meant, where are you from, originally?" Phoebe persisted.

"A small town you wouldn't recognize."

Phoebe's chin came up. "Try me."

Beau's eyes narrowed. "Are you so well-traveled that you would know a small town many miles away?"

Why wouldn't Beau give a straight answer? He must be hiding something. Either that, or he was annoyed at Phoebe's nosiness. Liberty extricated her arm from his grasp a little less gently this time.

Phoebe fell silent, although Liberty didn't count on that continuing. She sighed. The walk home was growing longer every minute.

The branches overhead parted as the path widened. Shafts of light broke through. The cabin in its small clearing backed up to tall trees. The windows stared out blankly, as yet unlighted. A wooden bucket waited near the stone well, and a side track ran to a second cabin. In the wilderness beyond, a bright ribbon of water wound through tall grasses, light gilded the leaves of a mixed forest, and distant mountains lifted into the sky.

Beau's footsteps slowed and came to a standstill. "How peaceful."

Liberty and Phoebe stopped also. Liberty shielded her eyes from the sudden sunlight. "The schoolteacher has the best view."

"Is that who lives there?" Beau nodded toward the second cabin.

"Yes." Liberty would normally linger in this spot. Today, she yearned to go home.

Phoebe turned her head toward Liberty. "You sound tired."

"I am, a bit."

"Let's hurry you home." Phoebe spoke briskly. "Are you coming, Mr. Hensley?"

Beau joined them on the wide turn into the cottonwood grove. Pointed leaves dangled from the rough-barked trees, and the flower spikes looked ready to burst. When they did, the wind would spread the cottony fluff far and wide.

Where is Jake at this moment? The stray thought intruded.

Beau's hand found its way to hers. "I would like the pleasure of courting you."

Liberty fought for words. "Mr. Hensley—"

"Beau." He stopped walking and turned toward Liberty but looked at Phoebe. "You'll excuse us, Miss Walsh."

"I think not." Phoebe sounded more than a little snippy.

Liberty recovered her composure. "No, it's all right."

Phoebe held Liberty's gaze. "Are you sure?"

Liberty wouldn't say that, but she'd rather get this over with. "I'm willing to speak to Mr. Hensley alone."

"All right, I'll remove myself—but only for a moment." Phoebe marched to the edge of the grove and stood with her back to them.

Liberty turned to Beau. "You astonish me." She spoke first,

a deliberate tactic. "We've barely met."

Beau smiled as if she'd said something funny. "Don't make that an obstacle."

"How can it fail to be one?" Liberty didn't share his amusement.

He stroked his chin, studying her with his eyebrows almost touching. "Is there someone else? That fellow Jake, perhaps?"

"No, but that's not the point. I've not considered courting anyone."

"It's about time you did."

This was harder than she'd imagined. The desire to escape returned, shaking her with its strength. She opened her mouth to make her excuses.

The snapping of wood drew her attention upward. Liberty blinked.

Jake stared back at her from the low branch where they usually met.

CHAPTER FIVE

LIBERTY'S FACE FLAMED. JAKE MUST HAVE heard every word they'd said. *Why hadn't he let on that he was there?* She could only assume that he wanted to remain hidden. That was fine with her. She didn't want to find out what would happen if the two men confronted one another.

Liberty pulled her attention back to Beau. He must not have noticed Jake. or he'd have said something. She couldn't resist a peek at Jake, who rewarded her curiosity with a roguish grin. Failing to see anything funny in the situation, Liberty jerked her gaze away. Beau droned on, but she stopped listening. She couldn't resist another glance at Jake. His scowl warned her that Beau must have said something amiss. Jake shifted, poised to spring from the tree. Liberty held her breath.

Something brushed her arm. Liberty jumped and turned her head to find Phoebe at her elbow.

Phoebe flicked a glance from Liberty to Jake, then glared at Beau. "I believe you have your answer."

Beau's face reddened. "You were eavesdropping, I suppose."

Phoebe stood taller. "I could hardly help hearing, since you carried on in my presence."

"*Please.*" Liberty intervened before Beau could respond. "I must insist that you leave, Mr. Hensley."

Beau furrowed his forehead then smiled more forcefully than usual. "I'll see you home first."

"There's no need. My house is within view."

His smile vanished. "Liberty—"

"I am *Miss Hayes*." Liberty corrected him without her usual civility. "And I believe you owe Miss Walsh an apology."

Beau jutted his jaw and scowled in Phoebe's direction. "I may have been a bit hasty. Forgive me."

Liberty didn't blame Phoebe her skeptical expression. As an apology, it didn't amount to much.

Phoebe pressed her lips together as if holding back words but nodded briefly.

"Good day, Mr. Hensley." Liberty felt the need to remind her unwelcome admirer of his imminent departure.

Beau engulfed Liberty's hand in his own. "I trust you'll feel better soon." He dipped his head and for an alarming instant, she thought he was going to kiss her hand. He treated her to his charming smile. "I'll return to check on your health soon."

Beau's swagger as he walked away from Liberty set Jake's teeth on edge. He wouldn't be surprised, after the man's bad manners, if both women found his departure a relief. It had cost him no small effort to resist the urge to challenge Beau. If Jake hadn't decided to stop interfering in Liberty's affairs, he might not restrain himself.

Jake wasn't given to spying, but overhearing Liberty fend off her admirer had been most informative. Why would she encourage Beau at the potluck, only to reject him a short while later? He wasn't vain enough to imagine she was trying to make him jealous, although she'd succeeded. No, his own possessiveness must have driven her to pretend interest in a rival. If true, that was one more reason to offer her an apology.

Jake swung down and dusted off his hands. The sooner he got this over with, the better.

Liberty spun about and faced him. "Why were you hiding?"

"Not for any reason but to stay out of your way. I had no time to leave unseen when you approached, so I stayed in the tree."

She narrowed her eyes. "Why would you do that after putting yourself very much in my way?"

Phoebe cleared her throat. "Do you want me to stay, or would you rather speak with Jake alone?"

Liberty summoned a smile for Phoebe. "Thanks for the offer, but you've spent enough time on my worries for one day."

"Don't think for a moment that I mind."

"Bless you." Liberty sounded close to weeping.

Phoebe patted her shoulder. "I'll go see what our cousins are doing." She set off toward the meeting hall.

"Well?" Liberty folded her arms. "What brought on this sudden desire to stay out of my business?"

Jake pulled in air. "Maybe I saw no point in taking up my argument with Beau."

"Why?"

"I had nothing to fight for. You'd made your wishes clear, plus I'm fairly sure the Almighty took me in hand."

She gave him a bewildered look. "You're giving up?"

"That's what you want. Am I wrong?"

"Yes—no."

"Well, that's clear. Beau should have asked your father before speaking to you, by the way. He failed to respect your father, Phoebe, and you."

"True." She crossed her arms. "But you were going to stop interfering."

"That doesn't mean I can't have an opinion." He couldn't help himself. "Why did you stand for it?"

She shook her head. "I didn't."

"Well, all right, maybe not—but you were far too polite."

"That is also true."

Jake cocked an eyebrow. "I'm glad you can admit it."

She took a step closer to him and lowered her voice. "How much did you hear of our conversation?"

"Once you reached the grove? Everything."

Liberty's cheeks flushed with heat. "I'd prefer a different answer."

"I never meant to eavesdrop, but I found it most informative."

She winced. "You must have enjoyed yourself."

"I found nothing about your conversation with Beau pleasant, especially hearing you deny me."

She gaped at him. "What are you talking about?"

"Let's just say that I found out what I needed to know."

"I can't try to sort this out anymore." She rubbed her temple. "My head is throbbing."

"You should go home, but take my apology with you. I acted badly, and I'm sorry. I'd like to say more, but I'll wait until you're better." Jake watched her walk away with a lump in his throat. He hoped she would give him the chance to speak his mind.

Will did his best to drag his thoughts from Phoebe and onto the conversation with his new boss. He'd lost his focus when Phoebe returned to the meeting hall, breathless and with color staining her cheeks. What had happened after she left with her friends? From all appearances, nothing good.

It was clear that everyone in her family adored Phoebe. He could understand why. She was both beautiful and lively. The attention this brought did her no favors, in his opinion. Phoebe struck him as a bit wayward. Today, she'd displayed interest in her cousin's suitor. Will had overheard her inviting herself to sit next to the man, and then asking him personal questions. She'd insisted on tagging along when her cousin left with her suitor.

Phoebe greeted several of her cousins at the next table and plunked down on the bench across from them. Seeing her out of his side vision didn't help Will's concentration. For some annoying reason that he didn't want to analyze, he noticed her every move.

Will shifted to remove her from his sight, but then fought the urge to turn his head her way.

Con Walsh appeared to be waiting for a response. Will forced his mind back to their conversation. What had Con said? He had no idea. Honestly, he needed to get hold of himself. Will cleared his throat. "I'm sorry. Would you repeat that?"

"I asked where you're from."

Judging by Con's glance toward Phoebe and his slight smile, he grasped Will's problem but was content to pretend he didn't. Will would happily do the same. "Tennessee, sir."

"That explains the southern drawl. What brought you west?"

"The same that brings many—the possibility of adventure."

Con laughed. "You're an honest man, I see. You may well find what you seek as my ranch manager. We've come up against our share of cattle rustlers."

Will smiled. "I'm grateful for the chance to ride the range. If once in a while I find a dry roof over my head, all the better."

Phoebe laughed, and the sound rippled over Will. He couldn't ignore his response to her, but he had no intention of following through on his feelings. Will returned his attention rather forcefully to his boss. It seemed more than clear that where Miss Phoebe Walsh was concerned, he shouldn't trust his feelings.

Phoebe slipped out early, leaving Liberty sleeping. She'd meant to go riding, but the sound of hoofbeats in the pasture drew her away from the open barn doorway. Her boots crunched on the road, and then on the worn footpath to the corral. Sunlight angled across the grass and sent her shadow ahead to touch Will, who stood at the rail beside her father. Her uncles, Con and Shane were looking into the corral nearby. Will swung about and pinned her with his gaze. The relaxed lines in his face tightened, and he glanced away.

Phoebe tried not to mind his reaction to her approach, but it still jarred. Why should Will, who barely knew her, show an aversion to her appearance? A movement beyond the fence distracted her. Uncle Nick's black hair gleamed as he tilted his head and gazed up at Chief, whose reins he held. Chief pranced and snorted, the veins standing out on his neck. Uncle Nick flicked his arm and the jacket settled over the horse's head, covering his eyes. Chief stopped prancing and tossed his head. The jacket flew, but by then Uncle Nick was in the saddle.

Phoebe rushed to the fence and curled her fingers against the railing. She hoped her uncle knew what he was doing. From what she'd heard, Chief wouldn't stand for being ridden.

The horse heaved his sides, flattened his ears, and pulled downward against the reins. A cord stood out in Uncle Nick's neck as they fought a battle of wills. Chief snorted, but with his head up, couldn't buck.

"That's the way." Uncle Con called his approval.

As if goaded by the remark, the horse charged toward the rail. Phoebe held her breath, well aware of Chief's intention to brush off his rider. She'd encountered this tactic herself while breaking horses.

Uncle Nick tensed before the moment of impact. Phoebe sucked in a breath, but her uncle pulled the leg that would have been crushed out from beneath him. He threw his leg over Chief's other side as the horse ground against the railing.

Phoebe let out her breath. She would never dare such a stunt, but her uncle seemed fearless.

The horse pulled away from the fence, and Uncle Nick straddled his back once more. Her uncle bent his head and murmured to the horse. Chief pricked his ears. Uncle Nick kept talking while the horse circled the corral and came to a standstill.

"Well, I never—" Uncle Shane breathed. "You accomplished more with that horse than I ever did."

Uncle Nick dismounted in a fluid movement. "Chief's had enough, I think. I'll try again before I leave, if I may."

"You may indeed." Uncle Shane grinned. "Ride my horse as many times as you like."

"That's fancy riding." Will burst out.

Phoebe nodded, although she didn't think he'd spoken to her in particular. "Uncle Nick is famous for his riding skill."

"I can see why." He turned toward her and adjusted his hat brim to shade his eyes. "It's quite early. I hope the noise we made didn't wake you."

She frowned. "Why do you assume I would linger in my bed?"

Will's face reddened. "I didn't mean it that way."

"I'm glad to hear it." She dipped her chin in a swift nod. "I was about to saddle my own horse. It's a lovely morning for a ride, don't you think?"

His blush deepened. "I suppose—" He squared his shoulders. "If you would like an escort—"

"I didn't mean to invite you." Phoebe felt her own cheeks warm. "That is, I—"

"It's all right." He chuckled. "I think we understand one another, Miss Walsh."

She smiled vaguely, not certain at all that they did.

Jake's boots crunched on the stone path. A rooster crowed. Smoke curled from the chimney above the house Gideon shared with his wife, Emma, and their two children. The barn door gaped, and hooves thudded inside.

Gideon, leading his palomino mare out of her stall, nodded at him. "Good morning, Jake. What brings you so early?"

"There's something on my mind—I wanted to ask…" Jake paused, not sure how to go on.

Gideon studied him. "Look, why don't you walk with us? I need to turn Goldie out to pasture, and she's fair to bursting." Goldie snorted, as if in agreement.

Jake fell into step beside his brother, grateful for the chance to collect his thoughts.

Gideon guided the horse along the worn path between the barn and fenced pasture. "It's a chore, taking the livestock back and forth every day, but they're healthier and happier for the chance to graze."

Gideon lived a country mile beyond the chapel, but Jake had a similar situation at Ma's place. Despite being closer to town, Ma's farm was too near the wilderness for Jake to dare leave the horses out at night.

Gideon rubbed a hand down his neck. "We've heard a panther yowling at night lately."

"That's an eerie wail."

"Oh, yes. Sounds like a woman screaming. It gives Emma shivers." Gideon swung the pasture gate open and removed Goldie's rope. The palomino took a running circuit of the pasture before lowering her muzzle to the grass.

"I'm thinking of moving," Jake announced off-handedly. "Maybe I'll mine for gold like Benjamin."

"Our brother caught a bad case of gold fever." Gideon clanked the gate shut. "I hope you don't suffer from it too."

"I want to try my hand at mining, that's all." Jake shrugged.

Gideon gave him a knowing look. "I don't suppose this has anything to do with Liberty."

Jake glanced away. "Living next door to her doesn't help."

"What about Ma? She'd be all alone if you left."

Jake sighed. "Do you think Ma would be all right without me? I doubt she'd want for company. You and Emma visit a lot. Ma's friends stop by too, and they come to those tea parties she likes to throw."

Gideon gathered Goldie's rope into a coil. "I can understand a man's desire to make his own way, but don't be hasty. Leaving your family is a decision worth pondering."

"It wouldn't be forever, but I do need to put a little distance between myself and Liberty."

"I understand how that can be. Who can say? It might be good for you, but I'd feel better if you weren't…"

"What?"

Gideon hesitated. "I'd hate to think that you're running away from your problems."

"When you're a magnet for trouble, avoiding it is next to godliness." Jake had learned that lesson the hard way.

"If you stood your ground, everything might work out in your favor."

Jake shook his head. "That seems unlikely at this point."

"Don't bet on it. Appearances can deceive, especially when it comes to matters of the heart."

Liberty breathed in the fragrance of wild roses overladen by the sharp scent of grass, glad she'd come walking with Phoebe. Early light bathed the road in a rosy glow. Meadow larks trilled in the brush, and a marsh hawk glided above fields threaded with bitterroot blossoms in shades of pink and purple.

Phoebe skirted a wagon rut that cut deeper than most. "What happened after I left yesterday? I hope Jake behaved himself."

"He apologized for the way he acted, which was more than I thought he'd do."

Phoebe glanced sideways at her. "Then what's wrong? It's plain that something is on your mind."

Liberty shrugged. "I don't feel good about my own part in what happened."

"You weren't responsible for the way Beau acted."

"No, but he wouldn't have lost his temper without my help."

Phoebe stopped abruptly. "What do you mean?"

"I shouldn't have encouraged Beau, and especially not in front of Jake."

"Hmm… Maybe Jake wasn't the only one who needed to apologize."

Liberty nodded slowly. "You're right, but it won't be easy."

"You'll never know until you try." Phoebe brightened. "It might go better than you imagine."

Phoebe's optimism could be maddening. Liberty shrugged. "I hope you're right."

They walked a while in silence. The situation hadn't changed, but Liberty felt better after confessing her guilt. She wanted so badly to live well and make her parents proud. Why did she so often fail?

Phoebe plucked a delicate pink blossom from the grass alongside the road and brought it to her nose. "Bitterroot flowers have such a mild scent. You have to pay attention to appreciate it."

Liberty glanced at Phoebe in suspicion, certain she was talking about more than Bitterroot flowers. "I see Uncle Con's new ranch manager came with them. Do you have any idea what he's like?"

Phoebe's cheeks blushed to match the flower dangling from her flingers. "He seems nice."

Liberty gave her a long look. She'd never known her talkative friend to say so little when asked to give an opinion.

The road ran through trees, and then burst into the sunlight. Liberty slowed her footsteps, savoring the scents of pine and cedar. A woodpecker drummed on a dead tree, then flew off in a flash of red, white, and deep gray.

"Did you see that bird?" Phoebe bounced on the balls of her feet as she spoke.

"Do you mean the Lewis's Woodpecker?"

"Yes!" Phoebe grinned. "I get excited whenever I spot one. They're pretty, and they have a sweet cry."

The bird's high-pitched alarm peeled through the grove.

Phoebe laughed. "Well maybe not that sound."

Liberty scanned the trees. "For being so colorful, he's hard to spot,"

"I don't think the little fellow wants company. He'll have to get over it, though. My feet need a rest." Phoebe plopped onto a fallen log by the side of the road. "Ouch!" She freed strands of her golden hair from the bush behind the log.

Liberty perched next to her, careful to avoid the bush. "Your hair looks pretty gathered into a hair clip and cascading down your back."

"Thank you." Phoebe grinned. "The curls were no trouble to achieve, of course."

Liberty smiled, remembering Phoebe as a young child complaining that her hair wound itself into tangles. Phoebe's curls might be difficult to manage, but they gave her an angelic appearance. "I wish I had them."

"Horrors!" Phoebe made a face. "You have no idea what you're saying."

Liberty laughed. "Be grateful you don't need to tie your hair up in rags like I do."

"Why you go to the trouble, I'll never know. Waves suit you."

Liberty watched the woodpecker climb higher in a tree. She didn't normally stop in this grove… She glanced about. "I didn't realize how far out we've come. Maybe we should head back."

"If we must." Phoebe yelped. "That hurt!"

"Are you all right?"

"Yes, but that accursed bush tore out my clip and some hair with it." She rubbed her head. "The clip must have fallen. Do you see it?"

Liberty peered behind the log and caught sight of the enamel ornament. "There it is. I just need— Oh, for goodness sake." Liberty straightened. "I accidentally pushed it further away."

"I'll see if I can reach it." Phoebe leaned across the log but came up empty-handed. "It's hard to see, the brush is so thick. I might have to leave it."

Liberty could understand Phoebe's skepticism. The log had a lot of brush behind it. "I'd hate for you to lose such a pretty clip. Let me try again." Liberty hiked up her skirt, and took a giant step over the log.

"Be careful!"

Pain lanced Liberty's leg. She cried out and fell against the log.

"What happened?" Phoebe bent over her.

"My leg—it grated against something sharp." Tears

squeezed from Liberty's eyes.

Phoebe supported her while she climbed back over the log.

Liberty inspected the damage. Her stocking was shredded, and blood trickled from a gash on her leg.

Phoebe stretched across the log. "I can't tell what happened."

"Be careful, or you'll fall."

"I'm all right." Phoebe sat up. "I'd better take a look." She reached for Liberty's leg.

"No, don't touch it." Liberty shifted sideways out of range.

"Let me help you. I'll be careful."

Liberty hauled in air. "All right, but go easy. It hurts." She pulled back her skirt and exposed the ugly gash.

"I imagine so." Phoebe examined her leg. "You have shards of wood embedded in your skin. Part of the log must have splintered when the tree fell."

Liberty gritted her teeth. "How bad is it?"

"Your wound doesn't look pretty, but it should clean up. I'll pull out as many slivers as I can."

"Give me a minute." Liberty closed her eyes.

"Let me know when."

After a moment, Liberty nodded. "All right, but stop if I tell you."

"Brace yourself." Phoebe bent over her leg.

"No, don't!"

Phoebe straightened. "I won't if you don't want me to."

Liberty stared at a patch of sky. "Just do it."

Phoebe dug her fingernails into Liberty's wound.

Liberty gripped the rough bark of the log and held her breath.

Phoebe held up a long splinter. "One down."

Liberty stared at her. "How many are there?"

"Several, but don't worry. That was the worst of them." Phoebe's fingertips probed her wound. "I'm not sure I can remove the others without a needle."

"Let me try walking." Liberty levered herself upright with Phoebe's assistance. She put weight on her leg and gasped. "I must have twisted my ankle."

"Let's hope you didn't sprain it." Phoebe supported her as she sat back down.

"It's possible." Liberty shook her head. "Much as I hate admitting defeat, I can't walk home like this."

Phoebe's forehead puckered. "I don't like leaving you, but I'd better go for help."

"There's no other way."

"I'll be quick as I can." Phoebe set off at a fast clip.

A sinking feeling came over Liberty. Sitting on the side of the road, helpless and alone, seemed a bad idea.

CHAPTER SIX

PHOEBE NORMALLY FOUND GOING AWAY SLOWER than returning. Today, the opposite seemed true. She pushed out of her mind the stories she'd heard about attacks by animals, not to mention certain two-footed predators. Phoebe gave herself a mental shake. Worrying would solve nothing. Liberty would be fine. Of course, she would.

A prayer never went amiss…

Phoebe ran most of the way home. She arrived at the barn breathing hard. "Pa?"

The only answer was a nickering from the stalls. After Phoebe's eyes adjusted, she could see that the horse belonged to Uncle Con's ranch manager. The other horses were gone. Maybe they were only out to pasture.

Phoebe hurled herself through the doorway and into the barnyard. "Pa!"

Her cry fell away into silence.

Hooves thudded on the road. A strange rider swerved into the barnyard. "Morning, miss." The roughness of his voice matched his appearance. Bearded and covered in dust, he looked like a man who hadn't seen a bath or shaved in a while. The piercing eyes trained on her gave the impression that he missed nothing.

"Sorry. I'm in a hurry—" Phoebe broke off. She could barely breathe, let alone speak.

He narrowed his piercing eyes. "I won't keep you long. I only want to know if I'm on the road to Liberty."

"You are indeed."

"Much obliged." He tipped his battered hat.

She decided against mentioning Liberty's plight to someone so disreputable looking. Hopefully, when Liberty saw him coming, she would find a way to hide. Phoebe wouldn't count on that happening, though. She needed to find help, and quickly. She ran for the cabin, hoping to find her father. Blinking in the sudden shade, she plowed into someone on the path. A scream broke from her.

"Miss Walsh?" Will steadied her. "What's wrong?"

She clutched the front of his shirt. "Where's my pa?"

"He went with your Uncle Shane, his boys, and your brothers to help one of your neighbors roof his barn. I'm on my way there myself."

"I thought you left this morning with Uncle Con and everyone else from his ranch."

"I don't start for a couple of days. I'm handy with roofing, so I volunteered to stay. Tell me—" He grasped her shoulders and held her at arm's distance. "Why were you running?"

Realizing that she'd been clinging to him, she stepped away with warmth stealing up her neck. "Liberty and I went for a walk, but she injured her leg and can't make it home."

"Where did you leave her?"

"On the road to town. She's a good distance by foot but not far on horseback."

"I'll saddle up and go after her." He stepped past her.

"Wait!"

Will looked back and tilted his head inquiringly.

"There's a strange man on the road."

"What did he look like?"

"He had uncombed dark hair, a shaggy beard, rough clothing…." Phoebe searched for the words to explain her alarm.

"There's a manner about him—"

"Does he bear arms?"

"Yes."

"I'll hurry." Will swung about and rushed off.

Phoebe let herself relax, just a little. Will seemed so capable, it was hard to imagine anything going wrong. Even so, she would feel better if someone followed him. Maybe Liberty's mother could suggest another person to send. Phoebe should tell her what had happened to Liberty, at any rate.

The cabin lay in silence. Her mother was probably at Liberty's house. Phoebe rounded the turn and plunged into the cottonwood grove without waiting for her eyes to adjust. She slowed her pace and felt her way through the darkness. The hissing of leaves crowded in, blocking other sounds. Phoebe emerged into the sunlight with a sense of relief. She slowed her pace, disoriented as shadows from the wind-tossed trees rushed across the path, only to retreat again. It was like walking through waves lapping a river bank.

Something moved in her side vision—Jake coming out of the Buckthorn barn. She hailed him and turned onto the side path that connected their properties.

Jake met her at the gate. "Something the matter?"

Phoebe caught her breath. "Liberty suffered a mishap."

He stiffened. "Is she injured?"

Phoebe nodded. "She has splinters in her leg, and I think she sprained her ankle. Will's gone to get her, but there's a scary man ahead of him on the road."

"I was about to ride to the post office, as it happens." He started for his barn but looked back to her. "Scout's already saddled."

"Thank you." Jake was already out of hearing, but Phoebe whispered more for God's hearing.

What was that thud?

Liberty's hand flew to her throat. Pulse pounding, she peered into the shadows under the trees.

Nothing stirred.

Liberty let out a shaky breath. She'd put on a brave front for Phoebe's sake, but this situation would unnerve the stoutest soul. Being unable to walk without pain hampered a person's ability to escape peril. The risk might be small on the road that connected the outlying properties with the township's Main Street, but that didn't mean danger didn't exist along the wilder stretches. She'd walked alone before but never at this distance from home. If she hadn't been deep in conversation, she'd have noticed how far they'd come and turned back sooner.

A bird's whistle peeled behind her. Liberty jumped, her heart racing. A plump bird with a snowy breast and brindled wings stood out against a cedar tree's shaggy bark. Relief washed through Liberty, along with annoyance at her own timidity. She'd started at the trilling of a brown creeper, a bird so familiar that she ought to have recognized its song.

I need to get hold of myself or I'll die of fright before anything else can kill me.

Liberty examined her wounded leg. Recovering from today's misadventure would take a while. Congealed blood ran along the gash and a rash of embedded slivers fanned over the chafed skin beside it. A fly fascinated with her wound posed an immediate threat. Liberty batted the insect away and pulled her skirt down over her injury. She was better off not looking at it anyway.

Hooves thudded in the near distance, raising dust. Someone was traveling at speed, hopefully coming to help her. Liberty strained to see but couldn't make out the rider. She would hate to be missed, here in the shadows. She struggled to her feet, ready to call attention to herself, if necessary.

The rider passed through the shade of willows bending toward the stream running at their feet. He reappeared in full sunlight, and Liberty shrank backward. This unkempt man was not anyone Phoebe would send.

Liberty cast about for somewhere to hide, but there was no time. She dropped down on the log, gasping from the pain caused by her swift movements. With her injury hidden beneath her skirt, she adopted a casual posture. She would do nothing to reveal her helplessness to the man who was almost upon her.

He drew up on the road before her. "Good day, miss. I'm surprised to see you all by yourself. Have you no companions?"

It must be obvious that she had no companions, but Liberty didn't want to admit it for certain. She drew a quick breath. "I decided to take the air but came a bit far. I thought to rest before going back home. If I don't arrive soon, Pa will be sure to come looking."

He smiled, but the lack of several teeth gave him a ragged appearance. "Your pa's a wise man, then. A pretty little filly like you should not go walking alone. There are dangers a girl of your sort won't have heard of. An Injun might tomahawk you and take your scalp—and that's if you're lucky. You wouldn't want to be made a bride—or worse. Why, an outlaw might come across you and do something dreadful."

"Please—don't go on."

The man turned his head and spat a stream of tobacco before Liberty managed to look away. That explained the lump in his cheek. He turned to her, grinning with stained teeth. "Scared ya, didn't I?"

Of course, he had, but not in the way he meant. Liberty decided to abandon politeness, which he might not understand anyway. "Sir, I am shocked you would broach topics of conversation no gentleman should mention in feminine company."

He laughed outright. "Well, la-di-da, ain't you swell?"

Liberty lifted her chin. "I really must insist that you leave me."

Hoofbeats interrupted whatever reply he might have made. The man pushed back his tattered hat and scanned the road. "I'd oblige you, but we have company. You won't mind if I wait and see who's come calling. Even an obnoxious coot like myself protects a woman, and that goes double when she fails to look after herself."

Liberty stared at the man in surprise. Perhaps she'd misjudged him. She found his looks off-putting and his behavior crass, but his bearing held a certain nobility.

Liberty pulled her attention from the man and put it on the approaching rider. She released her breath in a sigh,

Jake's horse ground to a halt in a spray of dust. "Good day to you." He nodded to the stranger. "What business do you have with this woman?"

"Greetings." The stranger tipped his hat. "I'm Deputy Sheriff Manchin. I came across this young lady out here all alone. She seems in need of help."

"You can leave her to me." Jake scanned Liberty's face. "She's my neighbor."

"Well that's a relief." The stranger took off his hat and wiped his brow with a dusty bandana. "I can't afford a delay."

More dust stirred in the distance. Liberty squinted and picked out a lone rider galloping toward them.

Deputy Manchin returned his hat to its place on his head. "This road is a mite traveled today. I'll just wait until the newcomer joins us so's I only have to ask once."

Liberty looked at him in suspicion. What could he possibly want from them?

The identity of the newcomer wasn't hard to guess once Will's sandy hair became visible beneath the brim of his hat. He rode up, and they exchanged salutations.

Jake's gaze settled on Liberty. "Are you all right?"

She nodded. "Mostly."

Jake's eyes narrowed. "Phoebe said you hurt yourself."

Liberty held back the ridiculous urge to cry. "It's a small matter, really."

"I won't keep you long. The lady looks plain tuckered." Deputy Manchin smiled at Liberty. "I'm on the trail of an outlaw. Have any of you met a man named Grady Bradshaw? He's tall, blond, blue-eyed, and has a southern drawl. He also goes by several aliases—Brad Shaw, Grady Shaw, Bradley Hereford and Lee Bradley. I'm sure he's come up with more."

"Sorry Deputy." Leather creaked as Jake shifted in the saddle. "None of them rings a bell."

Liberty shook her head. "I don't believe I've met him."

"Neither have I." Will chimed in. "What did this outlaw do?"

"You name it." Deputy Manchin squinted against the sunlight. "He's robbed stagecoaches, shot up towns, and murdered innocent people."

Liberty shuddered. "How does a person commit such acts?"

"Grady hails from a family of Confederate sympathizers." The deputy shook his head. "His older brothers went astray after they joined Quantrill's Raiders."

Jake whistled. "I've heard of that sorry group of bushwhackers. William Quantrill led them during the War Between the States."

Liberty didn't know what a bushwhacker might be, but she

wouldn't ask. That would remind the men they were discussing outlaws, crimes, war, and politics in her presence.

Deputy Manchin turned his head and spat. "Quantrill and 'Bloody Bill' Anderson corrupted the impressionable young men in their charge. I won't repeat their war crimes, but Quantrill's foot soldiers got so bad that the Confederate government disowned them. After the Confederacy lost to the Union, Quantrill's men formed gangs and continued to fight. That's how Jesse James and his brother Frank became outlaws. They started as preacher's sons, but their father died when they were small."

"May God have mercy on their souls," Liberty murmured. How horrible to think that men who might otherwise have lived honorable lives had lost their way because of the war.

"You have a kinder heart than I do." Deputy Manchin tipped his hat. "I'm in favor of the Almighty doling out the same measure of mercy such men give their victims."

"Deputy!" Liberty couldn't hold back her shock. "While men draw breath, they can beg God for redemption. Don't be so swift to wish them to perdition." His story illuminated the importance of her father's ministry.

"Well spoken, miss. The West needs more hopeful young women such as yourself. You almost persuade an old codger like me to believe in God's mercy."

"It is real, I assure you, and given to all who ask."

Deputy Manchin frowned at Jake. "Make sure this gentle lady doesn't venture so far on her own again. We wouldn't want her ideals shattered. As for Jesse James, a member of his own gang shot him just this spring." He pointed his horse toward town. "Godspeed to you all."

Liberty sat still until the clopping of his horse's hooves faded. She blew out a breath and turned to Jake. "I was never so glad to see someone as when you rode up."

A smile touched his lips. "I'll take that as a compliment. The reverse is true, in case you wondered. It gave me a turn, when Phoebe said you were hurt."

Will nodded to Jake. "So, Phoebe sent you after Liberty too?"

"She did. Meeting Deputy Manchin alarmed her so much that she urged me to check on you both."

Will's eyes widened. "I saddled my horse in record time. How did you reach Liberty before I did?"

"Scout was already ready to ride, plus I rode hard. After Phoebe's description of the good deputy, I was a mite concerned."

"He doesn't seem a bad sort, despite his manner." Liberty spoke out of fairness.

Will narrowed his eyes. "He didn't say so, but he's probably a bounty hunter. Deputies need to eke out their meager pay somehow. Begging your pardon, Miss Hayes, for mentioning such matters in your presence."

Liberty smiled.

Jake gave her a concerned look. "How is your leg?"

"Painful."

Jake dismounted. "Phoebe said you were having trouble walking."

"I twisted my ankle."

"May I see it?" He sat beside her on the log.

Liberty bit her lip. "I don't know." Jake had seen her legs when they were children at play, but this felt…different.

"I'll head back." Will spoke abruptly. "Phoebe and the rest of your family will appreciate knowing you're safe."

"Thank you." Liberty mustered a smile.

"My pleasure." Will tipped his hat to her and wheeled his

horse about. He sped off, stirring a trail of dust behind him.

"Let me look at your ankle, Liberty." Jake's expression held a hint of steel. "It might be broken."

"All right." Lifting her skirt, she exposed her injury.

Jake squatted before her and unlaced the top of her boot. His fingers slid over her ankle. "I can't find a break, but it's pretty swollen. How does it feel?"

Liberty released her breath. "Better than earlier."

"That's promising." Jake held up a pocket knife. "Phoebe mentioned splinters."

Liberty gave the instrument a doubtful look.

"My knife is clean."

"I don't know —"

"The sooner those splinters come out, the better."

"All right, but be gentle."

His face softened. "I'll try not to hurt you."

"Try? Is that the best you can do?"

"When the odds are against me, I prefer to hedge my bets." He bent his dark head and brushed his fingers over her wounds. "Most of these will come out easily."

Liberty glanced away. "Go ahead."

The blade slid across her skin. She gasped as the sharp tip scraped her raw flesh.

"All right?"

Liberty turned her head and found herself trapped in Jake's gaze. She nodded.

He smiled. "Only twelve more to go."

Liberty groaned. "I will never step over a log without looking again."

"Is that how you did it? Phoebe didn't say." He lowered the knife again.

"Ouch!"

"I've already failed you."

"No you didn't." Liberty smiled, despite herself. "You only promised to try."

He held up another sliver. "Do you want to save these—maybe as a collection?"

She laughed. "No thank you. You're improving, by the way. I barely felt that."

"I'm glad, but I won't count on competing with Doc Bailey for patients."

"That's best." Liberty was having trouble ignoring the fact that Jake's touches felt more like caresses.

He was all business, however, as he bent to his task. Liberty applied herself to her own job—hiding her pain. She'd forgotten Jake's soft-heartedness for a moment. She'd once watched him pull porcupine quills from his dog and couldn't have said which of them suffered most.

Jake smiled up at her, his hands still at last. "That should do it, apart from the smaller bits."

Liberty released her breath. "What a relief."

"How are you holding up?"

"All right. My leg feels better already."

"I can imagine." Jake stood and reached a hand to her. "I won't make you walk home today though. You can ride."

Liberty leaned on Jake and hobbled to Scout, but mounting the horse was beyond her. She turned to Jake in silent appeal.

"I've got you." He spanned her waist with his hands and lifted her. Liberty's feet left the ground, and she turned into his arms. Jake held her longer than necessary, but Liberty couldn't bring herself to complain. Was it her imagination, or did it take him longer than necessary to deposit her in the saddle?

Liberty gripped the saddle horn and adjusted to favor her

leg. She wasn't looking forward to her leg being jarred by the horse's swaying.

Jake grasped the bridle and led the horse toward home.

Liberty frowned. In days past, he would have ridden with her. That was one more thing that had changed between them.

CHAPTER SEVEN

THE TEA HER MOTHER MADE FAILED to soothe Phoebe. Twitching the kitchen curtains aside to look out would not bring Liberty home any sooner, but Phoebe couldn't help doing it. She hated to see Aunt America so tense. Although she sat at the table, drinking from her cup with quiet composure, her careful movements gave her away.

Phoebe couldn't stop picturing Liberty, vulnerable on the side of the road. She would have no warning when the stranger came upon her. Phoebe bowed her head to pray. *God, there's nothing I can do except trust you to watch over Liberty. I know you love her even more than me.*

Phoebe picked up her teacup and took a sip, feeling a little better.

A rapid knocking shook the back door.

Phoebe's cup clattered into its saucer. She jumped up, but Liberty's ma reached the door first. Phoebe peered unabashedly over her aunt's shoulder.

Will stood on the back porch.

"Come in." Aunt stepped back, colliding with Phoebe.

"Sorry." Phoebe gave her aunt a little more room.

Will came in but remained standing in the entryway. "I won't stay long, but I wanted to let you know Liberty is safe. Jake is bringing her back."

"Thank the Lord." Aunt America touched her apron to the corners of her eyes.

Phoebe released a sigh. "I'm grateful. I should have stayed with her until someone missed us."

He shook his head. "No, you did the right thing. She needed more help than you could provide on foot."

"Please accept my gratitude for helping my daughter." Aunt America spoke briskly.

He smiled. "I was glad to do it."

"Would you care for a cup of tea?" Ma gestured toward the table. "I just made a fresh pot."

"It's kind of you to offer…" His gaze slid to Phoebe. "I'd better turn my horse out to pasture though. Jud is tied outside."

Why hadn't he mentioned the stranger? Either nothing had happened, or he hadn't wanted to upset Liberty's mother. Phoebe wouldn't rest easy until she knew the truth. "May I have a word with you?" She avoided looking at Ma, who wouldn't approve of her forwardness.

Surprise flitted across Will's face, but he swiftly recovered his composure.

"Mr. Canfield wants to take care of his horse." Ma spoke before Will had the chance.

"That's all right, Mrs. Walsh." He smiled with a touch of gallantry. "Phoebe's welcome to come along."

Ma frowned. "All right, but only for a short while. She'll want to be here when Liberty returns."

"Sure, Ma." Phoebe smiled reassuringly. Her mother seemed to think she was chasing after Will. Nothing could be further from the truth. Sure, he was handsome—maybe too handsome. Phoebe couldn't deny that she felt exhilarated whenever he was around. That didn't mean anything though. Neither did the heady sensation of being in his arms…

She would head back as soon as possible.

Will held the door for Phoebe, wondering if he'd lost his mind. Phoebe stepped past him, too close for comfort, and he caught the clean scent of her hair. Giving himself a silent lecture, he untied his horse and started for the pasture. He should have let Phoebe's ma discourage her advances rather than tacitly approving them. This was how the charming young miss got her way so often. Whatever husband took her on would need a strong mind to match her strength of will.

"Would you please slow down?" Phoebe called from behind him.

"Sorry." He stopped and waited for her.

She caught up to him. "If you don't want to walk together, why invite me?"

"I'm fairly certain you invited yourself." Will recognized that he didn't sound welcoming. "Not that I mind."

"Really?" She gave him a doubtful glance. "I don't have to come if you want to be alone."

Will might not be the most perceptive person when it came to emotions, and even less so where women were involved. Even so, he could tell that Phoebe sounded hurt.

He sighed. "What's on your mind?"

"I was wondering--that stranger I saw—did he bother Liberty?"

"He was with her, but it turned out all right. That man may look rough, but he's a deputy sheriff." He set off, amending his pace for her.

"I'd never have guessed it. I suppose you didn't mention him because he's harmless."

"I don't know him well enough to say that, but he didn't lay a finger on Liberty. He lectured her, rightly in my opinion, for straying so far from home." He glanced sideways at her. "I'd say the same to you."

Phoebe's forehead creased. "We didn't mean to go so far, but we lost track."

"What an excuse." He shook his head.

"I suppose such a thing has never happened to you."

Will halted in the barnyard. "Was there anything else you wanted?"

"That's all, thank you." Her tone was so sharp it could have cut diamonds.

Phoebe's wounded gaze made him regret his curtness. It wasn't her fault that she roused feelings he'd rather not face.

He led his horse across the road to the pasture. Phoebe didn't follow, which was fine by him. Being with Phoebe felt natural, a fact heady enough to scare a man half to death. He'd already recognized all the signs he'd seen in himself once before. His romance had ended when his bride-to-be jilted him on their wedding day.

No, sir. He had no intention of falling in love again.

Scout's hooves clopped in a steady rhythm as Jake brought Liberty home. The morning dew had vanished from the fields, and the sun shone in a clear sky. The Bitterroot Mountains stood in sharp relief, making them appear closer. A flock of geese honked as they flew in formation toward the river. Liberty was safe in his keeping. How right that felt.

He would content himself with this moment, always.

"Jake?"

"Hmm?" Liberty's soft call roused him from his thoughts.

"There's something I need to say to you—about what happened at the meeting hall."

He frowned. "I'm not sure this is a good time."

"No, please let me speak. This isn't easy."

He relinquished the interlude of peace. "All right." Why Liberty wanted to revisit their falling-out right now escaped him. She seemed unaware of the toll today's ordeal had taken on them both. He must have lost seven years of his life worrying about her.

She cleared her throat. "I owe you an apology."

He glanced at her in surprise. "Why?"

"I encouraged Beau to put you off." She brought her words out in a rush.

He shrugged. "I figured as much."

"I'm ashamed of my behavior and so sorry it hurt you. It wasn't planned, if that's any comfort." She shook her head. "Beau deserves an apology too."

"Oh really?" He quirked a brow. "I doubt it would sink in."

He could tell from her expression that she agreed with his assessment but was too polite to say so.

Her eyes brightened, and she looked away. "I feel responsible for what happened between you and Beau."

He sighed. "Liberty, I'm accountable for my own actions."

"Yes, but I egged you on, and that was wrong."

"You wouldn't have done it if I hadn't crowded you." Jake shook his head. "I need to ask your forgiveness for that."

"I do forgive you." Her eyes sparkled with tears. "I hope you'll do the same for me."

Jake ached to embrace Liberty and kiss away her every sorrow.

"Before you answer, there's more." She heaved a shaky breath. "I pretended with you too."

Jake wasn't sure he wanted to know. "Maybe we should talk about it later."

"This shouldn't wait, and I'm leaving tomorrow for a couple of weeks with Phoebe."

He sighed. "Go on."

"I wanted so badly to keep your friendship that I didn't want to believe that it was impossible. I'm sorry, truly sorry, for how much I must have hurt you."

She'd left him with nothing to hold onto—not even a slender strand of hope. Even so, she deserved an answer. He would forgive her anything, even this blow, which she'd dealt in the name of kindness. "I will always forgive you, Liberty, no matter what."

Jake watched her tears fall, but there was nothing he could do to relieve them. He might not agree with her assessment, but she believed it. He walked on, giving her the silence she needed to compose herself. His state wasn't much better, and he was relieved when they reached her house.

He swung Liberty down from the saddle and gripped her arm while she struggled to climb the steps to the porch. She bit her lip, and her eyes shone with tears. It was hard to watch when he had all the strength she needed. He touched her shoulder. "Let me."

Liberty turned to him, and Jake lifted her. He carried her up the steps, lingering this last time he would ever hold her.

Liberty held Jake's gaze as he deposited her in one of the overstuffed chairs in the parlor. "Thank you for everything."

"You're most welcome." He positioned a footstool before her, then stepped back.

Ma, Phoebe, and Aunt Maisey rushed in.

Phoebe wedged Liberty into her chair with several cushions. "Is that more comfortable?"

Liberty nodded. "It helps."

Aunt Maisey studied Liberty. "I'll bet you could use a cup of tea."

Liberty smiled. "That sounds wonderful."

Aunt Maisey nodded. "I'll be right back."

Ma bent beside Liberty's footstool. "That shoe needs to come off."

Liberty winced in anticipation. Although Ma freed her foot with gentle hands, Liberty gasped in pain.

Ma stood up. "I'd better take a needle to those splinters."

Liberty nodded, accepting her fate. "Jake and Phoebe removed the worst ones."

Ma paused on her way to the door. "I'm surprised you let anyone near you."

"They talked me into it."

Jake shook his head. "Liberty had the sense to accept help when she needed it."

"I'm grateful for that." Ma smiled.

Jake walked from the room with Ma following. Liberty could hear them murmuring in the hallway but couldn't make out what they said. A moment later, the front door opened and closed.

Aunt Maisey returned a short while later. "This should fix you up." She lowered the tea tray to the table beside Liberty's chair. The fragrance of Earl Grey wafted to Liberty. She leaned against the headrest and let out a sigh. If she sat very still, her ankle didn't throb so badly.

A short while later, Doc Bailey came into the room and peered at her over his spectacles. "Jake Buckthorn tells me that you hurt yourself."

Liberty must have slumped in the chair while dozing. She pulled herself upright and sucked in her breath at the pain.

The doctor set down his bag and knelt beside her footstool. Freed from the confines of her shoe, Liberty's ankle had swollen further, and the bruise had darkened to deep red. "How did this happen?"

"A log I stepped over looked sound but was splintered on the back side. My foot caught in a gash in the wood hidden by the underbrush. I put my weight down, and my ankle twisted. I think it's sprained."

"That sounds painful." He prodded her injury. "I don't think you broke your ankle, but you do have a sprain."

Liberty groaned. "How bad is it?"

"Rest your foot as much as possible. I'd be surprised if it doesn't heal within a couple of weeks."

"That long?" She didn't want to be disabled the whole time at Phoebe's ranch.

He pinned her with another glance over the top of his spectacles "Be glad I didn't say six weeks. Let's take a look at that leg."

Liberty had little difficulty following the doctor's orders to rest. After he departed, leaving her with a newly bandaged leg and a wrapped ankle, she could barely keep her eyes open.

Ma offered her food, but all Liberty wanted was sleep. Pa would come home soon with her brothers, cousins, and uncles. She didn't want to explain her misadventure all over again for them. She would leave that to Phoebe, who liked to talk far more than she did.

Jake hadn't returned after fetching the doctor. He must have gone home. That was for the best—of course it was. Having Jake around confused her.

She'd worked out what to do about him while awaiting rescue. More than anything, she wanted to stop hurting him. That meant making a clear decision and abiding by it. Her choices could not be plainer—marry him or let him go. The first was impossible. She needed to bring a man into her family who would help Pa with his ministry. Pa hadn't asked this of her, but she considered it her duty.

Liberty couldn't even picture Jake as the man she should marry. Deputy Manchin's story of men going off to fight for their principles--only to become outlaws—broke her heart. There were so many lost souls in the world. Even a preacher's flesh-and-blood was not immune to corruption. That fact should serve as a warning to her. It was quite possible to want someone unsuitable, like Jake.

It pained Liberty to admit it, but only one choice remained to her.

Bringing Liberty safely home was reward enough, but the memory of her thanks sweetened Jake's walk home. He led Scout into his stall and poured an extra measure of oats into the feeding trough. His horse had earned his feed today.

Jake found his mother in the kitchen, stirring a steaming concoction that smelled wonderful. He would do his best to muster an appetite.

Ma's smile lit her whole face. "You're back in time for supper. I was beginning to wonder. Did you post my letter to Aunt May?"

"I'll mail it tomorrow. I forgot all about it, I'm afraid."

Her eyebrows drew together. "But that's why you went to town."

"I ran into trouble—or I should say it ran into me." Being clear about such things mattered.

She narrowed her eyes. "Have you been up to something?"

He sighed. "No, Ma."

Concern chased suspicion from her face. "What happened?"

"Liberty injured herself on the road to town, and Phoebe asked me to check on her. I wound up bringing her home."

"I see." She stirred the pot for a moment. "I'm sorry I

misjudged you."

"I wish you wouldn't have, but I understand." He truly did. Lost trust was hard to regain. Maybe his moving out of town would help her get over his early antics. He'd made his decision final somewhere between the barn and house. It made sense. Liberty would only be gone for a couple of weeks. He needed longer than that to get over her—much longer—perhaps a lifetime. He wouldn't stay away from home that long though.

He would speak to Ma about it, but not at the moment. Otherwise, she might conclude that he wanted to go because she'd wounded him. Besides that, he'd already dealt with enough emotion for one day.

"Is Liberty all right?"

He straddled one of the chairs at the kitchen table. "I think her main complaint is a sprained ankle, but even that isn't too serious. When's supper?"

"It's ready. Bacon stew and cornbread."

"I'll wash up at the pump."

"Jake?"

He paused at the back door and looked over his shoulder. "What?"

She offered him a smile. "I'm proud of you for looking after Liberty."

"Thanks, Ma." It didn't change much, but it was nice to know.

At the pump, Jake ducked his head under the spray, as if that might drive thoughts of the woman he loved out of his mind. He shook his head like a dog ridding itself of water and smiled despite himself. No more indecision. He'd decided his course. Ma would need a little time to adjust, but he had no doubt she would support his decision.

He didn't look forward to saying goodbye to Liberty. After

all they'd been to one another through the years, it wouldn't be right to leave without telling her. He'd stop by in the morning before she went to the ranch. That idea banished his appetite altogether.

CHAPTER EIGHT

LIBERTY WOKE AT DAWN, THE RESULT of falling asleep so early the night before. She yawned and stretched, instantly reminded of her sore leg. Doc Bailey's measures must be working, for the constant throbbing had dwindled.

She felt a bit foolish about all the fuss over her injuries. After attempting to stand, she revised her opinion. Liberty reached for the crutch the doctor had left. Hopefully, using it would alleviate any concerns her parents might have about her traveling to Phoebe's ranch.

For Jake's sake as well as her own, she needed to go away. Remembering their last conversation brought on pain of another kind. Her words had hurt him, but she couldn't take them back. Jake's look of sorrow had reduced her to tears but comforting him would have been heartless. Jake needed her to stay away from him. Only then could he forget her and find someone else to love. The thought of him marrying another was almost more than she could bear.

Liberty brushed away tears. She would never admit to Jake that she needed to recover from losing him. It wouldn't be fair to let him think she might welcome his advances when he'd never qualify as a preacher's son-in-law.

She pulled her thoughts from the edge of grief. Pining over what she couldn't have would provide no benefit. She busied herself with dressing, which proved a little tricky. She managed, however, without asking for help. Her mother was rustling about in the kitchen. The flour sack gaped open on the counter, and a wooden spoon waited in the large bowl Ma used to mix bread dough.

"I heard you thumping down the hallway." Ma placed a tin of salt next to the flour sack. "How are you this morning?"

"I'm doing well, considering." Liberty glanced down at her bandaged ankle. "I can't wear my other shoe. I'll pack it. Before I come back, it should fit again."

A crease appeared between Ma's brows. "Are you sure you want to go? Phoebe would understand if you didn't feel up to it."

"I'm fine, apart from being clumsy." Thankful Ma was leaving the decision to her, Liberty sank onto a chair at the table.

Ma measured flour into her bowl. "I'll change your dressing before you go and send the salve with you. Promise me you'll look after your injury."

"Don't worry, Ma. I won't neglect myself. Phoebe wouldn't let me anyway."

Ma smiled. "I'm sure you're right."

A light knock sounded on the back door. Ma looked out the window. "It's Jake. He must have seen the smoke from the cookstove."

"What does he want this early?" Liberty couldn't help sounding defensive.

"I have no idea, but there's one way to find out." Ma opened the door.

"Morning, Mrs. Reed." Jake looked past Ma. "Sorry to disturb you so early, but I'd like a word with Liberty. Since she's leaving today, I didn't want to miss her."

Ma smiled at Liberty. "Would you two like to visit in the parlor?"

No, she would not like an intimate meeting with Jake alone in the parlor. She thought they'd discussed everything yesterday. *On the other hand, if I don't let Jake speak his mind, I'll wonder ever after what he'd come to say.* Liberty stood with the aid of her crutch.

Jake watched her from bloodshot eyes. Her conscience pricked her. He looked like he hadn't slept well.

She led the way into the parlor, conscious of the awkwardness of her movements.

Jake waited until she was seated before lowering himself into the overstuffed chair opposite her. "You seem less in pain today."

"I am." So much for attempting to hide her misery from him yesterday. She had clearly failed. At a loss for further words, she waited for him to speak.

Jake cleared his throat. "I didn't want to leave without saying goodbye to you. I've decided to try my hand at gold mining."

"What?" She stared at him. "How did you decide this so quickly? You didn't mention it yesterday."

"I made up my mind last night, but I've been thinking about it for some time."

What about your mother? Your family?" Liberty stopped short of adding herself to the list of Jake's loved ones. "Won't you miss them?"

"I imagine so, but I'll come back in a year or two."

"That long?" The room darkened at the edges. Liberty passed a hand over her eyes.

"Are you all right?" Jake's voice came from far away.

"Not at the moment. This is quite a—a surprise." She'd almost called it a shock. "You don't need to do this on account of me, if that's the reason."

He shook his head. "You enter into it, but this is my choice."

Reminding Jake that his decisions often went awry wouldn't go over well. How had this happened? Only a few days ago, he'd kissed her and reminded her of their promises to marry one another. She found it hard to grasp that he would let go with such speed. Maybe he'd never really loved her. Liberty bit her lip, holding back tears. She'd cried a lot lately on account of Jake. Today would be no exception. "I hope you find lots of gold, if that's what you want."

Jake gripped the arms of his chair. "I can't have what I really want."

Seeing him so tortured did not bring Liberty joy. He should go. Discouraging him from his intentions would be selfish. She extended a hand to him. "Goodbye, Jake. May you find plenty of gold and even more happiness."

He caressed the back of her hand with his thumb. "I won't forget you."

Liberty nodded but couldn't speak. She would weep, and then he would know the depth of her devastation. That would never do.

Jake kissed her hand in the place where his thumb had lingered. "Goodbye, Liberty." He rose abruptly and strode from the room.

Liberty touched her cheek, where tears had begun to fall. Jake had lived next door since she could remember. Life without him near didn't make sense. She curled into her chair and cradled the hand he'd kissed.

She could still feel the imprint of his lips.

A knock at the front door made her jump. Who would call this early? She couldn't face anyone, but Ma was speaking to someone in the entryway. It was too late to slip away. Liberty picked up her crutch and stumped to the gilded mirror above the bookshelves. A masculine voice she unfortunately recognized joined Ma's higher-pitched tones. Liberty scrubbed at her cheeks to dry them. She turned as Ma led Beau into the parlor.

"Mr. Hensley has ridden from town to inquire after you."

Liberty wasn't quite sure what to do. Pa made everyone welcome, and she always tried to follow his example. Surely though, Pa wouldn't expect her to entertain someone who intruded on her.

Ma's smile faded, and a crease formed between her brows. "Perhaps this isn't a good time."

"What happened?" Beau ventured farther into the room, his bowler hat in his hand. "I left you complaining of a headache and find you on crutches."

"It sounds ridiculous, but I ran afoul of a log."

Beau frowned. "That is unfortunate. May I assist you in some way?" He looked genuinely concerned. Had she misjudged him, yet again? With a glint in his blue eyes and his black hair combed into smooth wings, he could turn a few heads. Liberty sighed. She didn't fancy Beau. Persuading herself otherwise would lead to grief.

She restrained the comment that he could help her most by leaving. She wanted to discourage Beau's advances without creating a fuss in her parent's front parlor. Her nerves were frayed from parting with Jake, but she would do her best. "Thank you, but I am well looked after by my family."

"Then I will leave you to their care." He stood, clutching his hat. ""I'll check on you in a couple of days."

Liberty released a sigh. It was high time she made herself understood. Having done so with Jake made rejecting Beau seem easier. "That won't be necessary, Mr. Hensley. You must place your interest elsewhere."

Jake met no one on the way to town, which was fortunate.

Sometimes a man needed privacy. Suspecting that would be the case this morning, he'd saddled and bridled Scout before saying goodbye to Liberty. The smoke curling from the town's chimneys told the story of happy families gathered around the table. Breakfast would be over by now, but a cookfire took a while to die out.

Like a smoldering fire, love might linger but finally extinguish. He hoped so, because he didn't want to go through life with this burden of sorrow. All he could do was carry it until it faded, if it ever would. He had his doubts.

Jake wondered, not for the first time, why so many counted romance essential. Except for the brief interlude of bliss when he'd believed Liberty wanted to marry him, it had felt more like a kick in the chest. Love caused people to act stupidly, himself included.

This was no time for self-reproach. He'd made mistakes with Liberty, but he'd tried his best to show her his love. That was all anyone could do.

You could try really hard to make Liberty like you, but she either does or doesn't.

Jake smiled at the remembered words. He'd love to have a conversation with his eight-year-old self. Solutions to his problems were clearer then. When Pa died, he'd lost his edge.

With an effort, he diverted his thoughts from their present course. He'd gain nothing by dwelling on what might have been. Ma's letter needed mailing, but the post office wouldn't open for a little while. He headed to the place in town that would welcome a visitor this early. Having grown up on a farm, Scotty Wells rolled out of bed before dawn from long habit. He brewed coffee on the general store's pot-bellied stove and unlocked the doors shortly thereafter. Any and all were welcome to join him for a cup. They might also expect an invitation to a game of chess on a board balanced atop an overturned barrel. Whenever Jake tried his hand, he lost. That didn't matter. He played not to win but to listen to Scotty's ongoing patter, which he found oddly comforting. Jake fancied that the world might end, but the stream of words would go on.

The general store's door rattled beneath Jake's hand as he shoved it open, and the floor creaked under his boots. He threaded through a maze of tall shelves displaying cast-iron cookware, tools, and tinned food. Scotty's pride and joy, a newfangled contraption he called a percolator, was heating on top of the potbellied stove.

"Good mornin' to you, Jake!" Scotty stood up from his stool by the stove. "You've gone to bed with the chickens and gotten up with the cows, I see. Wise fellow. The coffee's about to perk." On the high side of forty, he possessed the strength and stature of a younger man. His brown mane was thick although threaded by gray. The marks of time also showed in lines that creased the corners of his eyes and bracketed his mouth. "Grab a cup and have a seat."

"Thanks." Jake mustered a smile and followed his instructions.

"You look a mite peaked, on second glance. That coffee should come in handy. Did you go to bed with the owls, after all?"

Jake opened his mouth to reply.

"'Course, when you're young, you can get away with that. These old bones would never put up with such a thing."

Jake relaxed in his chair. He might have known his host would save him from answering.

"Trouble of the feminine variety—that's the only affliction I know what gives a man a frown like that." Scotty paused invitingly.

Jake didn't feel inclined to discuss his woes over coffee at the general store. A change of subject seemed in order. "I'm waiting for the post office to open. Ma wants a letter mailed."

"Your ma's a fine filly, and no mistake. If I wasn't set in my ways— Ah, but no one could replace my Margaret. A letter, did you say? Why, I recall a trip to the post office in heavy snow…"

Jake stopped attending but let Scotty's voice wash over him in a soothing tide. He would miss coffee and conversation by the pot-bellied stove. When he thought about it, he'd miss a lot more than the general store. Seeing the mist in the mountains after a rain could make a person feel new again. A flock of geese lifting off the Bitterroot River always put him in awe. Without the Creator, how would the birds know to fly in formation? Jake was used to hearing the bell in the church steeple ring out on a Sunday morning. No other would sound the same, assuming he heard any. Gold camps were notoriously low on church bells.

Noticing a lull in the monologue, Jake glanced up. His host must be waiting for a reply, although to what he had no idea.

Scotty smiled. "Got your head in the clouds, don't you? A woman can have that effect on a man." He chuckled, much taken by his own humor.

Jake saw nothing amusing in Scotty's words, but he kept his opinion to himself.

Scotty sobered. "I asked if you'd seen Beau Hensley lately."

Jake resisted the urge to scowl at the mention of Beau. "Can't say that I have."

"He went missing yesterday. I expect he'll show up with an explanation. Between you and me, he has a lot to learn as an employee."

"If he's not pulling his weight—"

"I know, I know." Scotty waved a hand. "I'll fire him if necessary, but not in haste. And don't go calling me tenderhearted. I get that enough from your ma."

Jake smiled, diverted despite himself at Ma calling this grizzled bachelor tender-hearted. The fact that Ma was right was probably why her suggestion annoyed him.

Jake finished his coffee and spent another half hour breaking away. He might not have managed so quickly, but the day's first customer provided a distraction.

From behind the post office counter, Martha Riddler showed her pearly teeth in a smile. "Nice to see you, Jake." Her honeyed tones let him know she meant every word.

"Morning." He gave her a grudging smile. Martha had become something of a beauty since her awkward school days. Her welcome salved his wounded ego, but he couldn't stomach the thought of romancing anyone but Liberty.

Martha weighed and stamped Ma's letter, and then accepted his payment. "Here's your mail."

His fingertips touched her palm as he took possession of several envelopes and a newspaper. "Thanks."

"My pleasure."

Jake couldn't miss the wistfulness in her gaze. A rush of sympathy warmed him. He knew all too well the unhappiness of desiring someone who didn't want you back. The reaction she drew from him was all the more reason to leave the post office, and quickly.

He was halfway to the door when he stopped short. Grady Bradshaw stared at him from a wanted poster on the wall, his bowler cocked at a rakish angle. A lock of curly hair strayed from beneath his hat, and the lips between his mustache and beard framed a mocking smile. It was hard to picture this character as an innocent young man following his older brothers into trouble—not when the tilt of his head conveyed supreme arrogance.

Jake stared at the poster. The likeness was poorly drawn, but Grady Bradshaw struck Jake as a tough character.

Liberty remained in the parlor with her foot up while Ma made breakfast with Maisey and Phoebe's help. She felt an odd detachment. At any minute, she might wake from a bad dream and discover Jake had never talked of leaving. Not wanting to believe it would happen, she pushed him from her mind—or at least she tried. Thoughts of Jake had a way of returning. Liberty leaned her head against her chair and tried to think of nothing at all.

"More tea?" Aunt Maisey stood before her, holding the blue willow pot aloft. "There's a drop or two still, if you want it."

"No thanks. Maybe Phoebe wants it."

"Phoebe is helping your ma with the dishes." Aunt Maisey sat in the overstuffed chair that faced Liberty's "If you're tired, go back to bed."

"I should pack."

"You can always do that later. Rob and I decided you need a day to recover from your ordeal. He and our boys started home after breakfast. We can't expect the neighbors to take care of our place too long. We ladies will travel tomorrow with Mr. Canfield. Con's new ranch manager stayed behind yesterday to help with the roof. He's happy to escort us."

"How sweet of you all." Tears pricked Liberty's eyes.

Aunt Maisey touched her shoulder. "Why don't you go lie down?"

"I'm not sleepy." Liberty sat taller in her chair. "I do feel sluggish though."

"A breath of fresh air on the porch would do you good."

Taken by the idea, Liberty maneuvered onto her feet and made her way outside without a hitch. Smaller than the back stoop, the front porch presented fewer steps to navigate.

Liberty closed her eyes, lifted her face, and savored the fresh air. The walkway lured her to the roses blossoming at the trellised gate. She breathed in their sweet aroma and found herself seized by the yearning to hide away, if only for a little while. She wouldn't stay away long enough for Ma to notice.

Walking with a crutch became easier with practice, and Liberty soon ducked into the coolness of the barn. While building the church, Pa had told her that barns often shared architectural styles with cathedrals. Maybe that was why the silence and light filtering through the high windows reminded her of a church during prayer. Aware all at once of why she'd come, Liberty knelt beside a bale in the hay mow.

God, please keep Jake safe while he's gone, and don't let him forget the way home.

"Do you want to explain why you've behaved strangely lately?" Pa's voice woke Liberty. Hay tickled her cheek. She raised up partway, but then lay flat again. Pa wasn't talking to her but to Ma, standing beside him near the barn doorway. With a quick glance, she located her crutch out of sight behind the stacked bales.

Liberty didn't want to eavesdrop on her parents' conversation. Neither did she want them to see her in such a state. Tears had followed her prayers, and then apparently sleep. She must look a mess. Her parents would ask questions she didn't want to answer. She might confide in her mother, but later—after the shock of Jake's news wore off.

"Is that why you dragged me into the barn?" Ma sounded miffed.

"I thought we needed privacy."

"I'm not sure we have it. Mr. Canfield might come in."

"He's gone to town. Stop stalling and tell me what's bothering you."

"I'm not stalling. In fact, I've been meaning to talk to you." Silence followed.

'Go ahead." A touch of humor crept into Pa's voice. "Here's your chance."

"Last time we went to the general store, I noticed a poster for Doc Woburn's traveling medicine show."

"I heard that it's coming. I'm not interested in that sort of entertainment. Seth wants to go, and I imagine Liberty would enjoy it. What does it have to do with anything?"

"Kyle Woburn's face was on the poster."

Pa didn't speak right away. "You can't mean Liberty's father?"

CHAPTER NINE

Liberty's stomach churned. *Why would Pa call someone else my father?*

"Yes, Liberty's father." Ma's voice shook. "I've agonized over whether it was wrong to keep Liberty from him."

"You didn't know his whereabouts, which is altogether different," Pa murmured.

"I might have tried to find him."

"Why would you?"

"For Liberty's sake."

Her parent's voices sounded nearer. After what Liberty had overheard, the prospect of being discovered took on even more horror. She curled into a ball, wishing she could vanish.

"America, you're not thinking clearly. Must I remind you that Kyle abandoned you and Liberty, not the other way around?"

"I haven't forgotten. How could I? Liberty's eyes are so like Kyle's. Sometimes looking at her brings him to mind. For all I know, he died while fighting for the Confederacy." Ma sighed. "Not knowing whether he was alive was easier than this."

"I'm sorry, sweetheart. Come here."

Time passed with nothing more spoken. Liberty risked a glance but ducked down as her parents broke apart from their embrace.

Ma sniffed. "I can't help thinking that Liberty should know about her father."

"I'm not sure I agree. Finding out she is illegitimate would destroy Liberty's confidence and complicate her life for no good reason."

Liberty restrained her gasp. She could hardly credit what she'd heard.

"That's the conclusion I always reach." Ma hiccupped. "Keeping secrets weighs on me."

"You don't carry this burden alone," Pa murmured. "Why didn't you tell me about the poster sooner?"

"I hated to trouble you."

"Darling wife, haven't you learned that whatever affects you never fails to touch me?"

Another silence stretched, so long that Liberty wondered if her parents had left the barn. She peeked over the stacked hay bales and glimpsed Pa holding Ma once more. He kissed the top of Ma's head. "The past is dead and gone, America. We need to leave it there."

Ma nodded. "I'm sure you're right."

"Come back to the house and I'll make you tea." Pa turned toward the doorway, his arm around Ma. She leaned on him as they left the barn.

Liberty waited a long time after their footsteps faded before moving. She didn't want a discussion with her parents. That might cause more sorrow, and Ma had suffered enough on account of her. Her parents hadn't seemed to fear being overheard, but they'd probably thought they knew the whereabouts of their children. Aunt Maisey could well have assumed Liberty had gone to bed. She should return home quietly and hide away in her bedroom. Liberty abandoned her hiding place and negotiated across the barn with the aid of her crutch.

A red-tailed hawk squealed as she emerged. The bird's eerie hunting cry raised goosebumps on her arms. Liberty shielded her eyes against the sun. The hawk sailed over the road and patrolled the pasture. The horses tore at the grass, undisturbed by the bird-of-prey spreading its wings above them.

Liberty couldn't pretend to be unaffected by what she'd heard. Carrying on with normal life felt impossible. She needed time before slipping into the house. Moments ago, she'd lost the only father she'd ever known. She'd acquired another, but one who seemed less worthy of the position. She had also learned the unfortunate circumstances of her birth.

The tunnel of trees on the way to the cabin swallowed her. The path made no sound beneath her feet, creating the sensation of floating in an endless dream. The cabin sat on its haunches, a wolf waiting to spring…

Liberty jerked her mind out of its odd fancies and continued past the schoolteacher's cabin into the grove. Her footsteps slowed. Cottonwood fluff formed drifts underfoot, and dangling flowers yet to burst perfumed the air. The remains of a treehouse Jake and Seth once helped her build peeked out from between gnarled branches. Liberty couldn't fit through the rough opening anymore, but her sisters and Liam still enjoyed it. She came to the tree where she'd given Jake her promise, the one where not long ago he kissed her. Liberty slid her hand along the rough bark, remembering. She climbed to the low branch. Sitting here without Jake stirred her misery, but she'd rather suffer than endure the wretched numbness she'd felt since learning the truth about herself.

About to sit down, Jake paused in front of the parlor window. The woman hurrying along the path into the cottonwood grove could only be Liberty, but he'd never seen her so unkempt. Having partly escaped its pins, her hair floated about her like a golden halo gone awry. Her clothing was disheveled, and her shoulders slumped as if she carried an invisible weight.

Why was she still here? He thought she'd gone home with Phoebe.

Jake headed for the front door. He couldn't stand by when Liberty needed help.

He found her in the tree, seated in her usual spot. "Are you all right?" he called up to her.

"It's—" Liberty shook her head. "It's hard to explain."

He climbed to the place he normally sat. "I have time to listen."

"I overheard my parents talking about me. I can't believe— oh what am I going to do!"

"Look at me, Liberty." He waited for her to comply. "Close your eyes and take a deep breath."

She lowered her lashes. Her chest rose and fell.

"Again." Jake watched as her breathing slowed. "Tell me what's on your mind."

She opened her eyes. "Do you know about the medicine show coming to town?"

"Yes, but why bring it up?"

"Apparently, Doc Woburn is my father."

He stared at her. "How can that be? Reverend Hayes is your father."

She gazed into the distance. "I wish that were true."

"Forgive me, but I'm having trouble taking this in."

"How do you think I feel?" She turned her head so quickly more pins flew. Her hair tumbled around her shoulders. "Everything I thought about myself was a lie."

"You're not reacting logically." He paced the words evenly, hoping they might steady her. "Wait until you have all the facts."

"What do you mean?" She watched him from wary eyes. "I just told you the facts."

"Overhearing a conversation won't inform you of every detail. I can't credit that your parents would do anything to harm you."

"I thought that too." Liberty nodded, and a lock of hair fell across her eyes. She poked at her tresses in a feeble attempt to restore order.

"What did your parents say to make you mistrust them?"

"It's what they didn't say. All my life, they let me believe Pa is my real father when he's not." Liberty looked away from him. "They never let on that I was born out of wedlock."

"Why would you want them to?"

"Because it's the truth." Tears fell to her cheek, and she scrubbed at them with the back of her hand.

He shook his head. "Your parents wanted to protect you. Don't fault them for that."

"It would almost be easier if I could, but I can't."

"Knowing the irregular circumstances of your birth might have marked your mind. Instead, you grew up feeling worthy as anyone else—which you are, by the way."

Liberty drew a shaky breath. "It hurts to lose your father."

"You haven't. You've gained an extra one."

"It isn't so simple." She bit her lip and waited a moment before going on in a calmer voice. "My natural father abandoned me once. I doubt he'd want me now."

"Then consider yourself fortunate to have two wonderful parents."

She frowned. "I thought you'd understand."

"Forgive me if I find it difficult. You're upset at having two fathers. Some of us have none." He would give anything to have his own pa back. Five years later, he still had trouble accepting that couldn't ever happen. He would see Pa no more this side of heaven. Reverend Hayes might not be Liberty's natural father, but he'd raised her as his own. In Jake's book, that counted for more. Hopefully, Liberty would come to the same conclusion.

Jake closed his front door rather firmly, but then regretted giving in to irritation. He should have been more tolerant of Liberty. She'd received a nasty shock.

The incident provided the springboard Jake needed to confide in his mother. He hoped she would take his leaving well and not think of Ben. Jake suspected he knew the reason his oldest brother had departed so abruptly. He didn't think it was coincidence that Ben had ridden out of town right after Gideon married Emma. Hopefully, Ben would find happiness and remember to come home once in a while. Maybe then Ma wouldn't look sad when she thought no one was looking. Jake had no intention of adding to his mother's sorrows. He would make sure she had plenty of letters and visits.

The house was too silent. He knew that at once. Ma's passion for cooking kept her busy. She should be rattling the pots and clanging pans as usual. He hurried down the hallway to the kitchen.

Through the archway, he caught sight of his mother lying motionless on the floor. Her eyes were closed, and a waxen sheen covered her face. He couldn't tell if she was breathing.

"Ma!" Jake rushed to her. He felt her pulse and found it light and fast, but present. She must have fainted.

Jake gathered his mother into his arms. He carried her into her bedroom and laid her on the bed. Her eyelids twitched, and she moaned. He loosened her collar and picked up a fan on the side table. Fanning the air stirred stray tendrils of her hair.

Ma's eyes fluttered open. "What happened?"

"You fainted."

"I did?"

Jake warmed her hands in his own. "How do you feel?"

"I—I don't know." Ma tried to sit up.

Jake pushed her down gently. "Lie still, and I'll get you some water."

"I won't argue with you." She settled back against her pillow.

Jake returned a few minutes later with a pitcher and a glass filled with water.

Ma sat up in bed as he approached. She seemed more alert, and her color appeared better. He held the glass to her lips. "Drink this down."

She grasped the glass with hands that shook.

Jake held onto it as she drank. After she drained the contents, he refilled the glass and placed it on the wooden coaster she kept on her carved rosewood night table. "I'll go for the doctor."

"Must you? I'm sure it wasn't serious."

"We'll let the doctor decide that." Jake set the pitcher within her reach on a folded copy of the latest newspaper. "I'll ask Mrs. Hayes to sit with you."

"I hate to impose."

"I doubt she'll mind." Jake looked back from the doorway. "Promise me you'll stay put while I'm gone."

She arched her eyebrows. "I don't plan to go any further than my pillow."

Jake smiled. His mother seemed to be recovering her spunk. Even so, he took the porch steps two at a time.

America opened the back door at Jake's knock. "Ma fainted. I need to ride for the doctor. Would you please sit with her?" He explained the situation in as few words as possible.

"I'd be happy to watch over Felicity." She untied her apron. "I'll be right over."

"I appreciate your help." Jake hurried to his barn and saddled Scout. He came out in time to see America going into his house by the front door. Thankful his ma would be well looked after, Jake sprang onto his horse.

The thudding of his horse's hooves reminded him of Ma's rapid heartbeat earlier. *Please God, let her be all right.* Losing his mother so soon after Pa's death would be too hard to bear. Doc Bailey lived about twenty minutes away down the road toward Liberty township. He probably made the ride in less time, but it seemed to go on forever.

Jake dismounted when he reached the Bailey house. He pounded up the porch steps.

The doctor opened the door before he could knock. "I heard you coming a mile away. What's wrong?"

"Ma fainted."

"I'll get my bag." Doc Bailey withdrew into the house but returned a moment later with a black valise in his hands. He gave Jake a kindly smile. "Go back to your ma, Jake. I'll be along as soon as I saddle my horse."

The journey home seemed even longer than the ride out. When he reached home, Jake stomped up the steps and into the house. He stopped short outside his mother's doorway.

Ma was sitting up in bed, by all appearances hosting a small tea party with America as her guest. She raised her eyebrows. "There's no need to come thumping into my room, Son."

"Doc's on his way."

"I hope you haven't pulled him away from important matters. I'm fine, as you can see."

"Then you won't mind him verifying that fact." Jake didn't miss a beat.

"You won't need me anymore." America stood up. "I would like to know the doctor's findings, if you don't mind."

"Of course not." Ma set her tea cup on the side table. "You're the same as family."

Doc Bailey arrived shortly after America left. He carried his medical bag into Ma's room. Jake waited outside the door for the doctor's verdict. Pacing relieved the strain of waiting. He didn't like thinking of his mother in need of medical attention. Despite Ma's protests of robust health, she'd been unconscious not too long ago.

Finally, the door opened, and Doc Bailey slipped into the hallway. "Let's go somewhere private, shall we?"

"Sure." Jake led the way into the parlor. He struck a match and lit the oil lamp on a marble-topped side table. Flocked birds that perched on gilded branches in the wallpaper jumped in the sudden light.

The doctor sat on the oversized rosewood sofa. "I'll come right out and say that I'm not sure why Felicity fainted. It could have happened for a lot of reasons."

Jake sank onto the straight-backed chair facing him. "Are any of them serious?"

"Yes." Doc Bailey glanced at him over his spectacles. "I have some questions to ask you. Felicity is not a well of information at the moment."

"Ma's determined that she's enjoying good health."

"Deciding on something doesn't make it so." Doc Bailey frowned. "Although, if anyone ever could, it would be Felicity."

Jake smiled at the doctor's apt assessment of his mother's character.

"Does she drink enough water?"

"I haven't paid attention, to be honest."

"Maybe you should. Has she seemed tired lately?"

Jake thought back. "I believe so, now you mention it."

"I suggest that you monitor her. If it happens again, we'd

have more of an idea of the reason."

"All right, but I'll have to watch her without letting on."

"I understand completely." Doc Bailey picked up his bag and stood. "Let's hope your ma only suffered from dehydration."

"I'll make sure she has plenty to drink."

"I'm counting on you to watch over your ma and report on anything you notice amiss." Doc Bailey clapped his shoulder. "If you'll excuse me, I have a very good supper waiting."

Jake saw the doctor out, and then looked in on his mother. Finding her sleeping, he listened at the door to her even breaths.

He wandered onto the porch. A mourning dove sobbed in the cottonwood grove, and he caught the faint sound of laughter from the Hayes's house. Jake doubted Liberty was one of the merrymakers. He pictured her hiding in her bedroom, hurt and confused. The yearning to comfort her washed over him.

Jake shut out the mental image. He'd stood here often, dreaming of Liberty. He would permit himself that pleasure no longer.

Dark clouds hovered overhead but allowed patches of blue to shine through. The sky blushed pink above the shoulders of the mountains. Trees brooded in the wilderness, and the stream shone like brown lacquer. In the garden, his mother's Moss roses closed for the night as if nothing had changed.

Jake gripped the porch rail, filled his lungs with cool air, and faced the truth. He might yearn to strike out on his own, but he couldn't desert his mother. If he went away and anything happened to her, he would never forgive himself. He'd already lost his father. He had no intention of taking chances with Ma's life. Until the doctor gave her a clean bill of health, he wasn't going anywhere.

CHAPTER TEN

PHOEBE PUT HER HAND IN WILL'S and allowed him to assist her up into the carriage. "It's kind of you to drive us home, Mr. Canfield."

"My pleasure." He smiled with obvious delight. "I'm looking forward to driving a landau behind a team of black Percherons."

Will's enthusiasm brought a flush of warmth that Phoebe feared would color her cheeks. She hoped he wouldn't think that his smile could make her blush. She settled against the red velvet upholstery beside Liberty, whose injured foot rested on a carriage stool. Shaped like an overturned harp, the stool featured a cushion covered in needlepoint roses stitched by Ma over many hours. Phoebe did not share her mother's ability or desire for needlework, a fact that made her all the more grateful for its beauty.

Ma had taken the seat opposite them, which meant she had to ride backwards. Phoebe would have yielded the forward-facing seat to her mother, but Liberty needed comfort. Ma would prefer Phoebe to entertain Liberty during the long journey home. This arrangement afforded Ma the chance to engage in her favorite pastime. She liked nothing better than to watch for birds. Ma had inspected a large variety of the feathered creatures through her field binoculars. Ever since Pa gave them to her last Christmas, traveling in the landau involved Ma hanging out the window and calling bird names over her shoulder. She'd identified willow flycatchers, great blue herons, Lewis's woodpeckers, marsh hawks, bald eagles, and numerous birds Phoebe couldn't remember.

Whenever Ma displayed her enthusiasm for feathered creatures in Pa's presence, a bemused smile crossed his face. The success of his Christmas gift had clearly exceeded his expectations.

The landau dipped and swayed as Will climbed to the driver's seat. He spoke to the horses, and the carriage rolled forward. Phoebe leaned against the backrest and sighed.

Liberty turned her head. "That was heartfelt."

Phoebe smiled. "I love visiting family, but going home sure is nice."

"That's how it should feel." Liberty closed her eyes. "For my part, I'm glad to get away."

Phoebe scanned Liberty's face, noting the slight pucker between her eyes and the tense line of her compressed lips. "I can't wait to put you on a horse."

Liberty's eyelids flew open. "You know I don't ride."

Phoebe grinned. "Sorry. I couldn't resist teasing you. But seriously—you should try again."

Liberty's expression changed to one of horror. "Perish the thought!"

"Why not? You'd move about the ranch better on horseback than with a crutch."

Liberty made a face. "I'll think about it."

"You really should." The scent of greenery wafted to Phoebe, and her gaze wandered to the window. The new day looked promising for travel. Night rains had washed the sky and banished dust from the road without leaving mud puddles. The few clouds floating in the sky showed gray underneath but fleecy white above. They reminded her for all the world of the accursed petticoats her mother insisted on her wearing.

Thankfully, Ma didn't mind Phoebe splitting the skirts on a couple of her dresses. Her riding outfits offered much more modesty when worn with bloomers beneath them. While seated on a horse, Petticoats had a way of bunching up and baring an ankle or calf, and keeping them white was impossible.

Would Liberty wear a split skirt? Phoebe somehow doubted it. Phoebe would loan her a riding outfit if she wanted to try one in the privacy of the ranch. Phoebe shook her head, guessing that Liberty wouldn't. She didn't like to do anything that might displease others.

Sometimes Phoebe wondered why God had given Liberty and her a deep friendship, and then turned them into cousins. They were so different. Whatever the reasons, Phoebe meant to look after Liberty well. She couldn't think of anything that fresh air and exercise wouldn't cure.

Phoebe wanted Liberty to ride in split skirts and bloomers for another reason. Sidesaddles, in her opinion, were uncomfortable contraptions that made remaining seated difficult and hampered a woman's performance on a horse. Riding astride was probably too much to expect of Liberty. Honestly, it would make Phoebe happy to see her on a horse, whichever saddle she chose.

"I think—yes, there!" Ma's cry broke into Phoebe's thoughts.

Liberty startled as if awakened from a sound sleep. Come to think of it, she'd been quiet for a little while.

Ma lowered her binoculars. "Look there!" She pointed toward a group of trees.

Phoebe peered through her mother's window. The trees went by without her noticing any birds. "What did you see?"

"A black-billed cuckoo—listen."

Phoebe held her breath and strained to hear. Above the

rattle of the carriage a tripled cooing warble repeated endlessly. "Are you sure?"

Ma gave her an indignant look. "Oma Wilhelmina pointed one out to me."

Phoebe knew better than to gainsay something Elsa's mother had said. The whole family rightfully revered her. Even so, accepting as gospel every word a person spoke didn't sit well with Phoebe. "That doesn't sound like a cuckoo clock." She couldn't resist making the observation.

"I said the same thing to Oma Wilhelmina. She explained that the clocks imitate the common cuckoo found in Germany's Black Forest, which is where the clocks are made."

"That sounds reasonable."

Ma sighed. "It must be wonderful to hear the common cuckoo in the wild."

Phoebe nodded. "Our black-billed cuckoo must be its cousin."

"That's right." Ma smiled at her as if she'd figured out something miraculous.

"Kind of like us." Liberty stifled a yawn. "We might sing different songs, but we're birds of a feather."

Phoebe closed her gaping mouth. It seemed to her that God had answered her half-formed question of minutes ago. How nice to think that she and Liberty didn't need to agree to meet on common ground.

Ma went back to bird watching, and Liberty returned to her nap. Through the window beside her, Phoebe watched the miles roll by. The town and this valley were the only home she remembered. She never tired of the graceful trees, flowing waterways, and snow-capped mountains.

The jostling of the carriage lulled her into shutting her eyes for a moment. Phoebe passed into a sweet dream in which she rode through a wildflower meadow beside Will.

Phoebe woke as the carriage slowed. She sat up, having slumped against her seatmate. Liberty grumbled, but her eyes remained shut. Phoebe poked at her hair but soon gave up. Tidying herself without a mirror was too difficult. Ma's head was nodding, and her binoculars dropped from her hand onto the seat beside her.

"Whoa!" Will called to the horses, and the landau rolled to a stop.

Phoebe looked through her window. Will jumped down from the driver's seat and went to speak to the horses first, something she would do in his place.

Ma stirred awake, then Liberty.

Will looked in through Phoebe's window. "I see you've survived my driving."

"You did well, Mr. Canfield." Ma snapped her binoculars into their leather case.

A smile flitted across Liberty's face. "Thank you for driving us."

"That was the best carriage ride I've ever taken." Phoebe gave her honest assessment. Will hadn't started off with a jerk, rounded corners too fast, or slowed too quickly. His ability to put the horses through smooth transitions surpassed even Pa's.

Will's face reddened, and he lowered his gaze. "Why thank you."

Phoebe's heart went out to him. Accepting praise could be harder than enduring criticism.

Ma leaned toward the window. "Have you picked a good spot for the noon meal?"

Will smiled. "I'll await your judgment."

"Then I'd better have a look." Ma reached for the wicker basket on the floor at her feet. She and Aunt America had packed enough food for three journeys. Phoebe's stomach growled a reminder that she hadn't eaten since breakfast.

Will helped Ma out of the landau, and then returned to lift Liberty down. Phoebe decided to spare him the trouble of coming back for her. She paused in the doorway to gauge the distance from the metal step to the mounting block. With her dratted petticoats hindering her, this might be harder than she'd imagined.

"Careful, Phoebe!" Ma exclaimed at the exact moment she began her descent.

Phoebe snapped her head toward her mother. Her foot landed on air, but she clutched the rail beside the doorway. She swung and thumped against the carriage. Ma gasped. Phoebe hung, suspended, giving herself a minute to recover before she dropped to the ground.

"I've got you," Will's strong hands gripped her waist.

"I hardly need rescuing." Aware of Ma's indrawn breath at her ill-mannered remark, Phoebe turned into Will's arms. He lifted her down and steadied her on her feet before stepping away. She offered him a smile. "Thank you, Mr. Canfield."

He lifted an eyebrow. "Even though you didn't need rescuing?"

She refrained from informing him that she'd jumped farther from the hayloft when having fun with her brothers. Ma didn't need to know that. "I regret my hasty remark."

"Think no more about it." Suspicion lingered on his face, despite his kind tone.

Phoebe bit back the observation that he seemed to doubt her sincerity. To be honest, she'd apologized for Ma's benefit. Her words couldn't be truer, though. Rushing into speech often landed her in situations she'd rather avoid.

His gaze swept over her. "I trust you've come to no harm."

Under his scrutiny, Phoebe resisted the urge to pat her hair into place. Her curls never minded anyway. How strange to feel self-conscious in front of a man. "I am quite well."

"Please bring the quilt packed in the boot then." Ma opened the wicker basket. "We'll all want something to sit on, especially Liberty."

"I'll do that." Will touched Phoebe's arm as he spoke, a quick gesture that meant nothing. Why did it send tingles across her skin? "You can see to Liberty."

Phoebe didn't care for the way he took charge. However, he'd selected the task she least wanted to perform and assigned her the one she most desired. She left him rummaging in the boot and hurried to Liberty, who waited in the shade of an alder. Will had picked a wildflower meadow on a slight rise above the river. Lupines rose above the grasses, forget-me-nots cascaded in an avalanche of blue, and bitterroot flowers lifted their faces to the sun. Alders formed a canopy above their heads, and a gentle breeze stirred the leaves into sibilance. The rushing of the river made a steady undertone beneath the drone of bees gathering nectar in the sunshine.

"Don't fuss on my account." Liberty's protest might have been more effective if she wasn't leaning on her crutch. "My comfort needs no special measures."

"You can stand through the noon meal if you like. I would like a quilt to sit on." A trace of irritation laced Phoebe's tone. She admired Liberty's selflessness, except when she found it annoying. Putting others first was simple courtesy, but your own turn should come at some point. Liberty's never seemed to arrive. Phoebe smiled to soften her words. "I'm a little grumpy."

"Travel can have that effect." Liberty stretched. "Spending time away from the carriage feels good."

"I agree." Phoebe watched Will carry the quilt to her

mother. "The landau is nicer than a wagon though."

Liberty sighed. "We still have to take our wagon, but I'm thankful for it. I can't imagine riding to your ranch or Uncle Con's on horseback."

"You'd get used to it." Phoebe smiled. "If you had to walk, you'd be thankful for a horse."

Liberty laughed. "That's true. It's all in your mindset, isn't it? Be grateful for what you have."

"Plenty of folks rely on wagons. Uncle Con only bought a carriage when Elsa's mother immigrated from Germany to live on the ranch. Oma Wilhelmina felt poorly back then, and he wanted to make life easier for her."

"I'm glad she's improved." Liberty shifted her weight.

"Is your crutch bothering you?"

Liberty's forehead creased. "It's chafing under my arm."

Will straightened from spreading the quilt for Ma in a shady spot and glanced toward Liberty. "Why don't you sit over here?"

"Yes, do." Ma looked up from opening a jar of pickled eggs. "You can keep us company while Phoebe helps me put out food."

"Thanks, Aunt Maisey." Liberty made it to the quilt, and Will supported her while she sat down.

Phoebe had to look away from the sight of Will's gentleness, which made him far too appealing. She gave her attention to setting out beans with bacon, biscuits, Johnnycake, sauerkraut, pickled eggs, and fresh vegetables. A jug held well water, and Aunt America's strawberry shrub shone ruby red in Mason jars. Phoebe relished the tartness of the syrup made by infusing strawberries into vinegar. Mixed with water, it provided a refreshing drink.

Ma asked Will to say grace, after which they filled their

plates. For a time, no one spoke. Phoebe was too busy chewing for conversation.

"Have you lived in the West long, Mr. Canfield?" Ma recovered her manners first.

"Not at all." Will paused for a swig of strawberry shrub. "I came west a little over a year ago."

"Do you like it here?" Phoebe wondered why the answer to her question mattered so much to her.

"I do, although it's dryer than Kentucky. That's my home state."

Ma smiled. "Kentucky is much greener, from what I hear. Do your parents still live there?"

"Yes, although most of their children located west of the Mississippi." Will bit into a biscuit.

"That must be hard." Phoebe shook her head. "I can't imagine my family so far from me."

Liberty looked away, but not before Phoebe noticed the sadness on her face. What had put it there?

"It happens too often these days." Ma picked up the mason jar in front of her. "Folks are so taken with moving west they forget to count the cost."

A brooding expression shadowed Will's face. "Some are better off leaving."

Ma sighed. "I find that sad, but I understand how it happens."

"I hope my pa will want to come west. If he doesn't, I'll return for visits. It's easier with the railroads going through, unless the Indians cause trouble."

"Do you know much about Indians, Mr. Canfield?" Ma's voice held that quiet note it took on when she had something important to convey.

"Can't say as I do, except what I've heard around

campfires."

"You should take those stories with a grain of salt. The railroads often invade ancient hunting grounds. That's a big reason the Indians fight. It's a matter of survival for their families."

Will frowned. "I didn't realize."

"Few do." Ma glanced at the jar in her hand with vague surprise. She put it down. "Have you considered that winning the West requires others to lose it? Settlers make the Indians out like animals to alleviate the guilt of taking their land and ability to feed themselves. It breaks my heart, Mr. Canfield. The Indians have a different tint to their skin, and they don't talk the same language that we do. But they are every bit as worthy to live as anyone else."

"Thank you for explaining that to me." Will put down his fork. "It puts a different light on the stories I heard."

"You have a good attitude." Ma smiled. "I'm sure that's why you've gone so far. Becoming Con Walsh's ranch manager is an accomplishment many would like to attain."

"I'll do my best to make him proud."

The conversation switched to other topics as the food on their plates dwindled. Liberty had grown quiet, and she refused a slice of cherry pie. Phoebe would wait for a private moment to ask what troubled her.

After the meal, Will went down to the river to rinse off their plates. Phoebe helped her mother clear the food away. Liberty tried to lend a hand without much success. She finally stretched out on the quilt and closed her eyes. Ma stifled a yawn, but then joined Liberty. Phoebe didn't feel sleepy, so she followed Will along the deer path he'd taken down to the water. She hoped he wouldn't mind her company.

After sitting so long in a carriage, it felt good to stretch her legs. The path ran beneath cottonwood trees so thick they shut out all but glimpses of the sky. She could hear water rushing below but the thick vegetation cut off any view. The trail skirted the rise a small distance before turning toward the river. The incline grew steeper, and Phoebe thought about going back. If she'd known the track went so far, she wouldn't have set off on it. She'd intended only to stretch her legs, not to go on an extended walk. It occurred to her belatedly that she'd left Ma and Liberty sleeping near a road where anyone might happen upon them.

An intriguing patch of light beckoned ahead on the path. That must be where the trees broke beside the river. If she continued, she could ask Will to hurry back. Phoebe hesitated, not certain what to do.

She struck a bargain with herself, deciding to continue that far but no farther unless she reached the river.

A few minutes later, the trees parted overhead, and Phoebe stepped into the patch of light. She shielded her eyes against the sudden glare. The river wallowed between its banks, glistening in the sun. Phoebe continued on to the riverbank, breathing in the sharp scent of foliage that crushed beneath her feet. Grasses waved fluffy spikes above the shining surface. Birds sang a bright chorus in the willows, and burnished dragonflies darted about on gossamer wings.

Will was nowhere in sight.

Phoebe could have sworn she'd taken the right path. She must have gone too far. Either that, or something had happened to Will. She pushed that idea from her mind before her imagination ran away with it.

The hair on her nape bristled, and Phoebe spun about.

CHAPTER ELEVEN

THE INDIANS WATCHING PHOEBE FROM THE trail were Salish. She could tell from their markings. They'd materialized out of nowhere, sauntering from the shadows beneath the cottonwoods into the patch of light. Phoebe counted two young men and two women, all carrying pails. The small group must be picking berries or digging roots. Phoebe ranked them in age from perhaps twelve to sixteen. She didn't recognize any of them from the Indian school where her mother had taught the Salish children.

"*Way' sl'axt.*" She greeted them in their own tongue.

"Why do you speak our language?" One of the braves glared at her with hard eyes. He wore western clothing, but the feather behind his head lifted in the breeze. "Who are you to greet us as friends?"

The anger in his face brought back images of Spukani's wrath. The desire to run gripped Phoebe, but she tamped down the impulse. She knew better than to display fear in the face of bullying. Oh, why had she wandered off by herself? She took a deep breath before answering. "I called you friends out of respect for the Salish people. My name is Phoebe. I attended the Liberty Indian School alongside the Salish children my mother taught. That is why I speak your language."

"I know about your mother." A young woman wearing a quillwork headband circled Phoebe. "She killed Spukani's daughter Rain."

"That's not true!" Phoebe was sick to death of that

accusation against her mother. Spukani had used it to justify his cruelty. Would this band do the same thing?

A tall youth with pulled-back hair and that made his broad forehead seem wider loomed over Phoebe. "Aren't you afraid to walk alone so far from safety?"

"Stop it, my brother." The youngest of the two women spoke sharply. "Can't you see you're scaring her?"

"If you don't like what I say, Singing Dove, don't listen." He swung back to Phoebe. "Your golden hair would look beautiful tied to a war-horse's bridle."

"I'm going to tell our mother what is going on." Singing Dove turned, poised as if to carry out her threat.

The woman wearing the quillwork headband grabbed Singing Dove's arm. "No you don't, little sister."

"Let go of me, Magpie!" Singing Dove jerked out of her grasp and darted away.

The brave with the feather headed her off before she could return down the trail. "Our mother will come soon. She only stopped to rest for a moment."

"I wish we'd stayed with her." Singing Dove folded her arms and nodded toward Phoebe. "Leave her alone. This isn't right."

Those were Phoebe's sentiments exactly. Heartened by Singing Dove's championship, she stared her tormenter in the eye. "Anyone who scalps a woman is a coward, not a warrior."

"I'm not going to hurt you." He stepped backward. "I only meant that someone else might."

"What are you doing, children?" A Salish woman with her hair in braids ambled down the path.

"Nothing important." The tall youth moved farther away from Phoebe.

"Ouch!" Singing Dove cried. "Magpie pinched me." She

hurried toward her mother, the others at her heels.

Phoebe crept as quietly as possible to a red willow with branches draping the ground. She slipped into the shadows beneath the tree but couldn't resist peering out between the leaves. From the look of things, Singing Dove was telling on her siblings. Their mother scolded her unruly children and urged them to continue along the riverbank.

Singing Dove remained behind while her family moved off. She ran to Phoebe's hiding place. "Come out. You are safe."

Liberty emerged from the tree. "Thank you for speaking for me."

Singing Dove's almond eyes warmed. "You are welcome. I am sorry my brothers and sister frightened you. They are angry because a settler challenged my brothers over a chicken. The bird was allowed to roam, so my brothers thought they could take it."

"My daughter, where have you gone?" The older woman's voice carried from a little way off. Her other children were no longer in sight, probably driven farther down the trail by their impatience.

"I am here." Singing Dove called, and then smiled at Phoebe. "*Nem eł wičtmncn.*"

"See you later." Phoebe returned the Salish goodbye in English.

Singing Dove joined her mother, and the two ambled out of sight.

Phoebe didn't normally favor hurrying uphill, but the fright she'd suffered lent wings to her feet. She would never, ever, wander off on her own again.

The path bent, and then straightened to reveal Will striding toward her. Phoebe shook with relief, so glad to see him that she didn't even mind the exasperation on his face.

Liberty stole a glance at Phoebe, seated beside her in the landau. Not speaking for several miles was unusual for Phoebe. Getting lost must have affected her. Either that or something had happened between her and Will. He'd marched off after her with an expression like thunder. Liberty could understand. When Phoebe gave in to an unfortunate impulse, it often had that effect on others. Phoebe always seemed surprised when her actions worried those who cared about her. Liberty found it impossible to remain angry with such charming thoughtlessness. Although thankful for Will's tracking skills, she hoped he'd calmed down before locating Phoebe.

Liberty leaned her head against the cushioned rest and let the swaying of the carriage lull her. She normally enjoyed Phoebe's banter, but today silence soothed her. Aunt Maisey abandoned her binoculars in favor of a book. She opened a worn copy of Jane Eyre and flicked her eyes back and forth as she read. Liberty admired her aunt's ability to concentrate. She found it difficult, especially when memories flashed through her mind. Her parting with Jake kept intruding. She couldn't bring herself to believe he was gone, and yet it must be true. That alone was enough to distract her without remembering the glance her mother had given her this morning. Liberty had never been able to hide her emotions from Ma. Thankfully, her mother hadn't asked what was bothering her. If Ma had, Liberty didn't know what she'd have said.

"Wagon ruts ahead," Will warned from the driver's seat. "Hold on!"

Aunt Maisey dropped her book and clutched the rail beside the window. Liberty and Phoebe both followed her excellent example. The landau bumped and lurched like a drunkard.

Thinking of potential mishaps was not beneficial at such a time, but Liberty couldn't help herself. Phoebe's past assurances that runaway horses rather than rutted roads caused most carriage accidents did not comfort her.

The landau shuddered a final time before settling to a smooth pace.

"Sorry about that," Will called. "I didn't see the ruts early enough to slow down."

Aunt Maisey leaned out the open window. "Don't you worry. You're doing a fine job." She retrieved her book from the floor and thumbed through the pages.

Phoebe turned to Liberty. "Are you comfortable?"

"Yes, but I'll be glad when we reach your ranch."

"I think we all will." A pensive expression crossed Phoebe's face. "This trip has been—eventful."

Liberty thought back over the journey but could come up with no reason Phoebe would say that. "How so?"

Phoebe glanced at her mother, who seemed lost in her book. "I'll tell you later."

Liberty nodded, glad to drop the attempt at conversation. She'd made the effort to socialize this morning to avoid dampening the journey for her fellow passengers. The puzzled glances Phoebe had sent her way indicated that she'd failed, at least in part. She doubted her angst could dent Phoebe's good humor for long. Very little could.

The carriage rolled through a clearing dotted with wildflowers. Liberty shifted her position so she could see out the window better. She spotted her favorite flower, a white snapdragon with orange-bearded flowers in shades of yellow. She'd learned its name as butter-and-egg, but others knew it as the less-whimsical yellow toadflax. The flowers didn't smell pleasant, but the plant possessed medicinal value. Folks used it for a wide array of ailments. Liberty glimpsed the pale-tipped violet spires of silvery lupines. The delicate blossoms close to the ground were the rampant flower of the bitterroot herb.

The branches of a mixed forest closed in. Liberty noticed pine, fir, larch, and cottonwood before she stopped paying attention. It must be late afternoon, judging by the angled light filtering through the trees. She nudged Phoebe, who was gazing out the window beside her. "How much longer until we arrive?"

"We still have a distance to go, I'm afraid." Phoebe shook her head. "My getting lost cost us time."

"That could have happened to anyone." For the sake of kindness, Liberty refrained from mentioning that not everyone would wander off alone.

"No, it couldn't, but thanks for trying to make me feel better."

Aunt Maisey glanced up from her reading. "I hope you've learned your lesson."

"I have, Ma." Phoebe recited the words Liberty had heard her say many times before. Phoebe never had to repeat life's lessons, but she always found new ones to study.

Liberty exchanged a wry glance with Aunt Maisey. Phoebe no doubt meant what she'd said. To back up her words, however, she would need to change her inquisitive nature. Liberty hoped Phoebe never tried. She doubted such a feat was even possible.

They polished off the food in their basket during a second brief stop. The daylight softened toward evening, a reminder that they would arrive by lantern light. Even Aunt Maisey abandoned polite conversation in favor of a speedy return to the carriage. Liberty had just taken her seat when a stranger hailed them from the road. She peered out from the window. The slender man rode a high-stepping black horse that looked strong enough to carry five of him. His stovepipe hat, striped vest, black trousers, and silk cravat seemed out of place in the West.

"Greetings to you." He tipped his tall hat, revealing slicked-back hair. "I'm Wilfred Faraday, assistant to Doc Woburn of medicine show fame. How delightful to find myself in such lovely company." He smiled at each of the ladies in turn.

Liberty shrank back, misliking the stranger's flattery and easy manner. He gazed at her for a moment before turning his attention to Will.

"May I trouble you for directions to Dillon? This is our inaugural circuit of Montana Territory, and I'm not used to finding my way. The roads aren't always marked around these parts."

"I know how frustrating that can be." Will smiled. "You'll want to travel the other direction."

"What? I must have gotten turned around once I left Corvallis. I was putting up posters and distributing handbills for the show. I hope you'll come and bring the ladies." He distributed another round of smiles. "You won't want to miss the magic tricks. There's a genuine snake charmer too."

"Thanks for the invitation, Mr. Faraday." Will handed Aunt Maisey into the carriage.

"You're most welcome. Be sure to look me up." The man tilted his hat and rode off.

Liberty sagged against the upholstery, exhausted from the encounter. Meeting someone from the medicine show made her natural father's existence seem more real. Whenever she tried to sort out what to do about him, her thoughts wheeled about like crows mobbing a hawk. Should she introduce herself? The prospect terrified her almost as much as keeping her distance. She could go to the medicine show just to look at him, but that might be worse. It would show her the father she'd never known, but with no hope of altering the situation. Did she even want anything to change? She couldn't imagine any other father than the one who had raised her. Pa wasn't perfect, but he'd done his best to provide for his family. Her earliest memory involved watching the road for Pa's return. He hadn't come that day or the next. Duty to his flock often called Pa from home, but he always made up for his absences with extra attention. She couldn't fault him as a father, but she held something against him all the same.

Pa shouldn't have pretended to be her natural father. She couldn't reconcile his deception with the man of integrity she'd always believed him to be. He should have wanted to tell her the truth rather than persuading Ma to continue hiding it from her.

Tears pricked her eyes, and she lowered her lids to hide them. The landau's swaying lulled her.

Phoebe shook her awake. "You're dreaming."

Liberty sat up out of her slouch. Darkness, somewhat lightened by the carriage lanterns, pressed the windows. Liberty sat straighter, wincing as she jarred her ankle. "How close are we?" She whispered to avoid waking Aunt Maisey, whose head had fallen to her chest.

"We just turned onto the drive. Ma, wake up. We're here."

Aunt Maisey opened her eyes. "I wasn't sleeping."

"Oh really?" Phoebe smiled. "What were you doing then?"

Aunt Maisey lifted her chin. "I was only resting my eyes for a moment."

The carriage traversed the wide turn that brought the ranch house into view. Warm light glowed from the windows. Uncle Rob flung open the front door the instant they drew up at the porch. The clopping of the horse's hooves must have announced their arrival. Phoebe's two brothers spilled onto the porch. Quinn was gangly at eleven, whereas Murphy's stoutness at nine reminded Liberty of Liam. The two brothers differed in other ways. Quinn's hair shone like molasses in the lantern light, and his eyes gleamed like pools of pale water. Murphy's hair matched his father's red tones, and his eyes glinted green.

Aunt Maisey embraced her husband. "I've missed you."

"Welcome home, Mrs. Walsh." Uncle Rob murmured against her hair.

Aunt Maisey stepped away from her husband and greeted her sons.

"I'm glad you're back." Uncle Rob grinned at Phoebe. "It's been too quiet without you." He winked at Liberty, and she couldn't repress a smile.

Aunt Maisey turned to Liberty and Phoebe. "You two must be ready for your pillow. Do you want something to eat or drink first?"

Liberty was only too happy to follow her aunt inside. "Not for me, thanks."

"Me neither." Phoebe stifled a yawn.

The thumping of the men's boots echoed on the porch but muffled when they reached the red, blue, and cream Persian carpet inside. Dark paneling and a gold chandelier added richness to the entryway. Uncle Rob, carrying a trunk in his arms, nodded to Will, who was equally laden. "You'll bed down for the night, won't you?"

"If I may, thank you. I brought my horse behind the wagon, but it's a bit late to show up at Con's ranch."

"He wouldn't mind, but I don't like sending a man alone into the night."

Liberty surprised an expression of relief on Phoebe's face. If Liberty wasn't mistaken, her friend nurtured tender feelings for Will.

"Let's get you settled." Aunt Maisey picked up a lantern from the foyer table and raised it aloft.

Phoebe trailed her mother but paused partway up the stairs and looked down. "Can you make it all right?"

Liberty peered up from the foot of the staircase. "Maybe I

should sleep on the sofa."

"Sorry." Aunt Maisey peered over the rail on the landing. "I forgot about your ankle. Do you think you can—"

"I'll carry you." Uncle Rob set the trunk in his arms against the wall.

"Thank you." Liberty had barely spoken when her feet left the floor. She felt, for a fleeting moment, like a little girl. Some of her fondest childhood memories were of Pa carrying her.

Uncle Rob put her down in Phoebe's room. The first night of any visit, Liberty and Phoebe liked to sleep in the same room. They did their best not to talk so loudly that they kept the household awake.

Phoebe seemed to discover her second wind, which involved a great deal of chattering. Liberty revived enough to brush Phoebe's golden curls until they shone. She submitted to the detangling of her own hair. After washing up, she changed into her nightgown and slipped between the cool sheets in the cot beside Phoebe's bed. Liberty sighed, content to lie still, although it felt like she was still rocking in the carriage.

Phoebe's mattress crunched as she crawled into her own bed. Candlelight carved hollows in her face as she leaned toward the candle on the side table. She blew on the flame, which bent and sputtered. The shadows swung, and the light scattered. Darkness fell. Phoebe's covers rustled, and she let out a long sigh. Quiet cloaked them like a velvet mantle.

The sensation of rocking faded into a floating feeling. Liberty drifted along with slumber washing over her in waves.

"Are you awake?" Phoebe's whisper intruded.

"Mmm…" Liberty wrestled with the impulse to say nothing more, but sleep had fled. She rolled toward her friend. "What do you want?"

"You seemed out of sorts today. Is something wrong?"

Liberty wished she'd played possum, after all. "It's hard to talk about."

"Has Jake upset you?"

Liberty grimaced in the dark. When had Jake upsetting her become a normal assumption for Phoebe? "Yes, but that's not the whole trouble."

"Does it have anything to do—"

"Please stop asking." Liberty kept her voice polite. "It's not anything you can guess."

"I don't mean to pry, but I'm concerned about you."

"I appreciate that." Liberty softened her tone. "I feel the same about you."

"What do you mean?" Phoebe sounded guarded.

"You've acted strangely ever since getting lost."

"Oh, that." Phoebe sighed. "I ran into some of the Salish out berry picking."

"Goodness. Were they peaceful?"

"Not really, but mostly."

Phoebe's words didn't make sense, but Liberty gave up trying to untangle them. "Do you know how confusing that sounds?"

"Never mind. It doesn't matter."

"Maybe you should tell your ma what happened."

Phoebe snorted. "She'd make sure I never went anywhere by myself again."

Liberty refrained from pointing out that Phoebe's ma never wanted her going off alone. Certain things were better left unsaid. "Did Will get onto you about it?"

"Not really, but I could tell he was displeased. I can't blame him. I didn't think it through, or I'd have stayed with you and Ma. I don't know why I didn't. I'm not proud of leaving you two sleeping on the side of the road."

"Don't feel guilty. No harm came of it."

Phoebe stopped talking for so long that Liberty suspected

her of falling asleep. After Phoebe's questions, it would take Liberty longer to reach that happy state. She needed to absorb what had happened before she gave Phoebe any details. She wasn't certain, for Ma's sake, that she should even talk about it. She didn't want to discuss anything that could damage her mother's reputation. The true issue remained unspoken.

Liberty didn't know who she was anymore.

Phoebe laid still as long as she could with birds singing outside the window. When she could stand it no more, she tiptoed from bed to avoid disturbing Liberty, who still slept. Phoebe slipped on a pink striped day dress and slippers. After pinning up her hair, she crept to the door.

Liberty peeked out from her covers. "What time is it?"

Phoebe peered at the clock on the mantel—a silver and white enamel confection decorated with enameled foliage, birds, and stags in bright colors. A Christmas gift from Oma Wilhelmina, it cheered her whenever she looked at it. "It's only seven. Do you want to go back to sleep?"

"No." Liberty sat up in bed. "I'm awake now."

"Sorry. I didn't mean to wake you. I'll bring you breakfast in bed to make it up to you."

"There's no need." Liberty yawned. "I must have slept well, I feel so rested."

Phoebe turned with her hand on the door knob. "If you're coming down to breakfast, I'll ask Pa or Quinn to help you."

"I was exhausted last night. Now that I've had a good night's sleep, I'm sure I can manage the stairs on my own."

Phoebe smiled. "No one would hold you to that, in case you change your mind."

Phoebe tried not to hover while Liberty navigated the stairs. She followed Liberty into the kitchen, where her friend perched on a stool at the counter. "Let me help with breakfast."

"It's just you and me. Pa and the boys are out doing the chores. Ma fed them hours ago." Phoebe passed her a bowl and the basket of eggs. She cut slabs from a loaf of bread while Liberty cracked eggs into the bowl.

After a quick breakfast of eggs and toast slathered with butter and huckleberry jam, Phoebe did the washing up. She hung up the flour-sack towel to dry and leaned on the counter beside her friend. "Come riding with me."

Liberty shook her head. "I don't think I can with my injury."

"That's why you should."

"I don't know—"

"Think about it. Would you rather glide about on horseback or struggle to walk with a crutch?"

"You almost convince me, but I'm nervous around horses."

"That's another good reason to ride. Facing your fear is the only way to overcome it."

"Sometimes fear is sensible."

"What am I going to do with you?" Phoebe shook her head, even while she held back laughter. "Come riding."

"I hate to admit it, but I agree with your last point. Playing safe hasn't protected me one iota. In fact, it just cost me Jake's friendship."

"I'm sorry to hear that, but give it time. You never know what will happen."

"He's leaving town." Liberty stopped speaking as tears gleamed in her eyes.

"Even that doesn't have to be the end. Look at my mother and father. He went away for three years." She blew out a breath. "I thought they never were going to get together, but they did."

"I remember." Liberty smiled. "I don't think Jake and I are

so inspiring."

"Time will tell about that too." Phoebe straightened. "Am I to understand that you've agreed to ride this morning?"

Liberty nodded. "All right, but I need the horse to go slow."

"I knew that already." Phoebe grinned. "This is going to be fun!"

Liberty's forehead puckered. "I'll try not to disappoint your expectations."

Phoebe put Liberty on the gray Palouse horse who had lovingly endured her brothers' early attempts at riding. She had no worries about Liberty's safety on Old Smokey. Her own chestnut Quarter Horse whinnied in greeting. Phoebe patted Nutmeg's neck and fussed over her a bit before putting on her tack.

Phoebe mounted Nutmeg and guided her horse to the path beside the creek. A glance behind revealed Liberty holding her own on Old Smokey. Despite her lack of confidence, she sat a horse well. Phoebe pulled in a breath of cool morning air that smelled like water. Rain clouds threatened but might blow elsewhere before releasing their load. The sky shone blue between the clouds, creating a dramatic effect. Whenever the clouds shifted, shadows raced across the ground. The creek reflected the roiling sky but burbled on merrily.

The thrill of being on horseback went through Phoebe. She felt most alive in the saddle. She'd needed an outing as much as Liberty. Life had become so emotional lately, what with meeting Will and dealing with Liberty's problems. Out in the open air, Phoebe could forget all of that. She envied Will his job on Uncle Con's ranch. Phoebe could think of nothing grander than living outdoors and riding most of the day. If she were a man, Phoebe would become a ranch hand. She had half a mind to apply, regardless.

Liberty clung not only to her horse's saddle horn, but to its mane as well. "I don't know why I let you talk me into this."

Phoebe, riding ahead on Nutmeg, smiled over her shoulder. "You're doing fine."

Liberty had a different opinion about that. Phoebe seemed to have no trouble managing her horse, but Liberty had yet to master her own. No horse took kindly to confusing signals or a fearful rider, but Old Smokey seemed to take her incompetence in stride. This might go all right, after all.

Riding did feel better than stumping about with a crutch rubbing her arm raw. The enforced rest of the carriage ride had stopped her ankle from swelling. She could wear her boots on both feet again. Liberty kept her injured ankle out of the stirrup to keep from putting pressure on it. Phoebe informed her that this was normally dangerous for a novice rider. However, Old Smokey was unlikely to do more than plod safely along. Liberty felt sure that staying off her feet could only benefit her, provided she managed to stay on her horse.

Phoebe acted so exhilarated that it was easy to understand why she spent so much time in the saddle. Whiling away an hour outdoors allowed a person to regain a sense of balance. The ability to think clearly dispelled the gloom that shrouded Liberty. She still didn't know the answer to her problems, but developing a little backbone was a good place to start.

She might fear meeting her father, but that was why she should.

CHAPTER TWELVE

Liberty leaned down and patted Old Smokey's neck. The gentle horse made traveling the open road a lot less frightening. Liberty couldn't relax entirely though. The need to give Old Smokey clear signals, maintain an upright posture, and simply remain in the saddle commandeered her attention. Also, the possibility of surprising a bear on the prowl in the early morning kept her peering into the woods lining the road. "I missed spending time with Katie and Fiona at Sunday Meeting," she called to Phoebe, riding ahead of her on Nutmeg. "This visit will make up for that." She almost convinced herself that she wanted to trade the quiet haven of Phoebe's ranch for the joyful chaos ahead of her.

"Don't worry. We can ride at Uncle Con's ranch."

Phoebe must have caught Liberty's reluctance and gathered she was worried about becoming bored. Liberty could think of no way to explain her difficulty without revealing secrets. She would normally welcome the chance to visit Uncle Con's ranch. However, since learning that she belonged to Pa's family only through adoption, she felt like an outsider.

Liberty had taken to riding during the past week, much to her own surprise. Her ankle had improved to the point where she could hobble without a crutch. Whenever Aunt Maisey saw her up and about, she insisted on Liberty sitting down. She found her aunt's concern sweet and well-intentioned but vexing. Liberty was a little relieved that Aunt Maisey had decided to remain home with the boys. Aunt Maisey planned to pitch in later by cleaning the house that Uncle Nick and Aunt Bry were vacating.

Uncle Rob would lend a hand moving heavy furniture to Uncle Nick's new ranch. Uncle Rob planned to spend the night before returning home, which was fine by Liberty. Doing her best to help Aunt Elsa in the kitchen would no doubt tire her.

Uncle Rob glanced back at Liberty. "Are you comfortable?"

"Yes, thank you." Her aunt must have prompted him to check on her during the ride. Aunt Maisey had almost persuaded him that Liberty should travel the short distance in the carriage. It was only through Phoebe's intervention that Liberty had been allowed to ride. With the day pleasant and the sky clear, Liberty was glad for the opportunity. The road wound through wild meadows and into shady groves, but always with the river in view. They rounded a curve and surprised a herd of deer grazing in a clearing. The deer froze and watched them with liquid eyes, noses twitching and ears alert. White tails raised, the frightened creatures bounded into the forest.

"Where are they?" Liberty stared into the underbrush. "The entire herd seems to have vanished."

Phoebe laughed. "They're long gone."

"It's amazing how fast they can go." Liberty shook her head.

"That's a fact." Uncle Rob chuckled. "I doubt they'll stop this side of the Continental Divide."

They stopped to water the horses at a stream that tumbled over large blocks of granite and splashed into a pool. The water frothed over a lip of stone and eddied around exposed tree roots before plunging over more boulders. Liberty breathed her fill of moist air that tasted like raindrops while Old Smokey drank his fill.

They arrived in time for the noon meal. Aunt Elsa spread out a feast on the dining table, no mean feat with two babies—year-old Meg and three-year-old Otto—clinging to her skirts. At fourteen, Fiona was the oldest of their five children. Twelve-year-old Richard came next, followed by little Wilhelmina, aged six. The gap between Richard and Wilhelmina had seen the funerals of a stillborn daughter and a son lost to pneumonia.

Liberty sank onto a chair between Phoebe and Fiona. Katie, who had escaped this morning's moving chores by spending the night with Fiona, sat on Phoebe's other side. Uncle Con and Will also joined them at the table. Uncle Con said grace, and they passed around the serving dishes.

No matter what Aunt Elsa cooked, it turned out well. Liberty enjoyed the German potato soup with a name she couldn't pronounce topped by green onions and bacon chunks. Thick slabs of brown bread dunked into the soup didn't fall apart and tasted delicious. A tangy beet salad nestled beside garden greens, herb leaves, tomatoes, and onions glistened with a creamy dressing redolent of dill.

Liberty ate her fill, letting the chatter roll over her.

"Are you going to the medicine show?" Phoebe leaned forward and spoke to Fiona across Liberty. "There will be all manner of acts—acrobats, banjo players, dancers, magicians, and I don't remember what else."

Katie's forehead furrowed. "What do acrobats do?"

"They throw themselves through the air but somehow land on their feet." Phoebe blew on a spoonful of soup. "Don't ask me how they do it without falling."

"Will you go when it comes to Corvallis?" Fiona's blue eyes shone with excitement. "We plan to."

"Can we go to the medicine show, Pa? Fiona said they're going." Phoebe turned pleading eyes on her father.

"Your ma mentioned it." Uncle Rob smiled. "I think it would be all right."

Phoebe, Fiona, and Katie cheered.

Liberty couldn't bring herself to rejoice about something she halfway dreaded.

Phoebe boosted Liberty onto Old Smokey, and then stepped back to admire the figure she made on horseback. "What a long way you've come. It's hard to imagine you were afraid of horses."

"I must have you fooled."

Phoebe smiled. "Fear makes the wolf bigger than he is, according to Oma Wilhelmina."

Liberty laughed. "Or the horse, as the case may be."

"The opposite is also true. Courage shrinks a wolf—or a horse—down to size."

"Which is still pretty big, if you ask me."

"True." Phoebe took her own horse's tack off a nail in the grooming stall. "It's important never to forget that, even with a gentleman like Old Smokey. Wait for me outside if you like. I'll be right with you after I saddle my horse."

Phoebe walked down the wide aisle between rows of stalls. She smiled as a whinny greeted her. Nutmeg lifted her muzzle and blew softly. Phoebe touched her horse's nose with the back of her hand, and then rubbed the mare's silken neck. She slipped the bridle over her horse's head and buckled it into place.

While tightening the rope girth to hold the saddle on, Phoebe caught Fiona's and Katie's voices. They'd agreed to meet for an early ride before Phoebe and Liberty left, but the other two hadn't appeared. Their absence might have something to do with Katie sleeping over a second night. Phoebe could recall Fiona and Katie talking until she fell asleep. Leading Nutmeg out of her stall, Phoebe aimed a pointed glance at her young cousins. "I almost gave up on you."

Fiona had the grace to blush. "Sorry to keep you waiting."

"Yes, sorry." Katie gave Phoebe a hangdog look.

Phoebe stopped herself from laughing. "Do you girls need help with your horses?"

"No, thank you." Fiona shook her blonde head.

Katie stood taller. "We saddle up all the time."

"I'll leave you to it then." Phoebe mounted her horse. "But hurry."

The girls headed to the tack room as Phoebe rode from the dimness of the barn into the soft early light.

"Good morning." Will strode across the barnyard carrying a coiled rope. "Going riding?"

"We are." Phoebe squinted his direction. The sunrise burning behind Will made him hard to see.

"Fiona and Katie are coming too," Liberty added. Old Smokey's hooves thumped the ground as she moved nearer.

Will stopped before reaching them and tilted his head upward. "Would you ladies care for company?"

Phoebe hesitated. *Why would he offer to go with them? He must have chores to do.*

"Of course, we would." Liberty answered him roundly. She turned her head toward Phoebe. "Wouldn't we?"

Unless she wanted to be outright rude, Phoebe could do nothing but agree. She couldn't name the cause of her reluctance, anyway. Maybe it was nothing. "You're welcome, although I should warn you that some of us can't keep up with you on a horse."

"She means me," Liberty inserted with wry humor. "I'm a novice in the saddle."

"Never you mind." Will smiled. "We all have to start somewhere."

Her face lit. "Bless you."

He grinned. "I'll get my horse."

Will reappeared a short while later with Fiona and Katie behind him. They rode single-file along the trail that traversed the river. Phoebe took the lead. She preferred her own thoughts but tolerated the girls' chattering. Liberty rode behind the younger girls, and Will brought up the rear.

Sunrise blushed the eastern sky and turned the river to molten gold. Larks trilled in the dark willows leaning out from the banks. Mayflies lifted from the water in a cloud of gossamer wings that glinted in the morning light. A trout jumped and fell in a bright plume of water. Phoebe yearned to cup her hands around this moment like a bright butterfly she chanced to catch. She knew from childhood that trying to cherish a treasure for too long only ruined it. Moments, like butterflies, needed to be released.

The river broadened in a place where the water ambled along. Uncle Con and the neighboring ranchers used this place as a crossing to reach common range land. Phoebe turned onto a track that led away from the river into tall timber. Pines, cottonwoods, spruce, and fir towered into the sky, casting deep shadows at the horses' feet. Liberty was traveling more slowly to spare her ankle, and Will had stayed behind with her. Phoebe stopped and waited for them to catch up. A hawk soared across the patch of sky between the treetops. The wild creature voiced a primeval cry. Katie and Fiona gazed upward, for once silent. A deer huffed a warning somewhere near. Phoebe assumed that their presence, and not the proximity of a predator, had upset the animal. None of their horses acted frightened. Even so, she breathed easier when Liberty and Will reached them.

Phoebe scanned Liberty's face for signs of strain and found none. In fact, Liberty appeared more at ease than Phoebe had seen her in a while. Her eyes shone and her face glowed with health. Will seemed relaxed and happy as well. A suspicion kindled in Phoebe's mind, but she couldn't bring herself to examine it.

The cautious expression Will normally wore around Phoebe settled on his face. "I think Liberty's foot is bothering her, but she doesn't want to say."

If so, Liberty was doing a good job of hiding her pain. "There's a meadow ahead. We can rest there before heading back."

She urged her horse onward, and Nutmeg lumbered down the trail. Her hooves crushed fallen pine needles underfoot, releasing their sharp scent. Phoebe peered into the deeper shadows, mindful of the deer's alarm. She saw no evidence of wolves, coyotes, mountain lions, or bear—predators that might prey upon deer or people.

The trail brought them to a meadow ringed by trees. The early sun slanting through the branches sent long shadows across the wildflower-tangled grass. Phoebe reined in near a boulder where Liberty could sit.

Will dismounted and hurried to Liberty. "May I assist you, Miss Hayes?"

"You are very kind." Liberty smiled. "I'd be grateful." She swung her leg, clad in bloomers beneath her skirt, over the saddle.

Will reached up and caught her as she leaned down. He carried her to the boulder and lowered her gently.

"Thank you, Mr. Canfield." Liberty gave him a dazzling smile. "I'm fine while riding but climbing on and off my horse is challenging."

Will returned her smile. "I'm glad to help such a lovely lady."

Phoebe's suspicions came knocking. The way Liberty and Will were acting made her misgivings impossible to ignore. An attachment between the two struck her as a mistake, although she couldn't explain why.

Phoebe pushed the riddle out of her mind and turned her back while Liberty and Will murmured together. She joined the two girls and soon found herself in a discussion about whether or not hawks attacked humans. Fiona gave the opinion, with a certain amount of relish, that they did. Katie vehemently denied the possibility. Phoebe wisely took the middle ground.

"Hawks don't normally, but they will dive at folks too close to their nests." Will spoke up. "That's how a neighbor of ours in Kentucky acquired a nasty gash and a lump on his head."

"See?" Fiona crowed. "Told you."

"Why don't we change the subject?" Liberty intervened. "Talking about such things isn't very becoming."

"Oh, pooh!" Fiona pulled a face. "Who cares about all that?"

"Mind your tongue. I'm sure your ma wouldn't want you to use that expression." Phoebe tried not to smile, but Fiona's china-doll face made her scowl look adorable. She reminded Phoebe of a spitting kitten, an opinion Fiona would no doubt scorn.

"You will care one day, when you're older." Liberty's mild reply cut through Fiona's protests.

Fiona's brow furrowed, and Phoebe sensed a storm brewing. She searched for a new topic. "I've been meaning to ask you, Liberty, are you coming to Oma Wilhelmina's birthday party?"

Liberty's expression went blank. "Her birthday is coming up?"

"Yes. It's in two weeks, in case you'd forgotten."

Liberty's face went pink. "I'm afraid I've been— preoccupied. I remember Ma saying something about her turning sixty."

"We're going to fuss over her as much as possible. I hope you can make it."

"My family won't want to miss it." Liberty's face brightened. "I'm sure you'd be welcome too, Will—Mr. Canfield."

"I go more by Will, so that's fine. When folks say, 'Mr. Canfield,' I think they're talking to my father."

"You can call me Liberty. Since you're working for my uncle, you're practically a family member."

"If everyone is quite rested, we should go back," Phoebe announced abruptly. She couldn't watch Liberty and Will making up to one another any longer. She wanted Liberty to be happy but could have sworn that involved Jake. Her own reaction to the idea of Will courting Liberty troubled her. How ridiculous to feel pangs of jealousy at the prospect.

Abandoning all dignity, the girls clambered onto their horses without a mounting block. Phoebe busied herself with checking the tightness of Katie's saddle girth while Will lifted Liberty onto her horse. She had no desire to watch. Phoebe hoped, after she returned home, that it would be a very long time before Will crossed her path again.

"Phoebe—Miss Walsh?" Will spoke from behind her.

"Yes?" Phoebe turned about but didn't meet his eyes.

"May I assist you onto your horse?" Will sounded strictly polite, so different from his tone when offering to help Liberty.

She glanced at Liberty, who smiled encouragement from Old Smokey's back.

If Will had only offered out of politeness, she didn't want his help. She would use the boulder as a mounting block. "No thank you, Mr. Canfield." Phoebe lifted her chin. "I can manage on my own."

Will coaxed his horse down the trail after the young women under his protection. Con had sent him out to accompany them after hearing of a skirmish with the Indians over a stolen chicken. The incident had happened days ago and farther north, but emotions still ran high. Ranchers didn't take kindly to challenges to their livelihood. Con made ranching look easy, but many struggled to survive.

They left the side trail in favor of the path along the river. The air felt cooler here and smelled of water. Liberty rode ahead of him on the old plodder well suited to her inexperience. A breeze tugged a blonde lock of her hair free of its pins. The way it whipped about must have annoyed her, for she tucked it behind her ear.

He should have fallen in love with a woman like Liberty. That would have spared him a lot of heartache. His mother hadn't liked Sophie from their first meeting, and she'd objected to their betrothal. Ma's reaction should have alerted him to impending peril. Pa hadn't expressed an opinion, which ought to have warned him too. If Pa had considered Sophie a good match, he'd have said so.

Will couldn't lay their failed engagement entirely at Sophie's door. He'd made his share of mistakes. He sighed. One day he might understand how women thought, although it seemed unlikely. Until and if that ever happened, he'd better steer clear of romance. That included his present company. Will had no trouble admiring Liberty or enjoying a pleasant conversation with her. He felt certain his parents would approve of her. She was in every way suitable to become an excellent wife for someone, but not for him.

The woman most likely to endanger his heart had decided to spurn him. He ought to thank Phoebe for doing so. Ignoring the ache this caused him, Will vowed to deliver the confusing woman to the safety of the ranch and keep out of her way from now on.

Liberty slipped out of the guest bedroom and pulled the door to with a click. She hobbled along the hallway, glad to discover that her ankle could bear more weight without pain. Liberty paused for a deep breath at the head of the stairs. Supporting herself with a hand on the railing, she began the laborious descent. After reaching the lower landing without mishap, she bore left toward the kitchen, guided by the light shining beneath the door.

Aunt Elsa looked up as she entered. "Good morning. Did you sleep well?"

"I did, thanks."

"Would you care for coffee or tea?"

"Tea for me, thank you." Liberty, slightly overwhelmed by her aunt's cheerfulness, plunked onto one of the stools at the counter.

Aunt Elsa matched a gold-edged tea cup blooming with pink roses to its saucer. She slid the china and a matching sugar bowl before Liberty. "You're up early."

"You were earlier." Employing silver tongs shaped like twin roses, Liberty carried a chunk of rock sugar from the bowl to her cup.

"I'm usually awake at this hour, unless one of the babies is teething or has the croup." Aunt Elsa reached for the teapot, which was already steaming. "It is my habit."

"My mother wakes early to bake our bread."

"Ja." Aunt Elsa sipped from her own cup. "When you cook, the morning hours are best."

Liberty nodded toward a pile of dough on the counter behind her aunt. "Don't let me stop whatever you were doing."

"I'm making *schmalzkuchens*." Her aunt began kneading the dough. "They are small pastries like doughnuts that contain no sugar."

Liberty tried to imagine such an item. "Do they taste good?"

Aunt Elsa smiled. "Don't look so worried, *Liebchen.* You'll find plenty of sugar on the outside."

"Can I help you make them?"

"In a bit. Meanwhile, drink your tea and keep me company."

The back door crashed against the wall, letting in a gust of cool morning air. Liberty could almost believe that the wind had blown it open. Another force was responsible, she learned as Aunt Bry rushed in, her cheeks flushed. "I have more vegetables, if you want them." She spoke in the same lilting Irish accent as Liberty's pa. Bry raised the basket hanging from her arm. "I'm trying to harvest as much as I can before we move."

"Don't worry about that." Aunt Elsa waved a hand. "I'll take care of the garden after you leave. You're welcome to harvest whatever you like later, after your move." She smiled. "Come in and have tea."

"That sounds lovely." Aunt Bry pulled out the stool beside Liberty. "I was too rushed to make any this morning."

"It's barely dawn, and you're already rushed?" Aunt Elsa smiled even as she shook her head. "Please take care of yourself, no matter how busy life makes you."

"What am I going to do without you next door ready to dispense tea and friendly advice?" Aunt Bry's eyes shone with moisture. She smiled at Liberty. "Look at me, getting emotional when we're not going far."

Aunt Elsa squeezed Bry's shoulder. "It won't be the same without your early morning visits. You must return often." She gave her attention to the basket. "Now what treasures have you brought me? Oh look, zucchini."

Aunt Bry grinned. "I took a chance that you'd welcome more."

"Of course. I'll make zucchinisuppe."

"Zucchini soup sounds much better in German." Aunt Bry lifted her cup and breathed the steam. She sighed. "That smells heavenly."

"It's from Ostfriesland."

"Where is that?"

"It's an area on the north coast of Germany. You may know it as East Frisia. It's where the best tea in Germany is celebrated. My sister, Liesel, sends it to me. I hoped she would come to live with us when my mother did, but her husband wants to remain near his own family." Aunt Elsa frowned, but then brightened. "She says they can come to see us next year."

"I'm glad." Aunt Bry's eyes grew suspiciously bright. "I know how much that means to you."

Aunt Elsa dabbed at her own eyes with her apron. "I treasure my family."

Liberty wished she hadn't heard her aunts' exchange. She loved her family too, but she didn't know where she fit anymore.

CHAPTER THIRTEEN

LIBERTY STARED INTO HER TEA CUP to hide the tears that gathered in her eyes. She waited until Aunt Elsa turned again to Aunt Bry's basket before wiping her eyes with the back of her hand.

Aunt Elsa lifted a large red onion. "What shall I make with this? I know. How about that egg dish with mustard sauce and vegetables that you like so much, Bry? You, Nick, and the children are welcome to join us for breakfast."

"We'd enjoy that, if you're sure."

Aunt Elsa beamed. "Of course. I like to cook, and I love all of you."

Aunt Elsa hadn't consulted her husband's wishes, but Liberty knew why. With Uncle Con, the door was always open.

"I'll let everyone know." Aunt Bry gulped the last tea in her cup.

"What's up?" Uncle Rob leaned against the jamb of the door that led into the front hallway.

Aunt Bry smiled at her brother. "We're having breakfast guests."

"Oh really? Anyone I know?" Uncle Rob lifted an eyebrow, but then broke into a grin.

"Perhaps you can guess." Aunt Bry gave him an arch look. "They are pillars of the community, and good looking besides."

Liberty giggled at their antics, but then stopped in surprise. The troubles besetting her had seemed so dark that she'd wondered if she would ever laugh again.

"I have it on good authority that your pillars are pulling up stakes in a couple of days and leaving their community high and dry." Uncle Rob grew serious.

"Ach no, me brother." Aunt Bry adopted her best Irish brogue. "The community will never get rid of them."

Uncle Rob's eyes lit with humor. "Would they like help with their move?"

"Any man who volunteers needs a day to spare and muscles to make a maiden weep."

"That's a tall order, and no mistake." He grinned. "I'll see what I can do."

"We'll count on it then. But look at me, talking with you when I should be hurrying home." Aunt Bry rushed out.

Uncle Rob grinned. "It's like a whirlwind blew out the door."

Aunt Elsa laughed. "That seems a family trait."

"What did I miss?" Uncle Con appeared in the back doorway. "I just passed Bry hot-footing it across the garden, and Rob said something about a whirlwind."

"Nothing out of the ordinary, darling." Aunt Elsa embraced him one-armed while keeping her floury hands away from his clothing. "I'm about to make coffee. I assume you'd like some also, Rob."

"Thank you, yes. I was after coffee when I came in." He looked at Liberty. "Where's Phoebe?"

"I didn't hear a sound from her room this morning. She must still be asleep."

"I'll go knock on her door." He started toward the doorway.

"Would you mind checking on the children, Con?" Aunt Elsa rolled out the dough she'd kneaded. "Meg is a sleepyhead, but Otto and Wilhelmina should be stirring. Richard and Fiona should tend their chores before breakfast."

How Aunt Elsa managed to put on a lavish breakfast with

everyone getting in her way in the kitchen, Liberty didn't know. She helped as much as she could, given her injury.

Phoebe traipsed in a little later and pitched in by chopping onions. Liberty shifted her stool away from the cutting board. Phoebe's ability to withstand the tear-inducing fumes struck awe within her.

Later, at the table, she bowed her head between Phoebe and Fiona while Uncle Con said the blessing. The eggs with vegetables in mustard sauce were delicious. Much to Liberty's relief, she enjoyed Aunt Elsa's doughnut-like pastry.

Aunt Elsa seated her mother beside her, which happened to be directly across from Liberty. Oma Wilhelmina's eyes gleamed. "So you like the *schmalzkuchens*." She leaned forward when she spoke as if fearful her words would not carry.

"Yes, ma'am." Phoebe replied. Liberty nodded with her mouth full, and the younger children cheered.

Oma Wilhelmina laughed in that soundless way of hers. "I remember eating *schmalzkuchens* as a child."

"Oma!" Six-year-old Wilhelmina, her namesake, stared at her grandmother from the deep green eyes she'd inherited from her father. "You were a child?"

Laughter went round the table.

"Willie!" Aunt Elsa's face went scarlet.

"It's all right, Elsa." Oma Wilhelmina smiled. "Imagine that, Willie! Even someone as old as me was once a child."

A look of satisfaction came over Willie's face. "And you ate *schmalzkuchens*."

Oma Wilhelmina's shoulders shook. "My mother—your great grandmother Frieda—also made *krapfen*, doughnuts with jam inside."

"Will you make *krapfen*, Mutter?" Eight-year-old Richard thumped the table.

Con scowled. "Do you have the manners of a monkey, Rick? Sit still."

"Will you, *Mutter*?" Fiona turned pleading eyes on her mother. "I'll help."

"Please?" Wilhelmina spoke with her mouth full of *schmalzkuchens*.

Elsa shook her head at her young daughter. "Don't talk with your mouth full."

At three, Otto could not follow the conversation, but he chimed in with a droning wail.

Aunt Elsa looked a little hunted. "I think you children need to appreciate what you have." She frowned at her mother. "See what you caused?"

Oma Wilhelmina did not look the least bit sorry. "Tell you what, *lieblings*, I'll make them the next time you come over."

"That will not be for a while." Uncle Con spoke quickly, obviously anticipating his children's next move.

"Thank you for the *schmalzkuchens*, Aunt Elsa." Even with powdered sugar covering her chin, Katie displayed impeccable manners. "They are very good."

"You're welcome, Katie." Aunt Elsa smiled her approval.

Aunt Bry gazed at her daughter as if she might be a changeling left by some mischievous elf. Liberty could only conclude that Katie didn't always act so gracious at home.

Liberty thought of Pa, who taught about honesty but kept secrets. Folks were so complicated it made her head ache. How did God sort any of them out, including herself?

Jake waited until the last possible minute before saddling his horse. He didn't know what he was so stirred up about. Martha Riddler might not even be working today. Even if he found her behind the counter at the post office, he was a grown man with no reason to fear a diminutive woman.

His mother had suffered no further fainting spells, and her weakness seemed to be gone. Even so, he didn't like leaving her. He wouldn't go to town at all, but she wanted him to check the mail.

Scout pranced as Jake led him out of the barn, obviously delighted at the prospect of an outing.

Jake stopped short at the sight of Beau's horse tied outside the Hayes's house. Liberty was still visiting Phoebe, but Beau might have called thinking she was home. Jake couldn't see Beau waiting inside the porch alcove. Perhaps he'd entered the house.

Uneasiness ran over Jake. Some instinct warned him not to trust Beau. Shane was out of town officiating at a wedding, which left his wife and most of their children home alone.

Shane had asked Jake to keep an eye on his family. The present moment seemed an excellent time to do just that.

Jake left his horse in the barnyard and let himself out through the gate. He walked down the narrow driveway that led past Liberty's house to the main road. Jake heard Beau before he saw him. The man sounded quarrelsome, but Jake couldn't make out his words. He edged nearer.

"I told Liberty I'd come back to see her. Why didn't she mention she was going away then?"

Jake could guess the reason without being told, but Beau seemed to lack the necessary imagination.

"I'm sorry you're disappointed, Mr. Hensley." America spoke in unruffled tones. "You do recall that she had suffered an injury? Perhaps her distraction caused the omission."

Jake thought he understood Liberty's motives, and they didn't in the least resemble America's theory. Beau's treatment of Liberty and Phoebe had shown Jake that Beau bullied women. Liberty had simply wanted to avoid his overbearing reaction to her going away. She might even have feared he would follow her. Jake wasn't entirely sure he wouldn't have.

"Or maybe her behavior signifies an omission in her upbringing," Beau sneered.

Jake slipped closer, ready to intervene.

"You have no call to say such a thing." America sounded shocked.

Jake picked up his pace. He didn't like the way this was going, although he cheered America's backbone in confronting the rude man.

"You should have taught her better manners."

Jake's jaw tightened. How dare Beau question the parenting of a woman he barely knew? He was singularly unqualified as a bachelor with presumably no children of his own.

Jake slipped onto the front porch but didn't need to knock. Beau, who had apparently meant his last remark as a parting shot, strode through the doorway, fury written all over his face. He halted, glaring at Jake. "Step out of my way."

Jake held his ground. "No." He infused the word with every ounce of anger he felt at this man's treatment of Liberty, Phoebe, and America.

Beau's eyes widened as comprehension dawned. "Get out of my way, I tell you! I've had enough of your monkey shines."

"You owe Mrs. Hayes an apology." Jake ground out the words.

"Don't make trouble on my account, Jake." America called from the hallway. "Let Beau go on by."

Beau jutted out his chin. "You heard the woman."

Jake fought an inner battle. He very much wanted to teach this rude man a lesson in manners, but he could tell America wasn't as calm as she let on. Her voice had held a note of panic. Fisticuffs would only upset her further, and probably the children as well. Liam or Seth might come to investigate, and that would introduce complications.

"Please, Jake."

The pleading note in America's voice caught at Jake. "All right." He stepped aside but held Beau's gaze. "You win—this time."

"You'd better hope there is no next time." Beau brushed past him but turned before reaching his horse. "I'll thank you to stay out of my business in the future."

"Liberty and her family are *my* business."

"Don't count on it." Beau's face twisted in an ugly smile. "Liberty told me she wants nothing to do with you."

"You're lying." Jake could almost convince himself of that, but Beau's statement landed uncomfortably close to the truth.

Scout's muscles bunched and stretched beneath Jake as the horse's hooves pounded the hard-baked surface of the road. The confrontation with Beau had eaten into the meager time he'd allowed for the trip to town. Pushing his horse was the only way to reach the post office before it closed. Jake had gone nowhere since his mother's fainting spell, and Scout seemed eager to run. Galloping helped the horse release pent energy, and it let Jake do the same. His encounter with Beau had left Jake shaking with frustration. He'd better take command of his nerves before facing Martha. A clear head would come in handy as well. For that, he'd need to exorcise Beau's last statement from his mind. Telling himself that the man had every reason and the lack of conscience to deceive him did no good. When it came to Liberty, logic went out the window.

Jake rushed into the post office with five minutes to spare. The lobby was empty, except for Martha standing behind the counter.

"Well, well." She ran her hungry gaze over him. "I didn't think I'd see you again so soon."

He shrugged. "Ma is expecting a letter."

"I hope she appreciates such an attentive son." Her face held admiration. "Not every man looks after his mother so well."

Jake couldn't deny that her words and glances salved his wounds. She obviously craved his attention, whereas Liberty did not. Why shouldn't he get to know Martha a little better?

"Neither you nor your ma have any mail today, I'm sorry to say. I hope her letter comes soon."

Jake didn't budge.

Her eyes widened. "Do you want something else?"

He cleared his throat, nervous all at once. "It's getting a mite late. Would you like me to walk you home?"

A smile spread over her face. "I can't think of anything I'd like more. Let me lock up, and I'll be right with you."

Jake left his horse tied to a hitching post while he walked Martha home. She didn't live far, so he kept his pace as slow as possible. Martha didn't seem to mind one bit.

Wind frisked the quaking aspen above them, setting the heart-shaped leaves trembling. A dog barked as they passed but didn't venture from the porch where it lay. The smell of cooking wafting from many houses explained why the streets were deserted. His own supper waited at home, but at the moment he wanted no other food than a woman's admiration.

"Tell me, Miss Riddler—"

"Call me Martha like you did when we were kids."

He smiled. "Have you forgiven me for teasing you unmercilessly?"

"Almost." The glare she leveled on him put her reply in doubt.

Jake regretted making light of his thoughtless remarks

about her. "Forgive me. I shouldn't have called you skinny or freckled or wooly-haired—"

"No need to go on." She scowled. "I remember every slur."

Jake had never realized how much he must have hurt her. "I'm truly sorry."

She pouted for a moment, but then smiled. "You might have to make it up to me."

"What do you have in mind?" He asked the question with great caution.

"Hmm…" She glanced sideways at him. "I'll think on it."

"Not too long, I hope." He grinned. "You'll make me nervous."

Her smile took on a flirtatious timbre. "Stirring your emotions is more than I could do before."

Jake caught his breath at her forwardness. He waited until they'd turned down the shady lane that led to her house before speaking. "May I ask you something?"

Her gaze assessed him. "Go ahead."

"Why are you working at the post office? Didn't you have ambitions of some sort?"

"I wanted to become a journalist." Sadness touched her face. "That was before Pa died and Ma needed me to earn my keep to support her."

Life had quenched Martha's burning dream. No wonder her eyes held such hunger. He'd mistaken her desire for a different kind. "You admire me for taking care of my ma, but you're doing far more for your own."

She shrugged. "I figure she deserves it, after all she's done for me."

"Do you think you'll ever become a journalist?"

"I still want to, but my leaving Liberty depends on Ma." Martha's face shadowed. "She's in poor health. I doubt I'll have her much longer."

"Oh, I'm sorry." Genuine sympathy halted his steps in the shadow of a weeping willow. He turned to her in sympathy.

Martha flung herself into his arms.

Jake didn't resist, although he knew he should. She rested her head on his shoulder. Jake knew he shouldn't hold a woman like this, but he couldn't tell if she was crying. With the lane deserted, what harm could there be?

Martha pulled away and gazed up at him, no tears on her cheeks. Her eyes gleamed. "I know how you can pay me back for all those mean things you said about me."

Whatever she had in mind, he didn't think he was going to like it. "How?"

"Prove to me that you find me attractive, and you'll erase every sting."

"I'm not sure I understand—"

She lifted her face to his. "Kiss me."

Martha was attractive, but kissing a woman in public during broad daylight seemed a bad idea. Why did the woman need so much assurance? With her lips puckered close to his, logic didn't have a lot to do with his reaction. He was a man and only human. It took an effort of will to hold her at arm's length. "I'm spoken for, Martha."

"Oh really?" Her eyes reproached him. "Who is she?"

He shook his head. Speaking Liberty's name would be wrong, since he had no claim to her affections. Martha sounded so bitter that the desire to ease her pain rose within him. "If it's any comfort, I do find you attractive."

"It's Liberty, isn't it?" His face must have betrayed him, because she nodded as if he'd answered her. "Do you know that you broke my heart?"

"I'm sorry. No, I didn't."

She crossed her arms over herself. "Go away, Jake."

"Are you all right?"

A bitter smile marred her beauty. "I always am."

Jake walked away from her, glad to escape. If he'd given in, she'd have bound him to her somehow.

Jake finished brushing Scout's coat and gave him a final pat. Soft light fell from the high windows and lit swirling dust motes. Time to air out the barn, a task he performed regularly to protect the livestock from developing heaves. Every creature deserved to breathe fresh air.

A scuffling footstep alerted Jake to someone behind him in the barn. He spun about but relaxed when he recognized his mother. Light from the window behind her turned the gray strands threading her blond hair silver, but her face hid in shadow. The set of her shoulders gave away her irritation.

"You're late for supper." Her chiding tone confirmed her annoyance.

"Sorry, Ma. I left it too long to go after the mail, and then dealt with a couple of—delays."

Her face softened from annoyance to sympathy. "Do you want to tell me what's wrong?"

"Does it show that much?"

"You jumped like a tomcat when I came in. What has you riled?"

He drew a deep breath and considered how to begin. "Beau Hensley called at Liberty's house today."

"Oh?" Ma spoke in guarded tones.

Jake sighed. His mother must be recalling the ruckus he'd caused on Sunday. "Liberty wasn't home. She's visiting Phoebe."

"And?"

"Beau was rude to America."

She closed her eyes. "Don't tell me you picked a fight."

"Your faith in me is downright heartwarming. Do I look like I've been fighting?"

Forehead creased, she studied him. "No."

"That's because I haven't."

"I'm sorry." She folded her arms. "I assumed the worst of you, yet again."

Jake nodded his forgiveness. "You'd have admired my restraint."

A smile crept to her lips. "I'm proud of you, Son, truly I am."

"Thank you." He drew a deep breath and spoke in a rush. "Beau said that Liberty wants nothing to do with me."

"Perhaps you should talk with Liberty herself."

"I did before she left. She told me pretty much the same thing." Noticing he still held the horse brush, Jake laid it on the work table in the grooming stall.

"I'm sorry to hear that." His mother followed him outside the stall. "I like Liberty. I hoped—"

"I know, Ma. I hoped too."

"Did she say why?"

"I'm not sure she really knows." He shrugged. "It's my fault, anyway."

"What do you mean?"

"I pushed Liberty to accept a change between us. I wanted to court her, but she wasn't ready." Scout nuzzled him, a gentle reminder that it was time for his oats. Jake led his horse into his stall.

His mother trailed behind him. "It might not be too late."

"I assure you, it is."

"I'm not convinced."

He shook his head. "Don't ask me to hope."

"Why not?"

"Because hope hurts." He clanged the stall door shut. "I've thought about going somewhere else for a while."

Ma nodded. "Maybe you should."

He stared at her. "I didn't expect that reaction after the way Ben left." Ma had never gotten over his brother going off without any goodbyes. She'd found out by reading the terse note he'd propped on the kitchen table. That had happened five years ago, with little word from him since.

"What your brother did has no bearing on your decision."

"It doesn't matter." Jake dumped oats into Scout's feeding trough. "I'm not going anywhere until Doc Bailey tells me you're all right."

"I'm certain that day will arrive soon."

"I don't mind waiting for it."

Ma smiled. "Don't let concern for me hold you back."

"Of course, it should. I love you."

"You're every bit as stubborn as your father." His mother chided him with a smile on her face.

"Thank you." Jake grinned. "Speaking of Pa, I'm certain he would want me to look out for you."

Ma fell silent, and Jake knew that mentioning his father had tipped the scales in his favor. He was determined to do right by his mother, with or without her support. He might have to stay until after Liberty returned, but he'd face that problem if it came.

CHAPTER FOURTEEN

Uncle Rob lifted Liberty into the carriage while Phoebe grasped her arms from above. Liberty winced as she landed on her sore ankle.

Phoebe steadied her. "Are you all right?"

"Yes." Liberty half-fell onto the bench seat with a soft moan.

"You don't sound all right." Phoebe perched beside her.

"Climbing into the landau defeats me, but my ankle is much improved."

"I'm glad to hear it." Aunt Maisey appeared in the carriage doorway. She completed the ascent and took a seat opposite them.

"I want to ride in the jump seat!" Murphy's request came through the open window beside Liberty. "Can I, Pa?"

Liberty glanced out to see Quinn shaking his head. "It's my turn, Pa."

"No, it's not." Murphy raised his voice. "You rode in it last time."

"No, I didn't." Quinn matched him for volume.

"Yes, you did." Murphy thrust his face close to his brother's. "It's my turn."

"Boys, boys!" Uncle Rob pulled the combatants apart. "Maisey, do you remember who rode in the jump seat last time?"

"Didn't Murphy?" Aunt Maisey called out her window.

"I thought it was Quinn." Uncle Rob shrugged. "We'll have to settle this with a coin toss. Agreed?" He peered into each of his son's eyes in turn. The boys nodded, although they continued to bristle like angry cats.

Liberty could understand the boys' fascination. Riding in the detachable seat at the rear of the carriage sounded like something they would enjoy. The seat's lack of a roof might make the reality somewhat less attractive, which only added to the adventure. That the family didn't normally use the jump seat only increased its appeal. The landau could hold Phoebe's family with Uncle Rob in the driver's seat, but Liberty's presence made one too many.

With the coin toss concluded, Murphy claimed the coveted jump seat with a swagger possibly meant to annoy his brother. Quinn accepted the place of defeat beside his mother.

Uncle Rob stepped into the landau, bumping into Liberty's sore ankle.

She gasped.

He flinched. "Sorry. Move over a little, would you Maisey? I want—to—" He reached up and unfastened the convertible top of the landau. The leather roof divided in the middle and folded back behind each seat. "There. It's such a short ride, we can all enjoy a ride in the open air." He smiled at Maisey. "Thank you, my love."

Quinn sat taller, brightening considerably.

Uncle Rob climbed into the driving box, took up the reins, and called to the horses. The matched Percherons tossed their black manes, and the landau sprang into motion. Murphy shifted sideways and kept up a running commentary on the sights falling away behind them. Quinn entertained his sister and Liberty with stories about bears—which Liberty felt sure he made up—until Aunt Maisey snapped her book shut. "Quinn, have you nothing else to talk about? You're frightening the girls."

Surprised to learn that she was scared, Liberty glanced at Phoebe, whose eyes danced with mirth. Quinn pulled a face at his sister, but he received no reprimand. His mother was too busy shaking her head at Murphy. "Young man, if you insist on dangling from your seat, you'll fall out. If you do, don't expect us to come back for you."

Murphy didn't turn a hair, clearly aware—as they all were—that his mother could never drive off and leave one of her children, however naughty.

Aunt Maisey turned her firmest face toward Quinn and Murphy. "I hope you boys are prepared to work hard today."

Murphy creased his forehead. "What kind of hard work?"

Quinn drew his eyebrows together. "I thought we were only helping Aunt Bry and Uncle Nick move."

"That's right." Aunt Maisey smiled at her sons. "It takes muscles to lift furniture, trunks, and crates."

"We can do it!" Quinn announced with utter confidence.

"It won't be much different from toting hay." Murphy matched his brother in bravado.

The boys had a point, Liberty decided. Ranch life made her cousins strong.

"Do we all have to lift things, Ma?" Phoebe sounded bored.

"You and Liberty will help Elsa and me in the kitchen. All the helpers will need food."

Liberty nodded. "I'm happy to make myself useful."

"Speaking of food, what will we eat at the medicine show?" Phoebe clasped her hands. "I can just taste the corn on the cob. I like mine with lots of butter and salt. How about you, Liberty?"

"I haven't given it much thought." Liberty doubted she'd have an appetite at the medicine show.

Quinn's eyes lit. "I want a candy apple, and I can't wait to watch the magician saw a woman in half."

"He's not going to do that." Murphy startled gaze flew to his mother. "Is he?"

"Not really." Aunt Maisey frowned at Quinn. "I'm looking forward to the variety show."

"I want to see the acrobats." Uncle Rob spoke over his shoulder. "And I'd like fried chicken."

"I wonder what food they'll have." Aunt Maisey tilted her head, a bemused expression on her face. "If I owned the show, I know what I'd offer."

Uncle Rob laughed. "Don't you have enough people to feed without wishing for more?"

She smiled. "I suppose I do."

"Gee!" Uncle Rob commanded the horses, making sure they bore right at a tight bend. He glanced back. "I wish Shane and America would have come."

Aunt Maisey frowned. "What did they reply to your telegram?"

He shrugged. "Only that they didn't plan on going."

"I wonder why." Aunt Maisey shook her head. "Oh well, we'll make the best of it."

"Sorry, Maisey. I know how much you and America enjoy one another's company." Uncle Rob faced forward to navigate the turn into the driveway to Uncle Con's property. They pulled up at the ranch house, a clapboard-clad building that rose two stories. The green shutters that bracketed the windows kept out the worst heat in summer and the wind in winter. Pillars supported the balcony above the wide porch. The front door burst open, and Fiona hurried out with Richard and Willie in tow. Aunt Elsa followed more slowly, hampered by Otto clinging to her skirts and Meg in her arms. Uncle Con waved from the barn doorway.

Uncle Rob jumped down and opened the carriage door.

Quinn held back, allowing the women to leave first. Uncle Rob helped Aunt Maisey, Liberty, and Phoebe disembark. Duty discharged, he met Uncle Con on the way from the barn and clapped him on the back.

Quinn joined Murphy in tangling with Richard on the porch. The wrestlers came within inches of knocking over a cobalt blue pot spilling over with forget-me-nots.

"Boys!" Aunt Elsa rubbed Meg's back while she glared at the offenders. "Play in the yard, not on the porch."

"Quinn! Murphy!" Aunt Maisey's voice beat Aunt Elsa's for volume. "You know better."

"Yes, Ma." They chimed in chorus.

Richard murmured something Liberty didn't catch, and the three boys sped across the grass toward the barn.

"We have a new colt" Aunt Elsa smiled, then hugged Aunt Maisey one-armed. "It's good to see you again. Come in, and don't worry about the boys. The men will round them up when they're ready to leave. Con hitched the wagon right before you came. It won't be long before they head to Nick and Bry's house for a load."

Aunt Maisey picked up Otto, who was reaching out to her. "Our carriage might come in handy if Bry prefers to ride somewhere other than the back of a wagon. The boot can carry more fragile belongings."

Elsa smiled as she led the way inside. "I'm sure your carriage rides smoother than our rickety old ranch wagon. Bry and Nick's is not much better."

The staircase in the entryway curved upward in a graceful arch. Lined with sleek paneling and padded by deep red carpeting, it provided a beautiful backdrop for the gold chandelier suspended from the ceiling. When candles burned in the holders shaped like cupped flowers, prisms dangling below them scattered dancing rainbows.

"Fiona, you're in charge of Willie and Otto." Aunt Elsa glanced at the baby she held. "Phoebe, would you be willing to look after Meg?"

"That's no hardship." Phoebe held out her arms, and Meg leaned into them.

Elsa blew out a breath. "Thank you. It's nice to cook with my hands free. What about you, Liberty? Would you like to help in the kitchen or watch babies?"

"I'd probably be of more use in the kitchen, provided I can sit while I work."

"Yes, of course."

Liberty spent most of the day peeling and chopping vegetables and mixing batches of dough. Keeping busy felt good. When she returned home, she'd offer to assist Ma in the kitchen more often. Cooking and cleaning demanded a lot of effort, as she was discovering. Ma attended her chores without complaint, so used to performing them alone that she forgot to ask for help sometimes. Liberty wouldn't let that stop her.

She fell into bed after an exhausting day, grateful to rest.

Where is Jake in this moment? The stray thought quickened her breath. *Is he thinking of me?*

The end of a difficult day was not the time to lie awake wondering about Jake. Tamping down all thoughts of him, Liberty folded her hands to sleep. Accomplishing this goal took longer than expected, since her mind insisted on dredging up memories. She couldn't forget the feel of Jake's lips on hers, the caress of his hands on her injured ankle, or the way he'd looked at her when she'd told him there was no hope for them,

Phoebe dragged herself from bed, worn out from watching her young cousins. Her heart went out to Aunt Elsa, who looked

after her children every day and made it look easy.

Phoebe took care of her grooming and dressed as quietly as possible to avoid waking Liberty. She pulled the door to behind her and tiptoed down the corridor. At the top of the stairs, Phoebe paused to listen. The ticking of the grandfather clock behind her was the only sound.

The kitchen, normally a busy place, still slumbered. Waking up earlier than Aunt Elsa felt like quite a feat. Phoebe slipped out the back door.

The first light of a new day gathered on the horizon and leached the sky, extinguishing the stars. The moon still glowed, but with faded glory. The remnant of the night wind brushed her cheek.

Phoebe bent in the garden and pulled a couple of carrots. She glanced about her, conscious that predatory beasts might still roam. Lurking at the back of her mind was the old fear of Spukani, but she understood it as irrational. At some point she needed to address it, but not this morning. Stirrings in the house reassured her that others would soon join her. Morning chores beckoned to Uncle Con, Fiona, and Richard. Phoebe hurried to the barn.

Today she would skip her morning ride in favor of cleaning the house Aunt Bry and Uncle Nick were vacating. She wanted to make up to Nutmeg for neglecting their morning outing.

The rooster crowed, and the laying hens began clucking. The side door creaked, and Phoebe stepped into the barn's cool dimness. She could see enough to find her horse's stall. Nutmeg whickered and blew warm breath against her hand.

Phoebe fed her horse the carrot she'd brought for her. She patted Nutmeg's neck. "Sorry, girl. No ride today."

Old Smokey whinnied from a nearby stall.

Phoebe smiled. "Good morning to you, sir." She scratched

the old horse's neck while he crunched a carrot.

After paying her respects to the horses, Phoebe turned to go. She'd left the side door ajar for additional light. Through the opening, she could hear Will's whistle. Phoebe stopped in her tracks. She didn't want to run into him, not while she felt exhausted and vulnerable. In her haste, she'd done a sloppy job of pinning up her hair. She shouldn't care what he thought of her appearance, but somehow, she did.

Will's whistle grew louder, an indication that he was headed for the barn. So much for avoiding him. Phoebe entertained the idea of concealing herself but discarded it. If Will found her hiding, she might have to explain her behavior. That might prove harder than facing him. Mind made up, she squared her shoulders and waited.

Will appeared in the doorway. He froze and his whistle died away. Will laughed and relaxed his posture. "Phoebe— Miss Walsh—you gave me quite a turn, standing there. I wasn't expecting to see you out here so early."

Warmth flooded Phoebe's cheeks. She'd already started on the wrong foot with him. "I'm sorry. I was trying not to startle you in the doorway."

His lips quirked into a smile. "You managed to do it anyway. Why are you here so early? Going riding?"

"Not today. I'm needed to clean."

"I suppose you'll lend your ma a hand." He leaned against the door jamb. "I heard she plans to clean your aunt and uncle's old place for them."

"Yes, I'm helping Ma do so."

"It's nice of you to pitch in."

Phoebe shrugged. "I was pressed into service, to be honest, but I don't mind."

"Acquiring a willing heart is the first step to contentment."

He laughed. "My ma used to tell me that when she wanted me to do something I didn't like."

She smiled. "Does it work?"

"It got me to stop dragging my feet. I accomplished more and finished sooner as a result. So, I suppose so."

"Did it lead you to contentment?"

"Contentment isn't so simple, but there's a certain satisfaction in completing a hard job."

"I've felt that."

"There's your answer." He straightened away from the jamb. "I have a question for you."

Phoebe tensed. "What do you want to know?"

"There's no need to look frightened." He advanced toward her.

"Do I?" She tried to sound unbothered.

"Don't worry." He stopped before reaching her. "I come in peace."

Phoebe wrapped her arms around herself, too nervous to grace his attempt at humor with a smile. "What do you want to ask?"

"When we went riding, I gained the impression you were angry at me. Did I somehow offend you?"

Phoebe had no idea what to say. Wild horses wouldn't drag out the confession that she'd disliked Liberty and him fawning over one another. Nor would she enlighten him to the jealous pangs she'd suffered. "No offense, but I prefer keeping my own counsel."

"That can only mean that I offended you."

"I just said—"

"I understand that you don't want to talk, but please accept my apologies for whatever I did."

"I'm sorry, but I can't discuss this right now." Phoebe

stepped past him. "My ma will be looking for me."

Will's face softened. "All right, Phoebe—Miss Walsh. I understand."

She turned back at the door. "It's Phoebe."

"Thanks." He smiled. "Call me Will."

Meg normally squealed with delight at the sight of Liberty, but today she darted into the kitchen and hid her face in her mother's skirts.

"Never mind." Elsa stopped stirring a pot of soup and picked up her tiny daughter. "She can stay with me."

"Are you sure?" Aunt Elsa had a lot to do, preparing food for all those involved in the move with only Fiona as cook's assistant. Aunt Bry was busy unpacking. Aunt Maisey and Phoebe had cleaning to do. It was too bad that her own ma and pa had sent word that a death in their congregation prevented them from leaving home.

"I'm sure. We're having plain fare tonight anyway. All the upheaval has upset Meg, I think. Bry dotes on the baby but can't come around as often. She's also taken some of Meg's playmates with her."

"Poor dear." Liberty dove after Otto, who was making a break for the back doorway. His mother left the door open in the mornings for cooling purposes, which proved an irresistible challenge for the mischievous tyke. Liberty's tender ankle hampered her efforts to capture her young charge, but Willie collared him at the moment of freedom.

"No, no, Otto." Willie led her brother inside.

"Stay with Liberty, Otto." Elsa frowned at her son but turned eyes shining with mirth toward Liberty. "Are you sure that you and my *mutter* are up to watching this rascal?"

"It will be all right. Oma Wilhelmina is spry for nearly sixty, not to mention that we'll have an excellent helper." Liberty smiled at Willie.

"All right then." Elsa pulled a jar of red jam from the shelf and extended it to Liberty. "Please give this to *Mutter*. I put up her favorite flavor—strawberry. It is our custom in Germany to bring gifts when we visit."

"Thank you for your thoughtfulness. I'll make sure she receives your gift. Are you ready to visit your oma, Willie?"

The little girl nodded, her china-blue eyes gleaming.

"Keep close to me." Liberty took Otto's hand and led him toward the back door. Willie trailed her.

"Don't let go of Otto until you're past the garden." Aunt Elsa called after them. "Otherwise, you'll never get him out of the dirt."

Located on a hill a short walk through the woods from the ranch house, the log cabin resembled a chalet. It was large enough to house Oma Wilhelmina plus the six children she'd brought to America with her. They had all moved away but often returned with their own children. "Come in and sit down, *liebchen*." Oma Wilhelmina opened the front door of the house Uncle Con had built for her.

"Aunt Elsa sent this for you." Liberty held out the jar of jam.

"How delightful." Oma Wilhelmina beamed. "We must sample some. I know. I'll make *Marmeladentörtchen*."

Willie brightened. "Jam tarts. Can I help, Oma?"

"Yes, of course, child. I hoped you would offer." Oma Wilhelmina's face shone with joy. "And we must find a spoon for Otto to lick."

A while later, with bellies full of scrambled eggs and jam tarts, the children submitted to the washing of their sticky hands and faces. Willie protested the need for a nap at her age but was the first to succumb. Otto rebelled with more vigor but also surrendered.

Oma Wilhelmina shared a smile with Liberty. "More tea? Another tart?"

Liberty plunked into the chair she'd occupied at the scrubbed oak kitchen table. She rubbed her stomach and sighed from a combination of relief and contentment. "I can't eat any more, but a second cup of tea would be nice."

"I'll make a fresh pot." Oma Wilhelmina ladled water from a metal pail into the cast iron kettle. She carried the kettle to the stove and lifted an exquisite tea pot from a cupboard shelf. A yellow rose adorned the white porcelain above the pot's frilly pedestal base. Gold decorated the handle, spout, pedestal, and lid. Liberty was glad Oma Wilhelmina hadn't asked her to measure the tea. The teapot, obviously an antique, looked too delicate to use.

Oma Wilhelmina brought out tea cups that matched the pot. She poured the steaming amber liquid and set a cup before Liberty.

"Thank you." Liberty picked up the delicate china confection gingerly. She breathed the vapors rising to her. "This cup is lovely, but I'm afraid of breaking it."

"What good is it to own fine things if you never use them?" Oma Wilhelmina shrugged. "It is only a cup, although it belonged to my mother."

"I'm honored you would share such a precious set with me."

"You brought me joy today. That is reason enough." She smiled. "When I remember how much my parents enjoyed my children, it brings them back to me."

"I'm glad." Liberty didn't ask whether Oma Wilhelmina's parents had passed on, but from what she'd said it seemed likely.

Liberty could barely recall a long-ago meeting with her own

grandfather. It did not stir fondness in her. Why did Ma never speak of her parents? Was there more she didn't understand about her background?

Oma Wilhelmina sighed. "I think too, of my Otto. He loved all the children but favored Elsa. I wasn't surprised. She has a way about her that, of all the children, is most like him. He loved music, you see, and gave Elsa that gift."

Liberty nodded, recollecting the times Aunt Elsa had played her treasured hurdy gurdy for them. Fiona had inherited a beautiful voice.

"We met at a Christmas party my parents hosted. I didn't like him at first, and he thought I was too young and awkward." She laughed. "I was at that age—just fourteen. He was intrigued by my cousin, Gretchen, but she married someone else. He enlisted as a soldier and didn't come back for several years." Her head lifted in a coquettish tilt. "When he returned, I wasn't gawkish any longer."

Liberty realized her tea was growing cold. She lifted her cup. "How did you know you were in love?"

Oma Wilhelmina smiled mysteriously. "I figured it out."

"But how?" Liberty barely contained her frustration. She wanted facts, not inferences.

"That is not easy to put into words."

"I don't understand." A pleading note crept into Liberty's voice. If she could figure out this one thing, maybe the rest of life would settle down.

"You can't use logic to understand the heart, *liebchen*."

Tears pricked at the back of Liberty's eyes. "If only I could."

"Ah, but that would take away the adventure it brings." Oma Wilhelmina smiled. "To learn about this strange emotion, you have to experience it. That's true of the feeling between a man and woman. It's also true of God's love."

"You are under arrest." A familiar voice spoke from behind Jake. He straightened from bending over Scout's hoof with a pick and spun around.

The barrel of a pistol stared him down. "I'd advise you not to make any quick movements," Deputy Hanson drawled.

"What is going on, Clifton?" Jake couldn't recall doing anything the deputy would have an opinion on lately.

Clifton turned his head and spat tobacco juice. The deputy's inattention gave Jake plenty of time to attack him, if he'd had a mind to.

"May I know the charge?" Jake kept his voice steady, despite his annoyance. No point in antagonizing someone whose good graces he might need to call upon. The odds of mercy extending Jake's way weren't great to begin with. He knew Clifton Davey from his school days and felt no fondness for him.

Clifton no doubt returned the sentiment, judging by his glare. "You're accused of forcing yourself on a woman against her will."

Jake stared at him. "What on earth are you talking about?"

"Just doing my job." Clifton shifted the plug of chaw from one cheek to the other.

"I appreciate that." Jake scratched the back of his neck. "May I know who accused me?"

"Martha Riddler."

Jake started. This was beginning, horribly, to make sense. "What does she say that I did?"

Clifton cleared his throat. "I'm not privy to the particulars. All I know is we have to bring you in since she has a witness."

"A wit—that can't be true."

Clifton cocked an eyebrow. "You might want to be careful

what you say."

"I meant that it can't be true because the whole thing, whatever she claimed, did not happen." Jake measured out every word.

"You'll have the chance to stand trial." Clifton's voice held satisfaction. It had been years since they'd tussled in the schoolyard over a girl. Jake supposed that the memory of Clifton's defeat must still rankle. Clifton thrust out his chest. "You can either come with me peacefully or in handcuffs, your choice."

"I'll come peacefully." Jake dropped the pick onto the worktable beside him. "Let me put away my horse and tell my mother not to wait supper."

Clifton's face worked, as if he would like to deny Jake's simple requests but could find no reason to do so. "All right, but make it snappy."

Jake rubbed Scout's neck, taking comfort from the familiar gesture. He murmured soothing words to his horse, who was fidgeting. He threw hay into Scout's feeding trough, occupied with how he would convey this turn of events to his mother. He could think of no good way.

Jake located her in the kitchen, stirring a batch of huckleberry jam. After he explained the matter, Ma rose to her full stature and stared down Clifton, who had followed him. "Deputy, there must be some mistake."

"That's for the judge to decide." Clifton sounded authoritative, but the veins stood out on his neck, and it was clear that he feared Ma as much as anyone.

Her face turned red. "You aren't seriously entertaining the idea of putting my son in jail."

Clifton's face turned a darker shade than Ma's. "We have to, Mrs. Buckthorn—sorry to say." He added the last part when

Ma's mouth opened as if she was more than ready to blast him.

Jake's suspicion that his mother would take the news badly had proven true, but he couldn't have anticipated her protecting him. In the past, that hadn't been her reaction to finding him in trouble. Somehow, their relationship must have shifted for the better. Although he would rather find that out differently, it felt rather good.

"Ma, please don't fret. I do have to go." He gave her his best attempt at an encouraging smile.

"If you must." She released a heavy sigh. "We'll have you out of there soon, I promise."

Jake nodded. He hoped she was right. Meanwhile, he had a reservation in Liberty's diminutive jail house. He'd yearned to be alone of late, From all appearances, he was about to get his wish.

CHAPTER FIFTEEN

Liberty peered through the window while the wagon rolled past the colorful tents and painted wagons that surrounded a tall platform on wheels. A red-and-white striped awning shaded the stage where a man wearing a bowler hat and suspenders strummed a banjo and sang. "Oh Susannah! Oh, don't you cry for me…" Beside him, a man dressed in similar togs fanned the harmonica he held to his mouth. Crowds swarmed the main stage while some purchased food and wares from vendors calling from the tents.

They'd left the ranch a little late in the morning, but Uncle Rob had put the horses through their paces. It was not yet noon. Uncle Rob turned the wagon into the field that was roped off for parking. The medicine show occupied a space beside Willow Creek outside Corvallis. Beyond the tents, clear water wallowed between grassy banks, a cooling sight against the dry grass. Willows draped leafy boughs into the water and cast welcome shade. Overhead, pale clouds mimicked the outline of the white-capped mountains below.

Liberty could hardly believe she was at Doc Woburn's Traveling Medicine Show. What would her father look like? What might he say? Could he possibly want anything to do with her? Today she would find out.

To meet him, she'd have to find a way to escape on her own. She'd never done such a thing before and had no idea how Phoebe managed it so often. Since the rest of the family had decided to skip today's outing, stealing away would be easier than if they'd come. Aunt Bry and Uncle Nick had declared themselves too busy with their move. They might drive to Stevensville when the medicine show traveled there. Aunt Elsa and Uncle Con were worn out from helping them move. They would wait and travel to Stevensville also. Aunt Maisey and Uncle Rob almost postponed going to the show for similar reasons. They'd decided not to disappoint Murphy and Quinn. The boys had complained of exhaustion, but a night's sleep miraculously revived them. Uncle Rob proclaimed that the whole family deserved a reward.

Phoebe had seemed a little quiet during the trip but perked up when she stepped from the carriage.

Uncle Rob collared Murphy before he could take off into the crowd. "Not so fast! Stay with the family."

Liberty pressed her stomach to calm its churning. If her uncle insisted on corralling them all, how would she ever manage to meet her father?

Aunt Maisey touched Uncle Rob's arm. "Don't you think that the boys could explore on their own if they stay together? They're excited, and we'd never keep up with their energy."

Uncle Rob smiled in that special way he reserved for Aunt Maisey. "I suppose it would be all right, but I'm not so feeble that I can't keep up with my sons."

She smiled. "I didn't mean it that way. We're tired, not old."

Uncle Rob chuckled. "You, my darling, look younger every year." He turned to his sons. "Quinn, you're in charge. I expect you and your brother to conduct yourselves like young gentlemen.

Quinn stood a little taller. "Yes, sir."

"Murphy, I'd better not hear that you ignored your brother."

"No, Pa." The expression Murphy turned on his father was

the very essence of innocence.

"We'll wait for you by the red tent in an hour. Here's a bit of pocket change for both of you. Don't spend it all in one place."

"We won't." The boys chimed in unison.

"All right. Off with you." Uncle Rob spoke with the air of a king granting a sacred charge to a pair of knights.

The boys walked off with perfect deportment.

Aunt Maisey smiled. "Well done, Rob."

Halfway through the parking area, Quinn and Murphy broke into a run.

"Slow down!" Uncle Rob called after them.

"Sorry, Pa," the chorus came back.

Uncle Rob shook his head. "We'll have a discussion on deportment later."

Phoebe stepped closer to her mother. "Liberty and I want to look around on our own too."

Liberty stared at Phoebe in surprise. They'd never discussed it.

Uncle Rob glanced at them doubtfully. "I'd rather keep you girls near."

Phoebe frowned. "That's not fair. We're adults, and we have better manners than the boys."

"She has a point." Aunt Maisey took the arm Uncle Rob offered her.

"I suppose so." Uncle Rob gave Phoebe and Liberty each a handful of nickels. "Meet us near the red tent after an hour."

Phoebe touched the brooch watch pinned to her bodice. "We'll be there."

Aunt Maisey gave them a stern glance. "Make sure you stay together."

"Don't worry, Ma."

Liberty was grateful that Phoebe answered because, she

couldn't have affirmed her aunt's wish. Her conscience pricked at the prospect of slipping away from Phoebe, but she had no doubt that Phoebe would be fine on her own. Liberty wove through the crowd beside Phoebe, watching for a chance to steal away. One hour didn't seem a lot of time to find and meet her father. Liberty would need every second she could snatch.

Phoebe tugged on her arm. "Look over there!" She pointed at a man in evening clothes and a top hat. He was easy to spot because he was walking on stilts.

Liberty stared at the man, who lifted his hat and bowed to passersby. "How does he do that without falling?"

"It must take lots of practice. I wonder how many times he took a tumble while learning."

Liberty shook her head. "You'd never catch me doing anything so foolhardy." Well, not anything of a physical nature, anyway. She seemed to have a penchant for other kinds of mistakes.

Could I be making one today?

Liberty still hadn't figured out how to introduce herself to her father, let alone how to speak of private matters in such a public place. Maybe she should abandon her plans.

Liberty drew a steadying breath. If she gave up, she would never know what might have happened.

"The food is over there." Phoebe's voice broke into Liberty's thoughts. Phoebe pointed toward a line of tents with smoke wafting from chimneys that poked through their roofs. Situated across a grassy aisle from the vending tents, they seemed to be doing brisk business. Droves of people waited in the baking sun for the chance to order.

Phoebe shaded her eyes and peered about. "I wonder if they have corn on the cob."

"Maybe. Do you want to take a look?"

A few minutes later, Phoebe joined the queue to purchase an ear of roasted corn on a spit. Phoebe breathed deeply. "It smells delicious. Are you sure you don't want one?"

"No, thank you." Liberty barely kept the horror out of her voice. Her stomach was already struggling to digest the small breakfast she'd forced herself to eat. "I'm not feeling very well," she said with perfect honesty. "The smell of food is making me queasy."

"Oh no." Phoebe turned a concerned gaze on her. "I hope you're not coming down with something."

Liberty saw her chance. "If you don't mind, I'll wait for you at the stage."

"Yes, do." Phoebe glanced at the line ahead of her. "This may take a while. Maybe you can find a patch of shade for us to sit in and watch the entertainment."

"I'll try." Liberty hurried away from Phoebe, nearly colliding with the man in a swallowtail coat who stepped in front of her. He forced his way through the crowd and climbed the steps to the stage.

Liberty pushed to the front of the crowd without her usual manners. She tilted her head for a better view.

Liberty's stomach roiled, and she came within inches of heaving. The man standing on the platform could only be her father. Wavy blond hair much like hers fell to the collar of his frock coat. The blue eyes with which he watched the crowd matched hers. Liberty had seen herself often enough in the mirror to know that his features were a masculine version of her own. No wonder Ma had told Pa in the barn that she had trouble looking at her sometimes. She was the spitting image of her father.

"How much do you value your health, ladies and gentlemen?" Doc Woburn sounded smooth, as if reciting a practiced speech by heart. "It's a priceless treasure, wouldn't you agree?" He paused, scanning the crowd. His gaze rested on Liberty briefly, moved on, and flitted back before roaming elsewhere.

"Pay careful attention, my friends. I'm about to let you in on a secret that will change your life." He paused once more, knees bent and head cocked in a listening posture. He held this position while the crowd leaned forward. Tension built until it fairly crackled the air.

Doc Woburn rose to his full height. "Two bits! That's all you need to restore your well-being. I'm here to tell you the plain truth, ladies and gents! It will cost you only *twenty-five pennies* for Doc Woburn's Natural Herbal Remedy."

Liberty edged away from the stage. Her heart thudded in her ears, and her hands shook. In this state, she would never manage to introduce herself to this man. That might not be possible anyway. He seemed determined to spend all afternoon cajoling the crowd.

"Why, this tonic succeeds where doctors fail. Only the Natural Herbal Remedy heals so well. Here it is, right here in this little bottle—the most powerful elixir known to man. The formula comes from God's own laboratory—nature itself, and it cures all manner of disorders. I mean cancer, diabetes, heart murmur, bad breath, wrinkles, baldness, and rheumatism. But that's only a small slice of what it can do, folks."

Liberty broke out of the crowd, ready to run, hide, be anywhere else. She turned and fled.

Doc Woburn's voice followed her. "Buy a bottle and find out for yourself what this wonderful medicine can do to put a spring in your step."

Liberty glanced back and stumbled.

"Careful there." An arm caught her around the waist. "Begging your pardon, miss, but I thought you might fall."

"I was about to, thanks." Liberty glanced up at her rescuer and started. "It's you."

Wilfred Faraday grinned. "Delighted to see me or was that a cry of dismay?"

"Neither." She pulled away from him. "I was surprised, that's all."

"I hope you find meeting me again a pleasant surprise." He swept the bowler hat he was wearing today from his head and bowed. "I must thank you yet again for helping a stranger find his way on the road. I am in your debt."

"Mr. Canfield Will did that, but of course you are welcome. My family believes in helping lost souls find their way." Liberty fought the urge to wretch.

"Say, you look a little green around the gills. Are you feeling all right?"

She shook her head. "I'm afraid not. My stomach troubles me."

"Why don't you sit down on this nice bench? Where is your family?"

"They're around." She waved a hand vaguely. "I stepped away for a minute to listen to Doc Woburn."

"He's quite a showman. The presentation will end soon. I'm here to ward off the crowd so Doc Woburn can retire to his tent." He shook his head. "I wish I knew how he mesmerizes people."

Since Mr. Faraday counted himself in her debt, maybe she should take advantage of the moment. If she asked, he might introduce her to Doc Woburn. To find out, all she needed to do was speak.

"I'd better get back to work." He frowned. "I hate to leave you looking so dazed."

"I'm all right."

He gave her a doubtful glance. "If you want my opinion,

you're better off keeping close to your family."

If she didn't ask now, it would be too late. Liberty stared at him, tongue-tied.

"Something on your mind?"

She couldn't do it. She'd gone to a lot of trouble, only to learn that she wasn't ready to confront her father. Maybe she never would be. Liberty glanced away to hide the tears in her eyes. "You should go."

Jake rolled over on the hard mattress and groaned as realization dawned. Waking up in jail was not something he'd expected at this point of his life, although not all that long ago it had felt possible. His hope of polishing his tarnished reputation died a painful death. If asked as a small boy what he wanted to be when he grew up, he'd have chosen something other than a black sheep. While watching the sunrise behind the barred window in his tiny cell, that fate seemed more than likely.

He was glad Liberty hadn't been home to watch the deputy arrest him. The sight would only have confirmed her low opinion of him. He didn't know what to think about his mother's reaction. He'd expected her to accuse him of wrong doing. Why had she defended him? Unable to come up with an answer, Jake tucked the riddle into the back of his mind.

He laid down again and covered himself with the scratchy wool blanket the deputy had tossed to him with a smirk. Jake closed his eyes and courted sleep. Memories swarmed into his mind instead. He saw again twelve-year-old Liberty tip her face with utter trust in her eyes as she murmured the words he'd yearned to hear. Jake had pledged to love and cherish her for life, and he was a man of his word. Whether or not she returned his affections didn't change that. Another hope he'd held dear—of marrying and having a family—had already perished.

Jake flipped onto his back and folded his hands behind his head. Dwelling on the past only drove home what he'd never attain in life. A spider spinning a web in a corner of the ceiling rose and fell while constructing its trap. One of the fat flies crowding the window would likely fall prey to the spider, much as he had to Martha's lies.

Jake threw back his blanket and jumped to his feet, trying to escape his thoughts. They came along anyway, unwelcome guests lacking the decency to leave an unwilling host. Martha's wounded eyes and reproachful words returned to him. He wasn't proud of teasing her as a teen, but his offenses had been minor compared to the ridicule lavished on her by other boys. That she had singled him out to suffer for all her tormentors was the only conclusion he could reach.

An apology could only free a person who accepted it. Instead of acknowledging his, Martha had expected him to make his offenses up to her. Was this what she'd planned all along?

He couldn't fathom how she'd persuaded someone to back up her false story. Who might the person be? Which of his enemies had taken the opportunity to punish him? He wished he knew so his mind would stop posing possibilities. It might be better not to find out, but life might not afford him that luxury.

Jake bowed his head. "My life is a mess, God. I hope you can see clear to helping me clean it up."

Light footsteps crunched outside the building. Jake sat up, listening. He could swear they belonged to a woman. He peered out the window, which framed the uninformative view of grass waving in the field behind the jail.

The sounds dwindled into quietness.

The mattress crunched beneath him as he lay down again. He thought of Liberty. Was she still sleeping? He pulled his mind from images of her stirring awake, fresh and lovely as the dawn. Instead, he pictured her helping her mother bake bread. Jake smiled and closed his eyes.

A while later, he opened his eyes to the chomp of heavier footsteps approaching. Jake pushed to his feet, not sure what to expect. The knob rattled and the jail door burst inward, letting in a flood of light. He blinked and shielded his eyes. The stout figure of Frank Harris came into view. His old school friend, now wearing a star, pushed through the narrow doorway. On the tray in his hands rested a steaming pot that smelled of coffee. A plate of flapjacks swimming in molasses, strips of bacon, and a couple of fried eggs nestled beside the pot.

Jake stared in disbelief. "Where'd you get my mother's best serving tray?" He didn't ask the second question niggling his mind. Why was it laid with his favorite breakfast?

Frank plunked the tray down on the worn oak table in the outer chamber. He had the look of someone who had just awakened, his crumpled clothing doing nothing to contradict the impression. Frank pushed a hand through his rumpled hair, which did not introduce an improvement. "That ma of your'n. She's a strong-minded woman, and no mistake."

It all came clear. Jake smiled. "No need to tell me that."

Frank produced the key tucked into the waistband of his pants. "You might be in jail, but by golly, you'll dine from your mother's china."

"This is hard on Ma. I hope you were polite to her."

"Of course. What do you take me for? She insisted on cooking my breakfast too, so who was I to tell her she couldn't use my stove?" Frank wrenched open the door, which clanged against the bars. "Sorry. I'm not used to this. In these parts, the jail doesn't see much use. You're one of a handful so far this year."

"Lucky me." Jake accepted the tray. "Thank my ma for me,

will you?"

"I will when she comes back. We haven't seen the last of her, or my name's Rumpelstiltskin."

"What did she say?" Jake spoke around a bite of flapjacks.

"Nothing much…" Frank clanged the cell door shut.

Jake wasn't sure whether to feel relieved or disappointed.

"Unless you count her swearing up and down that she's sure you're innocent." Frank grinned. "We barely kept her out of the jail, she was so determined to see for herself that you're all right."

"This is no place for her."

"Funny, she said the same about you." Frank lowered himself into the chair at the table. "I'll wait for that tray."

"Did she say anything else?" Jake crunched into a piece of bacon.

"Let me think a minute." He stroked his chin. "Oh, yes. Your ma said she'd go into worse places than jail for you or any of her children."

"That sounds like Ma." Jake swilled coffee that tasted like home. He'd never lost sight of his love for his mother, but he'd wondered how she felt about him. It was nice to know he hadn't put himself out of her graces.

"I'm going to be a juggler." Seated in the landau beside his mother, Murphy tossed invisible balls into the air.

"Stop flailing about, son." Aunt Maisey smiled. "You don't want to knock your ma out of the carriage."

"I'm going to be an acrobat," Quinn announced from the jump seat. "Imagine flying through the air without a care in the world."

"Except breaking your neck when you fall." Murphy made a face at his brother. "No thank you."

"Yeah? Well, your juggling balls will smack you in the head."

"Boys!" Aunt Maisey spoke mildly, but her reprimand had an instant effect. Murphy folded his hands in his lap and adopted an angelic air while Quinn was seized with a sudden interest in the road falling away behind them.

Uncle Rob glanced over his shoulder. "Is everything all right back there?"

"Yes, Rob." Aunt Maisey leaned against the head rest. "The boys had a good time."

"Glad to hear it." Uncle Rob faced forward.

"What about you girls?" Aunt Maisey stifled a yawn. "Did you have fun?"

"Yes, Ma." Phoebe beamed. "I enjoyed my corn and the juggling, especially. What about you, Liberty?"

Liberty roused herself to speak. "I liked most of the shows, but part of it felt—I don't know—"

Aunt Maisey nodded. "The menagerie with all those poor creatures in cages was sad. I didn't care for the ventriloquist act either. A puppet moving and talking like a person gives me shivers. And Doc Woburn seemed charming but ambitious."

Phoebe frowned. "I can't say I admired the way he pointed out people who didn't buy his product."

Liberty remained silent. The last thing she wanted to discuss was Doc Woburn. Having seen the man in action, she didn't blame her mother for falling under his spell. He wasn't particularly handsome, but he had a way about him. How could a vulnerable young woman, as Ma must have been, have withstood his charm when it caused entire crowds to part with their money?

Meeting him today hadn't felt safe, but Liberty couldn't

reconcile her decision. The man was her father, whatever else he might be. Jesus didn't require worthiness in exchange for love. Neither should she. Treating love like a prize to win through good behavior would take away its beauty.

She ought to have introduced herself.

Something else had held her back, while she was being honest with herself. Her parents probably wouldn't approve of her contacting her natural father behind their backs. Although she was grown, her parents were allowed a say in her life. Denying them that privilege wouldn't be right.

Liberty emerged from her thoughts to discover that the conversation had returned to happier impressions of the show.

"The clown was hilarious when he sprayed water in his face and started running into people." Murphy's eyes gleamed.

"That was an accident." Quinn leaned from the jump seat at an angle that rivaled the one his brother had adopted on the way out.

"No, it wasn't." Murphy jutted his chin. "He did it on purpose."

"I don't think so." Quinn held out his hand, catching at the wind of their passing. "The people got awfully mad."

Murphy scowled. "That was part of the act."

Quinn shook his head. "No, it wasn't."

"Yes, it was."

"Boys!" Aunt Maisey pinned each of her sons with a stern glare. "We'll never know the answer."

"We could find out next week." Murphy pressed into his mother's side. "Can we go again in Stevensville? Please, Ma?"

Liberty leaned against the headrest and closed her eyes. It wasn't too late. She could still meet her father in Stevensville—if she dared.

CHAPTER SIXTEEN

Aunt Bry grinned. "I'll do any chores that don't involve cooking."

Liberty snapped a green bean into the bowl before her and exchanged a smile with Phoebe, engaged in the same task. They sat at the kitchen table in Liberty's house, having arrived an hour ago. Preparing for Sunday Meeting involved a lot of cooking, but whenever Aunt Bry arrived early to pitch in, she found other tasks to do. Her remark didn't surprise Liberty. Aunt Bry's distaste for cooking, matched only by her lack of ability, was legendary.

Ma glanced up from kneading bread. "That can be arranged."

"It's always the same with you." Aunt Maisey paused while stirring soup. "Stop telling yourself you can't cook, and I think you will make a surprising discovery."

Aunt Bry's doubt showed in her face. "I can sweep and mop, do laundry, make beds, and watch children. Just don't ask me to cook."

Aunt Elsa rolled her eyes. "How do you survive at home? Your children look well fed."

"We—eat." Aunt Bry picked up two-year-old Delia, her youngest. "Nick sometimes likes to try his hand in the kitchen, but the rest falls to me."

"How do you manage?" Ma picked up a spatula and divided the bread dough.

"I may hate cooking, but I love my family." Aunt Bry

shrugged. "Fortunately, I am in the company of three wonderful cooks who don't need anyone else in the kitchen."

"Flatterer." Aunt Elsa's eyes gleamed.

"You can help Oma Wilhelmina set up beds in the schoolhouse." Ma shaped the dough into loaves.

Aisling peered in from the hallway with Shannon beside her. "Ma, what do you want us to do?"

"Would you please help in the meeting hall?" Ma covered the loaves she'd made with a damp flour-sack towel. "The men went over to set up tables and chairs, but the kitchen needs to be organized."

"You girls can walk over with me. I'm headed that way." Aunt Bry joined them.

"Oh, good." Shannon beamed. "You can finish telling us about the time you lived in Boston."

Bry laughed. "That was a very long time ago."

"What was it like, living in a mansion?" Aisling walked a little ahead as they set off together.

"The experience is quite different for a servant." Bry's voice drifted into the kitchen, followed by the creak and slam of the front door screen. "I remember a lot of hard work."

Their voices faded behind the crisp snap of green beans. Liberty and Phoebe had picked the beans a short while ago, and they still held the warmth of the sun. The rhythm of the simple task lulled Liberty, as it had many times before. She was glad to be home. The time away had changed her perspective. Her troubles still existed, but she no longer felt powerless in their grip.

A knock at the front door brought her head up. Most of the neighbors came to the back door since they knew Ma spent most of her time in the kitchen. This visit must be something other than neighborly.

"Liberty, would you please get the door?" Ma reached for a towel to dry her hands.

Liberty identified the caller before reaching the screen door. "Mr. Hensley, I'm surprised to see you." She blurted the first thought that sprang to mind.

"Why are you surprised?" He raised his eyebrows. "Surely you knew I'd come back."

"I'm afraid I didn't." Telling him to look elsewhere ought to have discouraged him. She almost said as much, but that would be rude. "I can't invite you in. We're busy preparing for Sunday Meeting."

"Is that tomorrow?"

"Yes." She shouldn't tell a lie, even to dissuade an unwanted suitor.

"I'll be sure to attend."

Liberty wanted to tell him not to bother, if his purpose was to captivate her. She refrained, certain the Almighty would take a dim view of discouraging him from attending church. "You're welcome to do so."

He produced a beguiling smile. "Can I tear you away from duty long enough for a walk in the sunshine?"

"Thank you, but I don't have time."

"Would you at least step outside with me long enough to give your opinion about something I read in the Bible?"

That was the last thing she'd expected him to say. She couldn't very well refuse the opportunity to speak to him about God's Word. Liberty opened the screen door and stepped onto the porch. "I can bide with you a moment."

Beau turned to her as they started down the path to the arbor gate. "Thank you, Miss Hayes."

Liberty repressed her surprise at his form of address. He'd disregarded her every effort to remain on more distant terms—

until now. Come to think of it, the arrogant tilt to his head was gone. She stared at Beau, speechless. Just when she thought she'd figured him out, he changed.

"I missed you while you were away." He turned the hat in his hands as he spoke, a telltale sign of nervousness. "You were on my mind a lot."

Liberty had not thought about him at all, but she refrained from enlightening him to the fact.

"I believe I owe you an apology." Beau went on doggedly. "I behaved like an insensitive lout."

"You did." She refused to let him off the hook.

"Will you forgive me?" The hat fairly spun in his hands.

"I must say, you made me uncomfortable."

He winced. "I'm sorry."

"And you insulted Phoebe, whom I love dearly."

"I owe her an apology too."

Maybe she had misjudged Beau. She would never have expected an apology from him. She paused beneath the arbor, where pink roses in bloom sent up a heady fragrance.

"I forgive you, but I must ask for better consideration from you in the future."

Beau caught her hand. "Can I ever hope to court you?"

Liberty shook her head and pulled out of his grip. "I'm sorry, but my answer remains the same."

"Do you think that will ever change?"

She gazed past him to the pasture where the horses grazed. "Probably not."

"I'll take that as a challenge."

The smugness in his voice was the last straw. "Mr. Hensley, I'm afraid I'm losing patience. You wanted me to give you my opinion on something in the Bible, as I recall." She spoke each word crisply.

"You're holding out for that Jake fellow, aren't you?"

"If you must know, Jake left town. Since you're avoiding the topic I agreed to discuss—"

"Jake is still in town. He's been getting into mischief."

Liberty's heartbeat picked up its pace. "Mischief?"

"Something to do with a woman named Martha Riddler." A satisfied expression settled over Beau's face. "I regret to inform you that Jake is in jail."

"Liberty?" Phoebe's whisper came out of the darkness. "Are you awake?"

"Yes." Liberty thumped her pillow. *How can I sleep after learning about Jake?*

"What happened with Beau today?"

"He said he was sorry about the way he treated me."

"He *what*?"

Liberty put her arms behind her head. "Beau asked my forgiveness for his insensitive treatment. He also said he owes you an apology."

"What is he up to?" Suspicion laced Phoebe's voice.

"I'm not sure. Maybe nothing."

"Do you honestly believe that?"

Liberty considered the question. Her parents had taught her to give others the benefit of the doubt. Even so, Beau's humility rang false. "Not really, but what if he genuinely apologized?"

Phoebe snorted. "Do leopards change their spots?"

"You might have a point."

"Is that what upset you—Beau apologizing?"

Moisture gathered in Liberty's eyes. "He told me that Jake is in jail over something to do with Martha Riddler."

"Oh."

Liberty let out a breath. "I don't know what to think."

"That's an improvement over jumping to conclusions. If you ask my opinion—which you didn't—Martha Riddler has a grudge against Jake."

"I wouldn't know why." Liberty cast back in memory. "Sure, he teased her in school, but so did a lot of boys."

"I don't think it was about that, at least not directly."

She couldn't begin to guess what Phoebe meant. "Would you please get to the point?"

"Martha was sweet on Jake."

"No."

"Yes."

Liberty wracked her brain. "She never let on."

"I could tell, whereas you were oblivious," Phoebe assured her. "She was jealous of you and Jake."

"I didn't notice. Sometimes I wonder if you and I live in the same world."

Phoebe chuckled. "I would take whatever Martha Riddler says about Jake with a grain of salt."

"She's quite beautiful."

"What does that have to do with anything?"

Liberty searched for words. "Men have—desires. What if Jake made a fool of himself over her?"

"Liberty Prudence—"

"You promised never to use my middle name."

Phoebe made a sound very like a snort. "We're the only ones in this room."

"That doesn't matter."

"Will you listen? What I was trying to say is that Jake is head over heels in love with you. That doesn't mean he couldn't be stupid, but it's highly unlikely."

"Do you really think so?"

"I just said so, didn't I?" Phoebe spoke with undeniable

logic. "Why not give Jake the benefit of the doubt? I'd rather trust, even if I'm wrong, than not trust when I'm not sure I'm right."

Liberty did her best to decipher the convoluted remark. Phoebe had a unique way of looking at the situation, but it made sense. "I want to ride to town with you on Monday. Do you suppose Will would escort us?"

"You're planning something, aren't you?" Phoebe sighed. "Never mind. I don't want to know what."

"I won't go into the general store with you and Will." Liberty held up Ma's letter. "I need to mail this." She'd been wondering how to slip away from her companions when her mother handed her the perfect excuse.

Ma couldn't have known that the post office was exactly where Liberty wanted to go. She needed answers, and Martha had them.

Uneasiness crossed Phoebe's face. "That's not the best place for you to visit."

"Sure it is." Will gave Phoebe a puzzled look. "Where else do you mail a letter?"

Phoebe eyed Liberty. "Maybe I should come with you."

"I'll be all right." Liberty emphasized every word. "It's only a little way along the boardwalk."

Phoebe looked unconvinced. "You'll be careful, won't you?"

"Don't worry about me." Liberty spoke with more bravado than she felt. She would rather do anything else than confront Martha over Jake. Doing so might not help, but it was the only way she could think of to expose the truth.

Will led Phoebe into the general store while Liberty set off in the opposite direction. Her footsteps rang on the wooden walkway. Reaching her destination too soon for comfort, Liberty hesitated with her hand on the doorknob.

"Pardon me, Miss Hayes." The deep voice of Gerald Wilmington, a member of her father's congregation, sounded behind her.

Liberty jumped. She must have been so sunk in thought that she'd missed the thud of his boots. Liberty offered him a weak smile and stepped aside.

He held the door. "Aren't you going in?"

"Yes, thank you." Liberty braced herself and walked into the building.

The grizzled postmaster looked up from behind the counter. Martha was nowhere in sight. Her stomach sank even as she shook with relief.

Gerald gestured for Liberty to go first. She smiled her thanks and went to the counter.

"Mailing a letter?" The postmaster accepted Ma's envelope and weighed it on a scale. "That'll be two cents."

Liberty counted out Indian head pennies. "Any mail for us today?"

"Not today. Anything else I can do for you?"

"That's all I needed, thank you."

The postmaster nodded. "You might want to pick up a parasol at the general store, if you need one. A new shipment came in last week. With this sunny weather, they're going fast."

"Thanks for the information. May I ask if Martha will be in later?"

His expression soured. "Martha doesn't work here anymore. She quit on Friday. That's why I'm behind the counter instead of at my desk."

"I hope you find a replacement soon."

"You and me both." The postmaster shifted his gaze. "What

can I do for you, Gerald?"

Liberty didn't need to buy anything, and she would rather not go into the general store since Beau worked there. Rather than wait outside for Phoebe and Will, she came up with a different plan.

Knowing pretty much where everyone in Liberty township lived, it didn't take her long to reach Martha's house. Liberty emerged from the shade of a grove of aspen trees and spotted the small white house Martha shared with her mother. The gate creaked open, and she went through. Uneasiness crawled up Liberty's spine. Feeling someone watching, she peered behind her. The tree-lined lane was empty. Liberty shrugged off the sensation and climbed the steps to the porch. The boards sagged and creaked beneath her feet. The paint on the door was peeling, and one of the windows sagged on its hinges. She'd known that Martha and her mother didn't have much money, but the state of their home made her sad. Martha and her mother had refused Pa when he'd offered to help, and they'd stopped coming to service. Maybe they'd been too embarrassed to show their faces.

Liberty's knock echoed hollowly. She waited on the porch while birds twittered in the bushes. A pair of white butterflies etched with black chased one another into the sky. Dogs barked in the distance.

No one came.

Liberty caught the crunch of footsteps and turned.

Deputy Manchen walked toward her down the lane. He lifted his hat. "Hello, Miss Hayes."

"Deputy." She waited for him to reach her before speaking again. "Why are you here? I thought you were following Grady Bradshaw."

"I lost his trail and doubled back." He shook his head. "I see you're out alone again."

"Liberty township is safe."

He frowned. "You never know when that might change."

"Thank you for your concern."

He cracked a smile. "In other words, mind my own business. Tell me, do you know Martha Riddler and her mother?"

Liberty had thought so once, but apparently that wasn't true. She shook her head. "Not well."

The deputy watched her face. "Why did you call today?"

Liberty's cheeks burned. "I wanted to talk with Martha about a personal matter."

"I'd like a word with her too." He shook his head. "Everything in the house is turned over, as if Martha and her mother left in a hurry. Folks saw them ride out of town in their wagon on Friday. They haven't returned."

Will stepped in front of Phoebe before they reached the door to the general store. "Do you want to tell me what you and Liberty are up to?"

Phoebe did her best to appear innocent. "What makes you think we're up to anything?"

He sighed. "You shouldn't try to keep secrets. Your face gives you away."

"Why would I keep secrets?" If he didn't know, she wasn't going to tell him.

"I can guess that you're asking questions to fob me off without fibbing."

Her face warmed. "All right. I'll tell you." She glanced at the general store. "Not here though."

He offered her his arm. "It's a nice day for a stroll."

Phoebe placed her hand in the crook of his arm and matched her footsteps to his. That took a little doing since his legs were longer, and his pace ate up the boardwalk. "Do you think we could slow down a little?"

"Oh. Sorry." He slowed down.

A dog barked from behind a house they passed but didn't appear. A wagon rattled down the wide street, and the driver lifted his hand. Phoebe recognized the man from Sunday Meeting. From the broad smile that settled on his face, he must think they were courting.

She studied Will's strong profile. What would that be like?

He turned and caught her staring. Phoebe looked away, too late. Will cleared his throat. "Well?"

Rather than gazing at him like a lackwit, she should have been figuring out what to say. "It started when Jake went to jail." She said the first thing that came to mind.

His stride checked for an instant. "This is getting complicated."

"I suppose so. Liberty is, well—fond of Jake. She took the news hard. When she decided to go to town today, I thought she might try to see him."

His eyes widened. "And you're in favor of that?"

"Not necessarily, but they've been friends a long time."

"Would her parents approve?"

"I'm not sure." Phoebe didn't meet his eyes. "They know Jake pretty well and wouldn't believe he belongs in jail."

"But would they want Liberty to visit him there?"

"Probably not." Forced to admit the truth, Phoebe recognized that she'd made a mistake. "I'm sorry to involve you in this."

Will narrowed his eyes. "Why did you invite me along?"

He deserved the truth, although it shamed her. "Our parents wouldn't want us to ride to town alone." Phoebe pulled in a breath. "I also thought you might enjoy the outing." That hadn't been her first consideration, but it had crossed her mind.

Will said nothing.

She stole a glance at him and found his expression shuttered. Regret twisted inside her.

The boardwalk ended but the road continued past fields of waving grass. After that, trees crowded in to shroud the foothills below the mountains.

Will faced her. "Are you and Liberty aware of the accusations against Jake?"

"Yes, but the person who made them—" Phoebe shook her head. "Don't get me started about Martha Riddler."

"I gather you're acquainted."

"We went to school together." Phoebe left it at that. There was no reason to go into Martha's jealousy or her bullying ways.

"I can tell she didn't make a favorable impression on you."

She shrugged. "Let's just say that I'm inclined to believe in Jake's innocence."

"That explains why you encouraged Liberty to visit him." His tone softened.

"Liberty needed no encouragement, but I don't think she's with Jake."

"But wasn't that why you seemed worried when she left us?"

Phoebe shook her head. "Martha works at the post office."

Will's eyes lit with comprehension. "You don't think—"

"I don't know. I've stopped trying to guess what Liberty has in mind."

"We'd better find out."

"Yes, let's." Will set off, and she hurried to keep up with him. "I'm glad I told you."

"I am too, although I should be angry you dragged me into this."

"I didn't mean to."

He stopped so abruptly she almost ran into him. "You'll recall that my employer is your uncle. Aiding and abetting you and Liberty puts me in an awkward position."

Phoebe lowered her gaze. "I'm sorry. I didn't think…"

"That's clear." He touched her lightly under the chin and tilted her face upward. "There seems a lot that you aren't sure about, don't know, or can't guess." The set of his jaw betrayed his annoyance. He released her abruptly and started off again.

Phoebe waited as long as possible before reminding Will that she couldn't keep up with him. In hindsight, it was clear that she and Liberty had taken advantage of his kindness. Phoebe wished she'd been honest with him from the start.

Liberty was not outside the general store, where she'd promised to meet them. Nor was she inside. They checked the post office.

"I'm sure she'll turn up." The postmaster leaned on the counter. "Liberty asked after Martha, if that's any help. Maybe she walked over to check on her."

"Thank you kindly." Phoebe summoned a smile.

Will steered her out the door. "I'm sure Liberty will be fine, but it wouldn't hurt to hurry."

CHAPTER SEVENTEEN

SHERIFF UNDERWOOD UNFOLDED HIMSELF FROM THE chair behind his desk in the sheriff's office and towered to his full height. "Nice to see you, Miss Hayes."

Liberty tilted her head to look up at him. "Good morning, Sheriff."

He gestured to a carved oak chair on the other side of the desk. "Won't you have a seat?"

"Thank you." .

He lowered himself into his own chair, a larger version of the one she occupied. "Can I help you with something?"

"Are you aware that Martha Riddler and her mother have left town?"

"I heard about that yesterday." He slid open a drawer at his desk and retrieved a small tin. "Care for a peppermint?"

"No, thank you." She clasped her hands in her lap. "May I ask why Jake Buckthorn is still in jail when his accuser has left town?"

"The wheels of justice turn slowly, Miss Hayes." He stuffed a peppermint in his cheek.

"I don't care about your wheels, Sheriff. There's a man in jail who shouldn't be there."

"No need to upset yourself, miss." He held up his hands in a placating gesture. "We can't release Jake. Martha Riddler may turn up."

"Have you asked yourself why she went away?"

He shrugged. "Your guess is as good as mine."

"I would think you'd be more curious. What if Martha was afraid of someone?"

"Jake?"

"No, not Jake." Liberty shook her head for emphasis. "What harm could he possibly do to anyone behind bars?"

His eyes widened. "Who, then?"

She leaned forward and lowered her voice. "What if someone put Martha up to accusing Jake?"

"Martha and her mother." He spoke around his peppermint.

Liberty blinked. "What did you say?"

"Martha's mother said she saw Jake when he—well—never mind." His face turned red. "It's an interesting idea, Miss Hayes. You realize it's only a theory?"

She looked him in the eye. "Do you have a better one?"

"Give me time." He ran his hand down the side of his face. "I only found all this out yesterday."

Liberty waited for the sheriff to compose himself before speaking. "Deputy Manchen told me that Martha and her mother left in a hurry."

"When did you talk with Deputy Manchen?"

"Today, at Martha's house."

His eyes narrowed. "What were you doing there?"

"I wanted to ask her a couple of questions."

"About Jake?"

"Yes." There was no point denying the obvious.

He pushed the peppermint to his other cheek. "It's best to leave inquiries to us, Miss Hayes."

"What is the extent of your investigation, if I may ask?"

"You may not. Those are confidential matters." He stood. "Is there anything else I can do for you?"

Liberty remained seated. "Martha and her mother might

have run away to avoid perjuring themselves."

A knock at the door interrupted whatever the sheriff was about to say. He gave her a harried smile. "Pardon me while I answer that."

She nodded.

He strode to the door and wrenched it open.

"Sheriff Underwood, we're looking for Liberty Hayes."

The speaker was unmistakable. Liberty jumped to her feet. "Phoebe!"

The sheriff stood back, and Phoebe dashed into the small room. "You had me worried." She embraced Liberty while Will exchanged greetings with Sheriff Underwood.

Liberty glanced past Phoebe. "I see you've brought Will?"

She nodded slowly.

Will pinned Liberty with a glance. "We've been looking for you."

"I'm sorry." Liberty divided her gaze between them. "A lot has happened, and I guess I lost track of time."

"Don't think of it." Phoebe touched her arm. "That's happened to me often enough."

"We'd better start back, if you're finished here."

"I believe we are." Sheriff Underwood's expression held relief.

Liberty opened her mouth to protest otherwise but closed it again. Pressuring the sheriff further might only antagonize him. She'd done her part and would have to trust God to free Jake. She took her leave from Sheriff Underwood with as much grace as she could manage.

"What did you tell Will?" Liberty murmured to Phoebe outside the building.

"Everything. I apologized to him, and you should too. I think we hurt his feelings."

Phoebe was right. Regret washed through Liberty.

"What are you two whispering about?" Will sent them a suspicious look.

"Phoebe was reminding me of my manners." Liberty took a breath. "Please forgive me, both of you. My actions weren't fair to either of you."

She'd been so concerned about clearing Jake that she'd asked too much of her friends. And for what? Martha had vanished, and Jake was still in jail.

CHAPTER EIGHTEEN

LIBERTY SWUNG HER LEGS, MAKING THE bough beneath her creak and sway. The sky lightened in the east, tinged with the first blush of morning. Roosters greeted daybreak, and birdsong swelled in joyous chorus. She'd risen early and crept out to watch the sunrise from the place she most often felt tranquil. Climbing into the tree's embrace carried her to an earlier time, when life was simple. She smiled at the memory of an earlier Liberty who didn't know the difficult path before her, or that she would walk it all alone. What if she could reach across time and warn her younger self what she would suffer? Would she still make the promise that the older, more sensible Liberty needed to break?

She couldn't face the answer.

She'd wanted to marry a man who would make a fine son-in-law for her preacher father. Having been born on the wrong side of the blanket changed all that. How could she marry someone upstanding? If her secret ever came out, it would tarnish her husband's reputation.

A bigger problem stood in the way. Her unruly heart insisted on Jake. She'd tried so hard to break their tie, but every effort failed. Even with distance between them and Jake behind bars, it remained. Sitting in the Promise Tree, as her younger self had called it, brought him close in memory. She could almost feel him gazing at the same sunrise and thinking of her.

How ironic that she'd finally convinced Jake to let go of her, only to discover that nothing stood between them. Not that it mattered anymore. Jake would never trust her again.

Liberty dropped from the tree. What was the point of sitting there if it only made her melancholy? She could hear Ma rattling pans in the kitchen. There wouldn't be a better time to talk to her. Seth often woke early, but he shouldn't stir for at least another hour. Everyone else was still sleeping.

Apologizing to Phoebe and Will had alerted her to an unpleasant fact. She'd let her principles slip. When had she stopped doing her best to live an honest life? She wouldn't allow herself to compromise any longer. Telling the truth, even if she suffered consequences, had to hurt less than hiding behind deception. She refused to slink away from the people she loved any longer. Nor would she drag them into a mess of her making.

Liberty pulled open the screen door and stepped into the kitchen. Ma glanced up from her breadmaking. "You're up early."

"I went out to see the sunrise."

Ma smiled. "Would you sprinkle flour over my hands? They're so sticky that I don't want to touch the scoop."

Ma held her hands above the bread board, and Liberty sprinkled flour over them as she had done many times before. "Thank you." Ma scrubbed at her floured hands, shedding dough.

"Can you spare a moment?" Liberty cleared her throat. "I want to talk with you about something."

Ma studied her a moment. "Let me finish kneading the bread, and we can sit down for a cup of tea."

"I'll put the kettle on." Liberty sprang into action, grateful for something to keep her busy while she waited.

By the time her mother covered the bread dough with a damp flour-sack towel, Liberty was ready. She poured the steaming amber liquid from the blue willow teapot into matching cups.

Ma untied her apron and hung it on its hook before sitting across from Liberty in a ladderback chair at the kitchen table. She lifted her cup with both hands. "Thanks for brewing the tea. I'm partial to Earl Grey."

"I know." Liberty let herself enjoy the gentle moment of harmony before she had to ruin it.

Ma blew on her tea. "What's on your mind?"

"I have a confession to make." Liberty stirred sugar into her cup. "I overheard you and Pa talking about me."

"What do you mean?" Ma's forehead creased. "Where were we?"

"In the barn. I was sleeping in the hay mow when you came in and woke me."

Ma's eyes widened. "What did you hear?"

"All you said."

"Then you know everything?"

"I know." Ma looked so sad that Liberty wanted to hug her, but she'd wind up crying if she did.

"I'm sorry, Liberty, to have harmed you before you were born." Tears shone on Ma's cheeks. "I hope you can forgive me."

"I already have." Liberty laid her hand over her mother's. "I love you."

Ma dashed away her tears. "Why didn't you let us know you were there?"

"I didn't want you to see that I'd been crying."

"Why were you crying?" Ma's voice softened.

"Jake told me he's leaving town."

"That must have been hard to hear. You two were close for a long time."

"Most of our lives." Liberty blew out a breath. "If only Jake had gone then, he wouldn't be in jail."

"I think he stayed to look after his mother. I sat with her while he went after the doctor." Ma shook her head. "I can't credit Jake with committing a crime worthy of jail time. His mischief was never very serious. Pa figured he'd outgrow it. We suspected you two might marry one day."

Liberty stared at her mother, startled to realize that her parents considered Jake a worthy husband for her when she had not. What a fool she'd been.

Ma glanced at the full cup of tea in her hands with mild surprise. She set it down. "I'm sorry you learned about your father that way."

"Why didn't you tell me?" The cry broke from Liberty.

"I thought to spare you the burden." Ma's eyes shone with what looked like tears. "I almost told you many times, but I always decided you were better off not knowing."

"Hiding it from me was what hurt."

"I'm so sorry."

"I've learned that secrets hurt others, and they increase my own pain. That's why I decided to tell you what I overheard."

"You've carried this burden for over a month. Why didn't you let on sooner?"

"I was afraid of hurting you." Liberty's lip trembled.

"Oh sweetheart!" Ma covered Liberty's hand on the table. "You made the same mistake I did."

"I suppose so. Keeping secrets seemed right to me, but that's where I went astray."

"I'm glad you figured it out."

"That was easy." Liberty grimaced. "Everything I did caused suffering for myself and others."

"I noticed the same thing before I made my own peace with God."

"It always comes back to that, doesn't it?"

Ma nodded. "There is no other way to live in harmony with

others but to seek it with God."

"Tell me what happened with my father."

Ma sighed. "I should have trusted my instincts where he was concerned. Kyle and I grew up in the same neighborhood in St. Louis. I didn't want anything to do with him for a long time. That changed when my parents went through a divorce."

"That must be why I can't recall them together."

"I'm surprised you remember them at all. I wish it could have worked out differently. My mother moved to Europe. I've seen a couple of society articles about her, but she doesn't reply to my letters. I believe I'm a painful reminder of the life she left behind."

"What about my grandfather?"

"Shane and I traveled back East to see him only once. We couldn't really afford to go, but I'm glad we went." She pulled in a deep breath. "My father was ill, and the doctors thought he would die. Pa read about it in the newspaper, which is why we went."

"Why was it in the news?"

"Your grandfather is a United States Senator. He pursued his interest in politics after divorcing my mother."

"What happened when you went to see him?"

"He acted pretty much the same as when I was a child. I don't know why I expected anything different. My parents' neglect made me vulnerable. I was lonely, and with Kyle, I felt special. He insisted on certain privileges that I shouldn't have granted. It's hard to explain..."

"I think I understand, Ma. I went to the medicine show in Corvallis with Phoebe's family and saw him onstage."

Ma's eyes widened. "You saw him? Did you introduce yourself?"

Liberty stared at the scarred oak table top. "I couldn't bring myself to do it."

Ma let out a sigh. "It's probably just as well."

"I'm not settled about it, though." Liberty lifted her gaze. "I can't help feeling that I'll regret missing the chance to meet him."

"It was probably for the best."

"Maybe, but I want to try again when the medicine show opens in Stevensville on Friday."

"I don't think that's a good idea."

"It might be a mistake, but if I don't go, I may never meet him at all. I don't want to wonder for the rest of my life what might have happened."

Ma hesitated. "Have you considered that he might be unkind to you?"

"I have, Ma." Liberty nodded. "I'm willing to take that risk."

The brush crackled as Liberty pulled it through her sister Aisling's hair. Spun strands of red-tinged gold shimmered in the light slanting through the girls' bedroom window. Liberty let out a long breath. The rhythmic task soothed her nerves after the conversation with Ma. Aisling often begged Liberty to do her hair when Ma was busy. Shannon only knew how to braid hair and twist it into a bun.

"Ouch!" Aisling rubbed her scalp. "That smarted."

Liberty frowned at Aisling's reflection in the mirror above the dresser. "Stop wiggling, and it won't hurt so much."

"All right." Aisling winced in anticipation. "I'll try."

Liberty gave her a sympathetic smile. Of her two sisters, Aisling had the most trouble staying still.

Shannon, sitting on the edge of her bed, lifted a length of cream ribbon from the box on her lap. "This would look nice tied across Aisling's crown."

Aisling made a face. "That one is boring. I'd rather wear the gold jacquard silk one."

"Ma said the jacquard isn't for every day." Shannon dropped the rejected ribbon back into the box.

Aisling caught Liberty's eye in the mirror. "Can't I wear it?"

"I'm not sure you should." Liberty paused with the brush suspended midair. "The green satin would match the flower sprigs in your dress and bring out the red in your hair."

"I'll wear that one then." Aisling's eyes shone.

Liberty silently congratulated herself for her tact.

Shannon pulled out the green ribbon and handed it to Liberty. "Will you do my hair next?"

"Certainly." Liberty picked up the comb to part Aisling's hair. Keeping busy would take her mind off her conversation with Ma. It had gone better than she'd expected. She wished her mother would approve of her meeting her natural father, but that might be too much to ask.

Pa's tap came at the door.

Liberty cracked it open.

Pa's gaze searched her face. "Come outside with me for a minute?"

Liberty glanced at her sisters. "I'll be back." From Pa's sober expression, this would take a while.

She followed Pa down the hallway and out the front door. She could recall walking with him many times, but never with an awkward silence between them. That Ma had told him about their conversation seemed obvious. He struck out along the road away from town. They passed the empty schoolhouse and the quiet church. Driveways leading to farms branched on either side. The town had spread along the road, but the farms backed to wilderness. Pines stood like tall sentinels at the edges of tangled meadows, and cottonwood, aspen, and alder branches meshed above the road. Liberty savored the beauty of this stretch, although she usually went the other way. The land was more open and the road better traveled on the way to town.

Liberty felt safe with Pa walking beside her, wherever they went. He'd always stood as a barrier between her and danger. The sight of bees lifting from the pink owl clover flowers on the verge brought back one of her first recollections. She'd stepped on a bee while crossing the yard in her bare feet. Her scream brought Pa running from the barn. He swept her up in his strong arms and carried her indoors, out of harm's way. She could still recall how loved and protected she'd felt.

The memory faded, leaving her to face the bitter truth. Pa's deception had shredded her trust in his ability to safeguard her.

Pa glanced sideways at her. "Ma told me what you talked about this morning."

"I gathered as much."

He cleared his throat. "She said you've taken it hard. I hope you know we never intended to hurt you."

She nodded but couldn't summon the will to speak.

"We meant only to keep you from harm."

"By lying?" Liberty shot back the question without considering her words, but they might as well stand.

Pa turned her to face him. "We didn't lie to you."

She tilted her face to meet his gaze. "Omitting the truth is the same as lying. You taught me that yourself."

"It's not so simple."

"A lie is a lie."

He sighed. "When do you believe we should have told you? Five was too young for such a burden. The knowledge could have damaged the confidence of a twelve-year-old. You found seventeen hard enough without dealing with that. Can you appreciate how difficult it was to determine and how easy the matter became to postpone?"

"You weren't going to inform me at all."

"I'll confess that was a temptation, but your Ma and I were still figuring out what to do. Maybe we waited too long. Can you blame us for delaying a difficult decision?"

When he put it like that, she could understand what her parents had gone through. It occurred to her that she had focused mainly on herself. The high-pitched chipping of a hummingbird drew Liberty's attention. The gray-headed bird dipped its long beak into the tubular flowers of a scarlet paintbrush plant. To hold it in place, the tiny bird's lavender wings beat almost faster than the eye could see. The hummingbird lifted from the paintbrush and darted about. Liberty turned back to Pa. "I suppose not."

"Thank you." Pa transferred his gaze from the hummingbird to her. "I understand that you hope to meet your—Doc Woburn. Your mother doesn't like the idea, but she left the decision to me."

"I would like to go with your blessing."

"She said as much and explained your reasons." Pa's eyes glinted. "I'm not sure I agree, but I'll think about it."

"Thanks, Pa." Liberty didn't press for a quick answer. The conversation must be as tough for him as it was for her. She wanted to tell him that she loved him, and that nothing could ever change that. The words wouldn't come. A chasm had opened between them that she didn't know how to bridge.

Ma shoved a jug into Liberty's hands. "Liberty, would you please take Pa some water?" She returned to shredding cabbage for slaw at the kitchen counter.

Taking Pa water had become a euphemism for checking to make sure he hadn't broken his neck while trying to tame Chief.

Liberty glanced at Seth, who was chomping on a handful of hermit cookies after raiding the cookie jar. "You could take Pa water."

"I'm busy." He flipped another cookie into his mouth and gave her a lopsided grin. "I'm sure it's your turn." Seth pushed his hand into the cookie jar.

"Stop or you'll ruin your supper." Ma spoke without lifting her head, lending credence to the idea that parents had eyes in the back of their heads.

"Don't worry, Ma. It won't." Seth headed for the door to the hallway.

Accepting her fate, Liberty followed her brother. While he turned toward the bedrooms, she walked to the front door. She wished Seth had been willing to go in her place. After their earlier conversation, the task would be awkward for her.

She rounded the path to the barn and crossed the road to the pasture and the corral Pa and Seth had built. The grass inside the fenced area had worn down, and a plume of dust shrouded Pa as he balanced on Chief's rounded back. The black horse bucked repeatedly.

Liberty pulled in a sharp breath and rushed to the rail as Pa went flying. She bent her knees, ready to jump onto the fence, but then Pa picked himself up from the dirt. The half-broke stallion ran in circles, snorting and bucking. Pa thumped his slouch hat against his leg before returning it to his head with quiet dignity. He limped toward her. "I stayed on longer that time."

"Are you all right?"

"I've hurt my pride, if you want to know." He shook his head. "I thought I followed Nick's advice, but I must have forgotten something."

"Probably the part about staying off wild horses." Liberty

couldn't resist the remark.

"There's no need to worry. I'm perfectly fine."

"I can't help it. I hold my breath every time you climb on that beast. Ma can't even watch."

"Chief will come around with a bit more coaxing. If you'll excuse me—" Pa turned and started after his horse.

"You're not going to try to ride him again?" she called after him.

"Why not?" Pa caught at the rope his horse was trailing. He missed, and Chief continued circling the corral.

"He threw you, not five minutes ago."

"That's the best reason I can think of to climb back into the saddle." Pa lunged, and the rope tightened. The stallion tossed his head and snorted in protest.

"I would think you'd want to rest."

"When opportunity calls is no time to sit idle."

Liberty stared at him in suspicion. "Did you knock your head when you went down?"

He grinned. "Not at all."

"Well then, what are you talking about?"

"The best thing to do when you fall off a horse is to climb back on quick as you can. Facing a thing you fear is the only way to overcome it."

"I'm sure you're right." Pa would get back on that stallion no matter what Liberty said. She might as well take advantage of the situation. "That's why I want to meet my—Doc Woburn."

"I was planning to talk with you about that. Since you've decided on meeting the man, at some point in your life you probably will. I'd rather be present." Pa levered himself into the saddle. "I've decided to take you."

Liberty opened her mouth to thank him, but his whirlwind of a horse whisked him away.

CHAPTER NINETEEN

LIBERTY STARTED. WHO HAD KNOCKED ON the front door? Everyone else in the family was occupied. Ma was in the middle of frosting a cake. Pa hadn't received enough of a bruising yesterday and had gone out to launch a renewed campaign to tame his willful horse. The girls were cutting out paper dolls and giggling in their room, and her brothers had gone fishing. That left Liberty to get the door.

She set her embroidery aside and dragged her feet as she went. Suspecting that Beau stood on the porch, she rehearsed what she might say.

The knocking came again, but it sounded familiar.

Liberty pulled in a breath and wrenched open the door.

Jake waited on the stoop. Clean-shaven, and with his hair damp, he appeared unmarked by the time he'd spent in jail—at least physically. The haunted look in his eyes told another story. "Hello, Liberty."

"I'm glad to see you." Liberty restrained herself from embracing him and stood back from the doorway. "Come in."

He stepped inside. "I won't keep you long."

Liberty winced inwardly. It was her fault that he felt the need to say that. Maybe she could undo some of the damage she'd caused. "Stay as long as you like."

His eyes flared in mild surprise. "Thanks for the invitation."

"You're always welcome, Jake. I'm sorry if I made it seem otherwise." She closed the door and walked with him into the parlor. "Please, have a seat."

Jake sat opposite her in an overstuffed chair. "They released me yesterday. I spent last night cleaning up and slept most of the morning."

"You must have been exhausted."

"Jail isn't exactly restful, but I'm in better shape today. I didn't want any more time to go by before I thanked you."

"For what?"

"Don't look so confused." Jake smiled. "Sheriff Underwood said that you spoke to him on my behalf."

"Oh that. I don't think he paid much attention to me."

"On the contrary. Your arguments led to my release."

"Really?" Liberty couldn't quite take it in. "I thought he found them quarrelsome."

"He said something of the sort, yes. However, the sheriff is a fair-minded man, and what you said made sense. He couldn't disregard it."

"I'm glad I was able to help you. You shouldn't have been locked up in the first place."

He gave her a surprised glance. "Thank you for believing in me."

"I'm sure others do, too."

He laughed. "That depends on who you ask."

She waved a hand dismissively. "The actual truth is what matters, not what people think is true."

"Well spoken—and something to keep in mind." He rose. "I should go. Gideon, Emma, and the children are coming over. Ma's baking a huge meal."

She smiled. "Enjoy your family."

After Jake left, Liberty went out to weed the garden. She dug her trowel in the loose soil and pulled out a dandelion. The quiet work soothed her.

She could hardly credit that her conversation with Sheriff

Underwood had done so much good. It showed what could happen when she valued truth above pleasing others. Not so long ago, she would never have pressed the sheriff to see reason and free Jake. She'd have kept her opinions locked deep inside, where they would gnaw away at her. Because she had spoken, Jake walked free.

Jake ate a large portion of fried chicken, corn on the cob, baked beans, and potato salad. He groaned but found room for a slice of apple pie. He'd taken the joy of sharing a table with his family for granted. Maybe he shouldn't be so hasty about leaving. It might be easier to stay than he'd thought, although he would try not to read too much into today's visit with Liberty. Having peace between them felt nice.

After supper, Jake gave Gideon and Emma's children piggyback rides, much to their delight. He thought the children's squeals might deafen him, but his hearing somehow emerged intact. Ma put up with the noise for a while before she lured the children away to read them a story. While Emma started the washing up, Jake collared Gideon for a talk on the porch.

"I'm riding out tomorrow to look for Martha."

Gideon stared at him as if he'd taken leave of his senses. "Why on earth would you do a foolish thing like that?"

"Funny. Ma used the same words."

"Maybe that's because they make sense, whereas you do not." Gideon paced the length of the porch and back. "Have you forgotten that the woman put you in jail?"

Jake gripped the rail before him. "I wish I could."

Gideon eyed him. "You're not doing this as some kind of vendetta, are you?"

"No, of course not. It may interest you to know that I feel

sorry for Martha. I want answers, not revenge."

"I don't know why your release from jail wouldn't resolve the matter to your satisfaction."

"It's hard to explain." Jake sought for words. "Call it a hunch, but something deeper than a woman's scorn put me behind bars. I'd rather face a threat head-on than have it jump me from behind."

"I may be as delusional as you, but that makes a strange kind of sense." Gideon clasped his shoulder. "You'll be careful, won't you? I have half a mind to go with you."

"That shouldn't be necessary. I overheard two deputies discussing where Martha and her mother went. They know a lot more than they let on. The trail she left leads to Missoula before it vanishes. That must be where she's hiding. I can reach it in a day if I ride hard, but I'd rather take it in two."

"Are you sure you don't want company?"

Jake would very much like his brother with him, but he wouldn't ask Gideon to make the sacrifice. "I'd rather not involve you. I don't have a wife and children. You do."

"All right, but promise me you won't do anything stupid. You can be hot-headed."

Jake summoned his patience. "I'm planning nothing more than to ask Martha a few questions."

"What will you do when she refuses to answer?"

"She might not." Jake watched the sun dip below the treetops. Rays slanted through the leaves and cast long shadows across the grass. "I think someone put her up to accusing me. I doubt she could afford to travel farther than Missoula. If I offer to pay her way elsewhere, she may be willing to talk."

"Since you're determined to do this, Emma and I will watch over Ma and the animals."

"Thank you. That takes a load off my mind."

Gideon gave him an uneasy glance. "Watch yourself with Martha, will you? A woman who put you in jail once might do it again."

Liberty didn't say much to Pa on the way to Stevensville. Any remark she made would seem stilted, under the circumstances. Pa didn't talk much either. This trip must be as hard for him as for her. Since Liberty had started noticing more than her own pain, she could understand what he might feel. He'd raised her as his own, whereas her natural father had abandoned her. She wanted to say that no one could ever replace him in her life, but awkwardness held her back. She would tell him that, but not today.

In Stevensville, the main street was given over to the medicine show. Pa pulled the wagon into the line for the livery, where their horses would receive care until they returned. He helped Liberty down from the wagon and caught her in a brief hug. "It's not too late to go home, if you change your mind."

She smiled in gratitude. "It's all right, Pa. I don't want to back out."

Disappointment showed in his face, but he took her hand and led her through the crowded streets. Liberty felt lost. How could she ever find Doc Woburn among all these people?

They followed a voice amplified by a megaphone to the stage where acrobats dressed in bright colors climbed on one another. They formed an impossible pyramid, and Liberty could barely contain her worry for the man on top, who unfolded his length to stand. He raised his hands high for good measure. The pyramid broke apart, making the crowd gasp, but each acrobat landed on his feet. The troop raised their arms in unison to much applause.

Liberty turned her head to search the crowd. She saw no

sign of her father.

Pa touched her shoulder, making her jump. His smile went all the way to his blue eyes. "Are you hungry?"

He sounded so normal that Liberty wished nothing had changed. How different she would feel if they had come simply to watch the show. She shook her head. "I don't think I can eat."

He frowned. "You should try, sweetheart. At least have something to drink. We can't have you fainting from thirst in the heat."

"All right." She let him guide her to the food booths. Overwhelmed by the selection, she couldn't make up her mind what to order. Pa took the choice from her, purchasing lemonade and a chicken pastry. They carried their food to an unoccupied bench. Liberty surprised herself by wolfing down her food. Her stomach didn't feel sick like in Corvallis. Pa's presence seemed to have a calming effect on her. Either that, or it was from not feeling guilty about deceiving anyone.

"Well, if it isn't Miss Hayes." Wilfred's voice cut into her thoughts.

Liberty turned her head and smiled. "It's good to see you again. Pa, this is Mr. Faraday. He's an assistant to Doc Woburn. Mr. Faraday, please meet my father, Reverend Hayes." Pa stood, and the two men shook hands.

"How nice that you came back with your father." Wilfred beamed at her.

"I'm glad we ran into you." Liberty returned his smile. "We're not really here to watch the show. We've come to speak with Doc Woburn."

"He's usually pretty busy. What do you want to talk about?"

"It's a personal matter." Liberty gave him what she hoped was a beseeching look. "Would you be willing to help us find him?"

Wilfred frowned. "It's a little difficult, not knowing what it's about." He hesitated and seemed to consider the matter, then gave a nod. "Come with me."

Liberty glanced at Pa, who nodded. Together, they trailed behind Wilfred. He took them behind the booths to an area where several nondescript tents were set up.

"Wait here." Wilfred disappeared into one of them, and Liberty heard murmuring voices.

Wilfred emerged and sauntered over to them. "You're in luck. He's curious about what you want. It helped that I vouched for you. Go on in."

Liberty heaved a sigh of relief. "Thanks so much."

"I owed you a favor, as you may recall. You and your kin helped me find my way. I guess we're even now." Wilfred touched the brim of his bowler and melted into the crowd.

Pa touched her arm. "Are you all right?"

Liberty nodded. Talking with Wilfred had kept her from fretting about what she planned to do. Liberty steeled herself for the task before her. Pa opened the canvas flap for Liberty and followed her inside.

The tent contained the bare essentials—a narrow bed, a trunk, and a couple of chairs at a table. It seemed a sad place for such a celebrated person to live. The man she sought stood as they entered. "I'm Doc Woburn." He looked down his nose at Pa but extended his hand to him.

Pa nodded but didn't shake his hand. "I'm Reverend Hayes, and this is my adopted daughter, Liberty."

It felt strange for Pa to speak the truth of their relationship out loud.

"Nice to meet you." Doc Woburn lowered his rejected hand. His gaze lingered on Liberty, and she could swear a spark of recognition dawned in his eyes. "My assistant said you wanted to see me on a personal matter."

The moment to introduce herself had arrived. Liberty swallowed against a dry throat. She couldn't think how to start, nor could she find her voice.

Pa rested his hands on her shoulders. "Liberty has something to say to you."

"I'm your daughter by America Warrington." She blurted out the bare facts, using her mother's maiden name.

Shedding his supercilious air, Doc Woburn stared at her with wide eyes. His face turned white, then red. "I'm sorry your mother left you in doubt of a father, but I have no daughter by America Warrington."

Pa's hands gripped Liberty's shoulders more firmly. "Liberty has given you the truth. Don't throw it back in her face. And I'd watch what you say about America, if I were you."

"What proof do you have?" He shook his head. "None, I'll warrant."

"Just look at her, man. She's the very image of you. What other proof do you need?"

Doc Woburn studied Liberty. "She does have the look of my mother…" He shrugged. "That could be an accident of nature. Even if it isn't, what's it to me? I spawned more than one mongrel child in St. Louis."

"I'll thank you for not referring to Liberty by that term." Pa bit out the words.

"Can I help it if her mother had the morals of a tart?" Doc Woburn smiled. "I would think a preacher, as you call yourself, would marry a virtuous woman."

Pa's hands convulsed on Liberty's shoulders. She wondered through a haze if the two men might come to blows. "No, Pa." Liberty thrust herself between them. "Don't let him pick a fight." She met the eyes of the man who had sired her. "He's not worth the trouble."

"Out you get." Pa reached up, and Liberty lowered herself from the wagon into his arms. Her feet swung free, then touched the ground. Pa held onto her, and she didn't move away. "You barely spoke on the way home. Are you all right?"

"Mostly." She drew away and peered up into his face in the dimness of the barn. "Thank you for taking me to meet Doc Woburn." She would never call that vile man her father again.

He stroked her cheek. "I'm sorry it didn't work out the way you wanted."

"I'm not sure what I hoped except to stop wondering."

"And have you?"

She nodded. "There's nothing more I need to know."

"Don't take the things he said about your mother to heart. She sinned, but we all do—even those who place themselves above others. God alone can judge us, but when we call upon His Son's name and repent, He chooses to show us mercy."

"I'm sorry Ma ever fell into that man's clutches. I'm glad she found you."

"That makes two of us. God gave her to me to love and cherish. I've never once regretted marrying her."

"I'm not sorry that she's my mother, never mind how that came about."

Pa's lips curved in a soft smile. "God has a way of giving beauty for ashes. Your mother lost her home, her family, and the father of her baby. But into her pain, God brought you."

Liberty smiled. "What a lovely thought."

Pa tilted her face. "Never forget that you are a treasure, formed to mirror the very image of God. Any man who marries you will gain a wonderful wife."

She closed her eyes as tears welled. "I wanted to find

someone who would make you proud. After I learned about my birth, I decided that wouldn't be fair."

"Why wouldn't it? God doesn't require perfection, and neither do I."

Liberty's tears brimmed over, but she didn't care if he saw them. "I turned Jake away because I thought he wasn't good enough."

Her tears flowed in a cleansing flood, washing away all the lies that had held her bound. She was not a lesser creature, but a beautiful treasure cherished by God.

Pa embraced her while she wept. "Liberty, darling, only one man was ever perfect—Jesus, who came in the flesh to save us from our sins. I'll never measure up to Him. If I needed to be worthy before preaching a sermon, the pulpit would remain empty, the pews would stand silent, and souls would be lost forever. God doesn't expect us to be anything but contrite and willing. Most of the time, I can manage that much."

She smiled. "Thank you for being my father."

His face softened. "I consider it an honor."

Something else needed saying. Liberty drew in a breath. "Even if Doc Woburn was less disappointing, I'd never replace you with him."

"That's good to know." Pa nodded. "I assume you won't mind helping with the horses, then."

CHAPTER TWENTY

JAKE REINED IN HIS HORSE BEFORE the Eddy-Hammond Company store. Missoula's mercantile occupied the end of a city block and featured a covered porch that wrapped around the building. The screen door shut behind him with a well-oiled click. The polished floorboards didn't sag or creak like the ones in Liberty township's general store. He walked down the wide aisles, exchanging greetings with clerks stationed behind the counters. Most wore vests and shirt sleeves. A stuffed deer head surveyed newcomers from above the jewelry counter. All manner of merchandise awaited the customer—hardware, furniture, cabinets, groceries, and more.

Jake carried a bottle of sarsaparilla to one of the counters. The clerk's lips tilted into a smile beneath his moustache. "Is that all for you today?"

"Yes, thank you." Jake laid a coin down. "Would you mind opening my drink? I don't feel like digging through my saddlebags to find a bottle opener."

"Are you traveling through?"

"No. I'm staying at the hotel for a couple of days. My name is Jake Buckthorn."

The clerk's smile widened. "Welcome to Missoula. I'm Gus Felton."

"Nice to meet you, Gus. I wonder if you can help me. I'm looking for a woman named Martha Riddler. She's slender and has dark blond hair. Her eyes are blue."

"A woman by that name and description inquired about

working in the store a couple of days ago. I don't think she applied, though." He picked up Jake's coin and dropped it in the till. "Sorry, but that's all I know."

Jake carried his fizzy drink outside. He stopped on the porch to tip the bottle to his lips.

"Fancy meeting you here." Deputy Manchen spoke from below him.

Jake lowered his arm and swallowed quickly to keep from choking. "You startled me."

"Sorry about that." Deputy Manchen climbed the steps onto the porch. In the countryside, his roughness had blended in. Here in the city, he stood out. "You look travel-worn and weary. Did you just ride in?"

Jake nodded. "I'm glad to finally arrive."

Deputy Manchen took off his hat and used it to fan himself. "It's hotter than blazes. What brings you to this neck of the woods?"

Jake hesitated to inform a member of the law that he was searching for the woman who put him in jail. On the other hand, Deputy Manchen didn't seem likely to jump to conclusions. If Jake won him over, the deputy would make a powerful ally. "I'm looking for Martha Riddler."

Deputy Manchen's steely gaze flicked over Jake's face. "Certain folks might object to your errand."

"I guess you heard what happened." A horse's hooves clopped, and a buggy rolled by in the street. Jake turned his head to peer inside. Martha wasn't among the passengers.

"I know what she accused you of doing." The deputy's eyes glinted. "I don't believe a word of it. I've been around so many lawbreakers that my stomach churns a warning when one draws near. I've never noticed the sensation around you."

Jake tried to picture Sheriff Underwood's reaction to the

deputy's method of determining guilt or innocence. "I know one thing for certain. In my case, your opinion can't be faulted. I'm innocent."

Deputy Manchen placed his hat back on his head. "What do you want with Martha?"

"I'm out to clear my name."

The deputy raised his eyebrows. "I wouldn't take you for a man who cares what others think."

"Life has taught me to care. Failing to protect my reputation destroyed my mother's trust in me for years. It cost me the kind regard of the woman I love. I'm not about to make the same mistake a second time."

The deputy stepped aside to allow a woman in a flowered hat to pass by. "Why don't we stand in the shade of that building over there?" He pointed to a squat brick building with darkened windows and a 'closed' sign on the door.

"All right."

Jake crossed the street beside the deputy. He remembered the bottle of sarsaparilla in his hand and took a long drink.

"That looks good." Deputy Manchen nodded toward Jake's bottle. "I might have to buy one. First, I should mention that I'm looking for Martha also. I've searched high and low. Unless I'm very much mistaken, she's not here."

"I thought you were hunting Grady Bradshaw."

"There may be a connection between the two. Any idea where else Martha would go?"

"None."

"Listen up. You haven't asked my advice, but I'm going to give it anyway. Go home. You have no idea what you're getting in the middle of. Trust me when I say that you don't want to find out. Go back to that sweet mother who loves you so much she'll cook your breakfast while you're in jail."

"You heard about that?"

The deputy's lips quirked. "Along with half the territory."

Jake shook his head. Something about being told to go home to his mother jarred a man. "Thanks all the same, but I need to clear my name, and I'm already involved. There's no point in warning me away."

"I was afraid you'd say that." Deputy Manchen rubbed the back of his neck. "You'd better work with me then."

Liberty said a prayer for Pa, who had gone out to ride his half-broke horse. She returned her attention to embellishing a flour-sack towel with roses and violets in an embroidered pattern. She could hear Ma humming "Amazing Grace" in the kitchen to the accompaniment of clanging pans. Liberty's sisters were chattering in their room, and she'd caught a glimpse of her brothers out digging in the garden.

The knocking echoed through the house.

"Liberty, will you get that?" Ma's voice drifted from the kitchen.

Liberty stood up and dropped her embroidery onto the overstuffed chair she'd occupied in the parlor. She hurried to open the front door, a greeting for Jake ready on her lips. He'd promised four days ago during his visit that he would come by again soon.

Beau waited on the other side of the screen. Liberty halted, a sick feeling in her stomach. It was too late to retreat and ask someone else to get the door. She could tell by the smug expression on his face that he'd already seen her.

"Hello, Liberty. How are you this fine day?"

"I'm well, thank you." *Why did he sound so chipper?*

"And your ankle?"

"It's much improved."

"I'm happy to hear it." His smile broadened. "Your injury has kept you cooped up long enough."

She peered at him in suspicion. "I get out more than you seem to think."

"Of course, you do. What was I thinking to suggest otherwise?" He spoke in animated tones. "May I have a word with you?"

Liberty sighed. The last time she'd stepped outside with him, he'd lured her with talk of the Bible. On the other hand, refusing to oblige him might bring Ma from the kitchen to back her up. Liberty wanted to avoid that, if she could. Ma had been through a lot lately without having to deal with her daughter's truculent admirer.

Liberty opened the screen door and stepped onto the porch beside him. "I only have a minute."

Beau's smile lit his face. He really was quite attractive with his tumbling blond hair and blue eyes. "Walk with me." He held his hand out to her in a beguiling gesture.

The contrast between Jake, whom she'd expected to see, and the man before her stood out a mile. Beau seemed bent on showing her better treatment, she'd give him that. Still, she couldn't ignore that he kept coming over after she told him she wasn't interested. A person could behave like a dandy when it came to the finer points of etiquette but still be a bully.

Liberty touched her temple, where the beginning of a headache throbbed. She couldn't do this. She must make him understand her, once and for all. "I'm not interested in walking with you, or in your visits, for that matter. Sorry to say, but I dread them." *There. If that doesn't dissuade him, nothing will.*

She reached for the screen-door handle, anxious to escape into the house.

Beau's hand clamped over her mouth. He pinned her

against him. "I've had about enough of you." Liberty fought to free herself, even as Beau dragged her backward down the steps.

Liberty dug her fingernails into his arm across her middle. Beau hissed and tightened his grip. She had trouble drawing breath with his arm cutting off her wind. Although light-headed from lack of oxygen, she fought as he hauled her through the rose arbor and along the path toward the barn.

What did Beau plan to do to her when they reached it? Liberty's irritation gave way to fear. She might have rejected him too strongly for his oversized ego to accept.

Pa is in the barn saddling Chief. Relief went through her at the thought. Pa wouldn't let anything bad happen to her. He'd send Beau packing, and she could return to the safety of the house.

Beau was breathing hard from exertion by the time he shoved her through the barn doorway.

Pa's boots protruded at an odd angle from one of the stalls. Chief was tied beside Beau's sorrel quarter horse. Why had Pa abandoned his boots and left Chief in the barn? A moan carried to her. Understanding dawned, and Liberty shuddered in horror. Pa was *in* his boots. He was lying in the stall, injured. What had Beau done to him? Tears blinded her. Pa wasn't getting up.

Please God, don't let my pa be badly hurt.

Stunned, Liberty stopped struggling. Beau took advantage of her inertia to gag her. Afterwards, he threw her over the back of his horse and lashed her down with ropes.

She raised her head in time to see Beau lift himself into Chief's saddle. With her mouth gagged, she couldn't warn him of his peril if she'd wanted to.

The horse beneath her swayed as it paced behind Chief. Beau sat the half-broke horse well, but she doubted he'd be a match for Chief. Beau turned aside into the wild lands, keeping off the road. Chief went along so tamely that Liberty was beginning to think he'd mastered Pa's horse.

A rabbit startled out of its hole and darted across Chief's path. A shudder rippled over the half-broke horse. Chief squatted on his hind legs and pawed the air, squealing. Beau clung to the flailing stallion's back, so helpless that Liberty almost felt sorry for him. Beau slapped the reins repeatedly against Chief's straining neck, and Liberty withdrew all sympathy. Chief's hooves thudded to the ground, and he bolted.

Liberty's horse had no choice but to follow, since Beau was holding the lead rein. She laid low across the sorrel's back to avoid branches. Tied to the horse, Liberty couldn't fall off, but she could still meet with an accident if the sorrel stumbled and fell.

Jake turned into the parking area for Liberty township's general store. Compared to Missoula's mercantile, it wasn't much, but he was glad to reach the place. He'd covered the longer leg of the journey yesterday so he could arrive home before noon today.

Jake saw right through the assignment Deputy Manchen had given him. The deputy had instructed him to return home and keep watch for Grady Bradshaw. Jake had gone along with the ruse, regardless. The deputy had helped him see that worrying his family in the hope of clearing his name was selfish. He'd had second thoughts about risking his neck to change what people thought of him. Somehow, he'd gone from caring too little about his reputation to caring too much. He needed to strike a balance. It was only natural to want others to think well of him, but not to the point of threatening his survival.

"Well, aren't you a sight for sore eyes?" Scotty came out from behind the counter and slapped an arm around him. "How are you?"

"Fair to middling." Jake felt grateful they were alone in the store, or Scotty's greeting would have drawn every eye. He wasn't ready to weather that kind of attention. He hadn't spent many days in jail, although it seemed otherwise. The ordeal had marked him, all the same.

"Are you free for good, or will you stand trial?"

Jake shrugged. "That depends on whether Martha turns up to accuse me. At this point, it seems unlikely, but who knows what will happen?"

"I never once believed you were guilty." Scotty touched his chest with his fist. "When you know a person, deep down, you don't have to wonder."

"Thank you. That means a lot to me."

"So—" Scotty heaved in a breath. "Did you come in to say hello or were you after something?"

"Since when are you waiting on customers? I thought Beau did that for you."

"Good luck, if you want Beau to wait on you." Scotty's laugh held a bitter edge. "He up and quit this morning. Last I saw him, he'd packed his saddlebags and high-tailed it out of town."

"Any idea why?"

"None whatsoever. I paid him a fair wage and let him buy what he wanted at a discount. A lot of folks are happy with less."

"I doubt Beau would understand something like that. Did he say where he was going?"

Scotty shook his head. "Mind you, I'm not worried about Beau. From what I've observed, he has a quick mind and faster reflexes. I've never met anyone more likely to land on his feet."

Beau flew over Chief's head and plowed into a prickly pear. His curses scorched the air. Chief lowered his muzzle to the grass as if nothing momentous had happened.

The sorrel sidled up to Chief. Liberty started, aware all at once that Beau had dropped the lead line. Preoccupied with removing the cactus spines bristling from his arms and chest, he hadn't seemed to notice. Liberty caught her breath as the prospect of escape loomed before her. She had a little mobility left, despite her bonds, and could probably induce the sorrel to take off.

Liberty's shoulders slumped. The thought of being tied to the back of a runaway horse held no appeal whatsoever. It would be better to bide her time and attempt an escape with better odds of success. She had to believe she would find a way out of this mess.

"Don't get any ideas," Beau growled.

Liberty found herself staring down the barrel of his gun.

Beau holstered his pistol and stomped over to capture Chief. "You're a sorry excuse for a horse." He raised his hand.

Liberty averted her eyes as a slap rang out.

Chief squealed and snorted. He pawed the ground.

Beau drew back his fist, but then lowered it. "I'd love to have time to put you in your place."

The possibility of pursuit must weigh on Beau, as well it might. If Pa wasn't too badly injured, he would come after her. Jake would search for her too. Friends and neighbors were sure to ride out also.

Beau untied Liberty's bonds. "You can ride that devil horse. I'm not getting on him again."

Liberty's muscles were so cramped and sore, she could barely stand. Even tied into the saddle, how would she ever ride Pa's spirited stallion?

Beau lifted her and dropped her into Chief's saddle. The

half-broke horse reacted with quick fury, no doubt upset from the treatment Beau had meted out. Beau jumped out of the way in time to save himself.

Still choked by the gag, Liberty couldn't scream. She hung on for dear life as the horse beneath her bolted.

Jake stopped by the post office. He might as well check the mail before heading home. Going into Martha's place of work didn't feel entirely comfortable. She no longer lay in wait behind the counter, but he couldn't help wondering what she'd said about him to her fellow employees.

"Hello, Jake." The postmaster greeted him mildly from behind the counter.

Jake returned his salutation. "Do we have any mail?"

"You're out of luck. Gideon stopped in yesterday, and nothing came for you today."

"I wanted to check. You never know when something will turn up."

The postmaster smiled. "Take care of yourself, Jake."

"Thanks. I intend to." On his way to the door, Jake stopped in his tracks. Beau's eyes stared at him from a wanted poster.

"What is it?" The postmaster leaned across the counter.

Jake covered the lower half of the face in the poster with his hand. Without the mustache and beard, the pictured man was clearly Beau. He might have noticed the resemblance before, if it wasn't for Beau's clean-shaven face and blond hair. In his picture, Grady Bradshaw had dark hair and a beard. Hair could be dyed and a beard shaven. The man in the poster could be Beau. "Nothing much." Jake glanced over his shoulder at the postmaster. "He reminds me of someone."

"If you have any information, notify the sheriff. Bradshaw is one of the worst."

"My thoughts exactly." Jake pushed the door open and stepped into the fresh air. It took a couple of breaths to clear his head. He'd spent time in the sheriff's office a couple of days ago and wouldn't relish a repeat visit. The only thing he despised more was letting Beau escape. Deputy Manchen's return to the area must have spooked him into running off. If they didn't catch Beau before he hid somewhere else, he might continue to wreak havoc on unsuspecting people.

Jake walked the short distance to the sheriff's office. Sandwiched between a millinery shop and a bakery, the diminutive building seemed too small to shelter a man of the sheriff's height. Although the rough building was not large, it was a good sight more comfortable than the even smaller jail where he'd cooled his heels.

"Good morning, Jake." Sheriff Underwood answered his knock. He stepped back and allowed Jake entrance. "I'm surprised you want to renew our acquaintance so soon."

Jake smiled ruefully. "That makes two of us."

"Have a seat and tell me what's on your mind."

Jake chose one of the two chairs facing the sheriff's desk. "This shouldn't take long."

"Certainly." Sheriff Underwood's chair squeaked as he sat down. He folded his hands on his desk. "Go on."

"I believe that the picture on Grady Bradshaw's wanted poster is of Beau Hensley."

Sheriff Underwood gaped at him. "That's a serious accusation."

"It's more an observation. The poster bothered me before, but I couldn't figure out why until today."

Sheriff Underwood jumped up and paced a couple of steps. He came to rest before what Jake thought of as the 'Wall of Infamy.' Rank upon rank of outlaw faces stared out from wanted posters plastered above the unfortunate floral wallpaper that was mercifully faded. Belle Starr, Doc Holiday, Jim Miller, John Wesley Hardin, some of the worst outlaws in the West, peered out from the same wall as Grady Bradshaw. Some, like Jesse James, had gone to their eternal reward. Most still lived and could be counted on to raise trouble.

Sheriff Underwood gazed at the poster. "You're right, the picture looks like Beau. I don't know how I missed it before."

"He disguised himself well enough to fool the eye, and he hid in plain sight."

"Hold on there." The sheriff held up his hand, palm out. "I'm not certain it's really Beau, but it wouldn't hurt to ask him a few questions."

"You'll find that a little difficult. Beau left town this morning." His errand accomplished, Jake stood up. The sooner he departed this building, the better he'd like it.

Sheriff Underwood opened his mouth, but Jake spoke first. "That's all I know. Smitty might be able to tell you more."

"Thanks, Jake." Sheriff Underwood held out his hand. "I'll pass the information along to interested parties."

Of course, he meant Deputy Manchen. Jake smiled as he shook the sheriff's hand. He hadn't thought much of the deputy's assignment, but it was working out well, after all.

"He that dwelleth in the secret place of the most High shall abide under the shadow of the Almighty...." Liberty recited Psalm 91 as Chief's hooves ate up the ground. "I will say of the Lord, he is my refuge and my fortress—my God—in him will I trust."

She had Phoebe to thank for teaching her to ride. Otherwise, Liberty would never have overcome her fear of horses. She'd mostly overcome it, anyway. Chief still terrified her. Even so, she'd fallen into the horse's rhythm, and had so far remained seated. That could change at any moment. She couldn't imagine surviving on the stallion's back any longer than Pa. That wasn't very long, she realized with a sense of shock. By some miracle, she'd already outlasted him.

Liberty choked on her gag and fought to pull in air. It had to come off. Keeping one hand on the saddle horn, she untied the knot behind her head. She jerked the offending cloth from her face and gulped air that tasted of wildflowers, grass, and sagebrush.

Chief's back rounded and lifted beneath her. Liberty grasped the pommel with both hands and held on for all she was worth. The horse's bucking stopped at last. Liberty barely had time to recover before Chief ran at a clump of tall sagebrush. She flung herself low and clung to the horse's rough mane. The horse turned at the last minute, scouring her against prickly branches. Fabric ripped, and Liberty gasped in pain. Her sleeve fell open to the elbow. Blood oozed from the long welt on her forearm.

"Surely he shall deliver thee from the snare of the fowler, and from the noisome pestilence. He shall cover thee with his feathers, and under his wings shalt thou trust. His truth shall be thy shield and buckler." She recited the words with fierce concentration.

The thud of other hooves alerted her. Beau must be coming up behind her.

The impulse to urge Chief on faster took hold of her, but she resisted its pull. Moments ago, the stallion had tried to eject her from the saddle. After failing at that ploy, he'd done his best to brush her off. What harm might the horse cause at a higher rate of speed? The ground was already whisking by at a dizzying pace. The prospect of breaking her neck in a fall didn't seem far off. On the other hand, if she did nothing, Beau would catch up to her. She couldn't decide which fate would be worse.

CHAPTER TWENTY-ONE

JAKE POINTED SCOUT HOMEWARD ON THE road from Liberty. While rounding a bend, he surprised a marsh hawk riding the air on brindled wings. The bird of prey sailed to a bough partway up a large fir tree and folded its fan-shaped tail as it perched. The bough dipped and swayed. If Jake hadn't seen the bird land, he'd have taken it for a branch of the tree.

Things weren't always what they seemed.

What lay behind Martha's false accusations? He was inclined to believe himself a victim of something more sinister than the wrath of a scorned woman. But what? Did a connection exist between Martha and Grady Bradshaw, as Deputy Manchen suspected?

Jake couldn't feel sorry about Beau's departure. There had been a rash of robberies by road agents since he'd come to town. Jake doubted it was a coincidence. Hopefully, the information he'd provided the sheriff would lead to Beau's capture. Jake had a feeling that he sorely needed to be brought to trial.

Beau's likeness to the image of Grady Bradshaw explained Jake's gut feeling about the man. The resemblance must have bothered him for a while. Intuition wasn't the only reason he mistrusted Beau. His cavalier attitude toward Liberty and Phoebe still rankled. Remembering Beau's fascination with Liberty, Jake clicked to his horse, urging Scout to pick up his pace.

The last leg of Jake's journey home turned from pleasant to annoying. He couldn't shake his unease. He would feel better after assuring himself that Beau wasn't anywhere near Liberty.

Jake turned off the road onto the track that led past Liberty's house to his own. After turning Scout out to pasture, he hurried to Liberty's house. The back door stood open, but he knocked at the screen.

Voices murmured inside the house, and then America came to the door. "Jake! Thank the Lord you're here." She looked up at him with tears in her eyes.

"What's wrong?" he asked in sharp alarm.

"Reverend Hayes has suffered a blow to the head. Seth went for the doctor." Her tears spilled down her cheeks.

"I'm sorry to hear that. What happened?"

"I'm forgetting my manners." She brushed the tears from her face and heaved a breath. "Won't you come in?"

"Maybe for a minute. I don't want to keep you from your husband." Jake stepped past her into the kitchen, finding it strangely quiet. America should be preparing supper for her family, not weeping at the door.

"Thank you. Aisling and Liam are watching over him, but I would like to return to his side."

Something seemed very wrong. Liberty should have been the one who answered the door. She would want her mother to remain with her father. Either that, or she'd be keeping vigil over her father. "Where is Liberty?" Fear jerked the words from him.

America's face crumpled, and her shoulders shook with sobs. "Beau took her."

The fear that had driven Jake to Liberty's door stared him in the face. If Beau hurt her—

Jake quieted his thoughts. Giving way to panic would befuddle his mind when he most needed his wits. Come hell or high water, he intended to find Liberty and bring her home.

Liberty tried to scream but no sound came. Chief's hooves left the ground, and her legs lost their grip. For a weightless moment, it felt like she could fly. The stallion cleared a fallen log and came down. First the front hooves thudded on the ground, then the rear ones. Liberty landed hard in the saddle.

"Thou shalt not be afraid for the terror by night, nor for the arrow that flieth by day…" She panted the words.

Chief would tire at some point, but the powerful horse gave no sign of flagging. He'd stumbled only once while splashing through a river bed. For a horrifying moment, Liberty thought he would go over with her beneath him. She cried out in fear at the prospect of being simultaneously crushed and drowned. When the horse recovered his footing, she sobbed with relief.

The stallion might not be weary, but Liberty's strength was failing. She held on with difficulty and adjusted to the horse's movements more slowly. After surviving sagebrush, low-slung branches, a fallen log, and a river, Liberty didn't have much resilience left. It was only a matter of time before she couldn't hang on any longer. Her throat went dry at the terrifying thought. What would happen to her if she fell?

The question led to a number of conclusions, each capable of propelling her sagging body upright in the saddle. She would not finish without a fight. "Nor for the pestilence that walketh in darkness, nor for the destruction that wasteth at noonday."

The hoofbeats grew louder, warning her that Beau approached. She looked over her shoulder. Beau's hair glinted gold in the sunlight, and his sorrel horse gleamed like copper. He was thrashing the poor creature with the reins. The sorrel's chest heaved as its forelegs pumped.

Liberty would rather take her chances with an untamed horse than an unruly man. She tapped her heels against Chief's flanks. The effect was like a shot going off beside the horse. Chief reared, and the ground receded a long way below her. The stallion pawed the air, trumpeting. Liberty flung her arms as far as she could around Chief's neck. She kept her seat but when the horse came down felt herself slipping. If Chief reared again, she would fall.

Chief launched into a canter, and the rocking motion pushed Liberty back into the saddle. The horse stretched out his legs in a gallop. A glance behind revealed Beau a little way behind.

Liberty faced forward and sucked in a sharp breath.

She'd ridden to the end of the Earth, with nothing ahead but sky. At the last minute, Liberty embedded her hands in Chief's mane and hid her face.

The stallion seemed to take a long time to cover the achingly short distance to their doom.

CHAPTER TWENTY-TWO

THE SADDLE BENEATH LIBERTY TILTED AT an alarming angle. She screamed as Chief plunged down the steep gulch in a running slide. Panting with fear, Liberty forgot everything Phoebe had taught her about negotiating an incline. Her training on Old Smokey had involved nothing this dangerous. She leaned back to counterbalance the horse, hoping that was the right thing to do.

Chief reached the bottom without mishap and started down a dry river bed. Shaking with relief, Liberty closed her eyes and heaved a breath.

The stallion lurched sideways, squealing. Liberty went flying, and the ground rose up to strike her. Aching in every muscle, she rolled over. The sun-washed sky glared down on her, and a bee buzzed somewhere near. Three quick hoofbeats followed by a pause repeated down the gulch—the sound of Chief galloping to freedom.

Liberty sat up and scanned the cliff the stallion had carried her over. Broken sagebrush and tumbled stones gave silent witness to their passing.

Hooves rang out from above. Liberty pushed onto her hands and knees, sucking in her breath as pain tore through the side where she'd landed. She struggled to her feet, searching for a hiding place. The river bed offered little protection. The trees stood too far back from the grassy banks to reach them in time. Her throat went dry. She couldn't find a way to conceal herself.

An unmistakable whirring rattle alerted her. Liberty

snapped her head sideways. Not a foot away, a coiled rattlesnake's beady eyes were fixed on her. The forked tongue flicked up and down while the end of the striped tail vibrated furiously. Liberty backed away to a safer distance. The snake's presence explained why Chief had shied.

Beau and his horse stood in silhouette against the sky. Liberty could have wept. A spooked horse and a moment's inattention were all it had taken to leave her stranded. Riding Chief had been an ordeal, but she would willingly endure it longer to escape Beau. She couldn't hide, and there was no point running. Liberty lifted her chin and waited for him to reach her.

Beau kicked the sorrel's sides, but his horse didn't budge. He kicked again, harder. The sorrel took several steps backward. Beau lashed the horse with the reins and renewed his pummeling of its flanks. The sorrel reared, screaming. Beau's curses rang out as his horse bolted away from the edge.

She hoped that the sorrel and Beau would soon part company. Thinking back over Beau's behavior, Liberty marveled that she had noticed his selfishness but missed his cruelty. Beau had pushed himself into her company, but he'd also delighted in offending Phoebe and rejoiced at Jake's arrest.

She hurried down the dry bed away from Beau, keeping an eye out for snakes. She had a lot of walking to do. Before Chief had carried her into the gulch, she'd seen its length. If Beau couldn't bully his horse over the side, he'd have to navigate an interweaving network of gulches to reach her. The odds were good that he would give up, but she wouldn't put it past him to try.

Liberty would do well to remember that Beau wasn't the only threat she faced. She needed to find her own way out of the maze—and she'd have to do it on foot.

Jake reined in at the top of a hill and scanned the basin below. Grasses waved in hues of green and gold. Sparse trees lined a river that reflected the pale sky. Gulches gashed the valley floor, and gullies wrinkled the rock faces that rose above it.

The shine had gone from the day. The smoky grayness of dusk gathered at the edges of the valley, ready to creep in soon. The rough landscape before him wouldn't be safe to travel by night. Before he holed up, Jake was determined to close as much distance as possible between himself and Liberty.

He'd worn out his own horse this morning, but his mother had lent him her mare, Lady Gray. He sent the sure-footed Quarter Horse downward alongside the fresh hoofprints that had guided him from the Hayes's barn. He didn't have much skill at tracking, but these marks were obvious. He couldn't figure out why Beau wasn't being more careful. He seemed to have thrown caution to the winds. Considering that Beau had stolen a horse, kidnapped a woman, and was being pursued by a bounty hunter, his carelessness made no sense. The erratic course the horses had taken also troubled Jake. Why would Beau give the horses their heads? Maybe he'd had no choice in the matter. Beau hadn't inquired whether the horse he was taking was broken.

Jake urged Lady Gray onward. He wouldn't rest until Beau came to account, and that went double if Liberty came to harm.

He should have spoken louder when he'd voiced his first concerns about Beau. He shouldn't have discounted his own opinion. From here on out, he would listen to counsel but trust his instincts. If he'd persisted in communicating his mistrust of Beau to Liberty, this might not have happened. He'd failed her by letting his jealousy get in the way. She'd refused to listen after that.

The pursuit led Jake through grassland to the edge of a

wide, shallow river. Even in the dying light, he could see impressions in the sod on the other side. Jake dismounted and studied the surface of the water, debating whether to take a chance. It was safer to cross an unfamiliar river in the daylight. That meant spending the night here. It galled him to stop, but with dark lowering, he'd have to settle for the night soon anyway.

Jake ate a cold supper of elk jerky and biscuits before climbing into his bedroll. He rolled onto his back to watch the stars. Gazing at them brought the Creator, who had hung them, near. Jake closed his eyes. "I'll trust you to watch over Liberty tonight God, but please help me find her tomorrow."

Even though Liberty was wearing sturdy boots, her feet ached. The heat in the gulch was nothing compared to the temperature inside her boots. Her mouth felt parched, and swallowing was difficult. Whenever she turned her head, dizziness followed. Aching beyond measure, Liberty trudged onward. She needed to find water soon or perish.

The sky caught fire as the sun plummeted below the surrounding cliffs. Liberty slowed her steps. Twilight brought relief from the heat but made it harder to see. The shadows of dusk lengthened and connected as full dark came on. The moon shimmered behind wisps of cloud and turned the dry bed into a glowing river.

"Thank you, dear Lord." The night wind whisked Liberty's words away, but nothing could steal the peace that settled over her like a warm quilt. It defied all reason. Her circumstances could not be more dire. She was lost, and no one knew her whereabouts but a man she feared. *God sees you.* The thought wafted over her like a sweet fragrance. *He knows where you are.*

Something rustled behind her.

Liberty turned, the hair on her arms prickling. She peered down the dry bed and stared into the darkness beyond its banks.

Nothing stirred.

Liberty stumbled onward, feeling oddly detached from her body. It seemed she might float down the gulch on a breath of air. Pulling free of the strange sensation, she looked behind her again.

Glowing eyes stared back at her.

Heart racing, Liberty struggled to draw breath. *God, help me.*

Whatever stalked her might spring at any moment, but she knew better than to run. Acting like prey would send the wrong signals. Liberty stared at the creature, letting it know she saw it. "For he shall give his angels charge over thee, to keep thee in all thy ways." She spoke between panting breaths. "They shall bear thee up in their hands, lest thou dash thy foot against a stone."

The creature crept nearer. It turned to flank her, and the outline of a mountain lion gleamed in the moonlight.

Meeting the cat's glowing gaze, Liberty raised her voice. "Thou shalt tread upon the lion and adder."

The mountain lion gathered itself for a leap.

Liberty stifled a sob but held her ground. "The young lion and the dragon shalt thou trample under thy feet." If she was going to die, she would do it with Scripture on her lips.

The mountain lion sprang.

CHAPTER TWENTY-THREE

A GUNSHOT RIPPED THE AIR. THE mountain lion screamed and crashed to the ground, but it kept coming. Liberty threw herself sideways, out of the wounded beast's path. A second shot rang out. The mountain lion fell back. Liberty stared at the motionless creature, half-expecting it to rise.

"Killing it with two shots isn't too bad for shooting in the dark." A voice she recognized boasted behind her.

Liberty spun about. The moonlight picked out Beau on his horse. "What are you doing here?"

"I save your life, and you still can't give me a kind word."

"It's your fault I needed saving." Liberty spat the words, too bone-weary to care how he reacted.

"You're tempting fate, darling." His voice turned silky.

The click of his gun barrel brought her head up. "Don't aim that thing at me."

"You're bossy, all of a sudden."

"Maybe I'm sick and tired of being threatened by you."

"I should shoot you, ransom be hanged," Beau growled.

"Ransom?"

"You're worth a lot of money."

"What can you possibly mean?" Liberty wailed in bewilderment. It was all too much. Her head hurt, hunger gnawed her stomach, and her throat burned. She'd survived a runaway horse, a rattlesnake, and a mountain lion—only to fall once more into Beau's hands.

Beau chuckled. "Senator Warrington should pay a pretty

penny to free his granddaughter."

"Is that what this is all about?" It was the last thing she'd expected Beau to say.

"Did you think I fancied you? I was biding my time. Sorry to disappoint you."

"You are one of the most arrogant—"

"Shut up before I change my mind about shooting you."

Liberty might have replied, but a coughing fit seized her, forcing her attention onto more pressing matters than quarreling with Beau. "Do you have water?"

"Get on my horse and I'll let you drink from my canteen."

His wheedling tone grated on her nerves. Liberty hesitated, but she would die without water. She climbed up behind him, promising herself to find a chance to escape.

Beau dropped the canteen into her hands. "Don't drink it all."

Liberty was beyond listening to him as great gulps of tepid water slid down her throat.

"That's enough." Beau jerked the canteen away.

The horse swayed into motion. Certain that sleep would come instantly the minute she closed her eyes, she stared owl-eyed into the moonlit darkness. The night passed in a confusing kaleidoscope of sights and sounds.

God had answered her prayer for rescue in a way she wouldn't have chosen. Beau thought he could trade her for money, but why would the grandfather who ignored her existence pay for her freedom? She shouldn't mention that to Beau. Once he found out, she wouldn't give much for her life.

Lady Gray went into the river with the high-stepping grace of a filly, although she was getting along in years. Jake sat on the mare's back, searching the water for hazards. Lady Gray stumbled but recovered before he had a chance to react. She heaved out of the river on the opposite shore, and Jake pointed her toward the tracks he'd spotted.

He felt better for having slept. It hadn't taken long for him to feed himself this morning, although he'd wanted to skip the meal. During the challenging day ahead, he would call upon the strength it provided. That seemed more likely when the tracks went over a cliff edge into a deep gulch. He reined in his horse and considered what to do. Scout would have been equal to the task, but Jake wasn't sure how Lady Gray would fare. He shouldn't need to ride into the gulch if he could find a route to its mouth. As long as the tracks came out, he'd know Liberty wasn't there any longer.

Jake decided on a course that skirted the cliff top before descending at a gentler angle. That would give him a bird's-eye view most of the way. It also meant that anyone nearby would see him, but he doubted he'd find Beau and Liberty still there.

He noticed something unusual lying in the dry bed below. Jake caught his breath as the bloated carcass of a mountain lion came into view. He didn't need to see the dead animal at close range to recognize the cause of its death. Jake didn't want to imagine what had happened here. He was grateful that Liberty's mauled body wasn't lying there.

He dropped into the gulch and rode to its mouth, where he investigated a confused muddle of tracks. One set led in, returned, and bent eastward. The other, made by a galloping horse, turned westward. Liberty could have escaped on Chief, but he couldn't quite believe that Beau would let her go without giving chase. It seemed more likely that Chief had run away without his rider.

Jake followed the eastward tracks. If his errand had been more pleasant, he'd have enjoyed riding through the open plain with wind ruffling the grass and the sky wide above him. He stopped at a river for water. While he bent to fill his canteen, Lady Gray waded into the shallows and drank deeply. Jake straightened and stretched, idly watching trout jump. He lifted his head at the sound of hoofbeats, approaching from the east. Jake stood at a familiar sight.

"You're a hard man to catch up with." Shane pulled up on Archibald, the horse that had seen him through many years as a preacher.

"Sorry, but I'm bent on bringing Liberty home before much more time goes by."

Shane took off his hat and dusted it on his pant leg, raising a small cloud of dust. "I hope you can use a bit of company, because you have it anyway."

Jake smiled. "I suppose Doc Bailey couldn't persuade you to stay home and recover."

"I'm well enough to search for my daughter, as I informed him."

Jake sobered. "I gather you've read the tracks they left."

Shane nodded. "Liberty was on Chief when he went over that cliff."

"What makes you think so?"

"Because Beau must have been on the horse that traveled in and out of the gulch. He would ride in after Liberty, but I doubt she'd go looking for him."

"Liberty and Chief parted company, which means she took a fall." Jake sucked in a breath. "You don't think she's still in the gulch?"

"No, but I checked to make certain. She's not there. It looks very much as if the mountain lion stalked her. Beau must have shot it."

Jake shook his head. "I never expected to feel grateful to

Beau for anything, especially not for being handy with a gun. I guess that's a necessary skill for an outlaw."

Shane's gaze pierced him. "*What* did you say?"

"I believe that Beau is Grady Bradshaw. Beau has no beard, and his hair is different, but the upper part of his face matches the image in Grady's poster."

"Did you let the sheriff know your suspicions?"

"Yes, but I'm not sure whether he took them to heart."

"I hope, for Liberty's sake, that you're wrong about Beau. I'd hate to think she's been kidnapped by a cold-blooded killer."

"I feel the same. That's why, as you put it, I was hard to catch. Speaking of which—"

Shane gave a curt nod. "Once I water my horse, I'll be ready to ride."

"You can drink from the stream while I fill my canteen and water the horse." Beau swung Liberty down from the saddle. "But don't forget that I'm keeping an eye on you."

Eager to stretch her legs and still thirsty from her ordeal, Liberty rushed ahead to the stream. She knelt and drank handfuls of cold water. The sorrel waded into the water downstream from her, and Beau bent nearby to fill his canteen.

Water seeped under the ropes binding Liberty's wrists, and she gritted her teeth against the stinging pain. Beau had bound her wrists and ankles before going to sleep in a cave during the heat of the day. She'd scraped her wrists raw trying to free herself while he slumbered. Before continuing on the journey, he had freed her ankles but not her wrists.

Beau wouldn't tell her where he was taking her, but the journey to reach his destination seemed unending. Her existence dwindled to throbbing pain and the urge to fall asleep in the saddle. Any lapse might cause her to tumble to the ground.

Liberty sighed. Her life before Beau captured her seemed a lot simpler to her now. Would she ever return home? That became less likely as the day wore on and no riders appeared behind them. Where were Jake, Pa, and the others from Liberty who must be searching for her?

Her shoulders slumped. Perhaps Chief had out-distanced them. He'd traveled a long way before pitching her off. Liberty couldn't be angry at the horse. Chief had only wanted his freedom. She could understand the feeling.

Liberty traveled through a second night of half-waking agony. After her encounter with the mountain lion, the darkness seemed alive with danger. Deep-throated wolf howls and the yipping ululations of coyotes did nothing to put her at ease. Her position behind Beau made her vulnerable, should a predator attack from behind. Liberty's skin prickled, but casting uneasy glances behind them made it worse. She could think of only one way to ease her fear.

"He shall cover thee with his feathers, and under his wings shalt thou trust. His truth shall be thy shield and buckler. Thou shalt not be afraid for the terror by night," Liberty murmured the words of comfort under her breath.

Beau glanced back in the moonlight. "What are you saying back there?"

"I'm reciting Psalm Ninety-One."

"You mean from the Bible?" He sounded incredulous.

"That's the one."

Beau chortled. "It figures. No sooner do I make off with a woman, then she starts saying her prayers."

Liberty frowned, failing to find his brand of humor funny. She bit back the cutting remark that pressed her lips, however. All she wanted tonight was peace, not a fight with Beau.

By the time dawn lightened the sky, Liberty could barely

hold her head up. The sorrel had climbed through the night to a bench edged by firs and pines. They passed through a narrow canyon to a meadow where a cabin hid among tall firs beyond a gurgling spring. Liberty thought the log building small, but the closer they came, the larger it grew. Smoke curled from the chimney and drifted through the branches of lofty firs. The cabin seemed rooted in place, as if it had sprung from the soil like the trees hiding it.

Beau dismounted at the spring and threw himself down. He raised the water with cupped hands to his mouth, and then lifted his dripping face with a grin. "Come and drink."

Liberty dismounted with difficulty. Beau led the sorrel downstream while Liberty staggered to the spring. Her legs ached from riding, and as she bent down every muscle in her body protested. Sweet water burst against her tongue and moistened her parched throat. It washed the grit from her face and comforted her burning eyes. She stood, feeling a little more human.

Beau carried his saddlebags across one arm. He held the other out to her. "Let's go inside. I'll introduce you to everyone."

Liberty held back, fearful of the change in him. As soon as they'd entered the meadow, he'd gone from mean to kind. She was beginning to wonder about the soundness of his mind. Whether or not his reason was impaired, his spirit had to be. Otherwise, he wouldn't think it was all right to commit crimes. Beau rapped on the door three times, paused, and knocked four times more.

Metal scraped, and the door cracked open. A pock-marked face appeared, and so did the barrel of a pistol. "It's about time you got here. Come inside." The face and the gun withdrew.

Beau opened the door for Liberty. She hung back, having no desire to go through the opening and find out the kind of company he kept.

He gave her a puzzled glance. "I smell coffee, and someone's cooking bacon inside."

Liberty yearned to run away from Beau, not sit down to breakfast with him. The smell of food made her want to wretch, but her stomach growled for sustenance. If she tried bolting, she wouldn't go far on her shaky legs. Beau was bound to catch her.

Liberty lifted her head and walked past him into the building. An earthy scent that reminded her of rotting leaves overlaid the food odors. The feeble light straying through the windows did little to relieve the dimness. A single large room with a loft above it comprised the living quarters. Four rope beds, stacked two at a time with a window between them, lined one wall. The rumpled bedding consisted of thin wool blankets. Sleeping in those beds must be uncomfortable, but the men who looked up from their plates at the scarred table seemed equal to the task. They struck Liberty as rough in ways she couldn't at first define. One peered at her from beneath black hair not well acquainted with a comb. Another had tawny hair in a similar state. A long scar ran down one man's cheek, and the man who had unbolted the door possessed a face marred by pockmarks.

The man lifting a copper coffee pot from the pot-bellied stove raked her with an icy grey gaze. His handsomeness failed to relieve an impression of toughness. He shot a glance at Beau. "Who's this?"

Liberty straightened her spine. "My name is Liberty Hayes." She refused to be talked about while present.

"Well, well." The icy gaze penetrated her. "The little lady can speak for herself."

"She's made that plain since I took her." Beau pushed her farther into the room. "I've had an ear full."

Several of the men chortled. A red cast crept up Beau's neck.

Embarrassing him any further might lead to dire consequences, but Liberty couldn't resist rewarding his bullying with a glare.

The pockmarked man leered at her. "If you don't want her anymore, I'll take her."

"Na-uh, Jared. I will." The scarred man saluted Liberty with his chipped mug.

"You'd have to fight me for her, Kid." The tawny-haired man piped up.

"You and me both, Slade." The man with black hair grinned. "She's not hard on the eyes."

"Shut up, all of you," Beau snarled. "She's not for any of you, or me for that matter."

"What do you mean, Grady?" The man at the stove finished pouring coffee into a mug and thumped the pot down on the stovetop.

Grady? Liberty stared at Beau in confusion. Why would the other man refer to him by the name of Deputy Manchen's outlaw unless… She caught her breath. *Now everything makes sense.*

Beau slung his saddlebags down on a trunk against the wall. "She's Senator Warrington's granddaughter, Logan. He should pay well to free her."

"A senator's daughter, you say?" Logan took a slow drink of his coffee. "How did you find that out?"

"I was going through the mail after robbing the stagecoach and noticed a letter addressed to him from America Hayes. I was curious what the preacher's wife in Liberty township wanted by writing a senator, so I opened it. Turns out, he's her father."

"And just how do you plan to take Liberty to her grandfather?" Logan gestured with his coffee mug. "Washington D.C. is a long way from here."

"So it is." Beau grinned. "It's a good thing the Senate isn't in session. I only need to go to Missouri, where Senator

Warrington lives."

"That's still a long way to transport a woman without getting caught." Logan shook his head. "Count me out."

Beau fisted and unfisted his hands. "I didn't plan to involve you."

"You shouldn't have brought her here." Jared glared at Beau. "A senator's granddaughter has no business in our hideout. Lawmen are like to follow her."

Logan's gaze flicked to Liberty. "Does she know the way here, Grady?"

"I blindfolded her." Beau uttered the falsehood without batting an eye.

Liberty controlled her surprised reaction. She didn't like deceiving others, but if she let on that Beau was lying, she might pay with her life.

Logan plunked his cup onto the counter. "Where's the blindfold?"

"She wasn't wearing one when they rode up, Logan." The black-haired man spoke up. "I saw them through the window."

"Is he telling the truth, preacher's daughter?" Logan returned his attention to Liberty. "Yes or no?"

Liberty's breath caught in her throat. A single word could save or cost her life, and her lips had to speak it. A verse from Psalm 91 ran through her mind. *Because he hath set his love upon me, therefore will I deliver him. I will set him on high, because he hath known my name.*

Liberty knew the name of God. Jesus had borne all her sins to the grave with Him out of love. She couldn't blatantly add to their weight. She raised her chin. "No."

Beau flinched beside her.

Logan's gun appeared in his hand. "No need to draw, Grady, but here's where we part ways. Others are bound to follow you here, and I don't want to stick around to meet them." He glanced at the others. "Anyone else who cares to ride with me, grab your stuff and meet me outside."

"I'll go." Jared pushed his chair back.

"I'm with Logan." The black-haired man jumped to his feet.

"Not me." Kid shook his head. "I don't see nothing wrong with taking advantage of a situation."

"I'm with Beau." Slade mumbled.

"All right, go," Beau snarled. "But leave the spare horses. They belong to me."

"You're welcome to them. I didn't want to steal them in the first place. I'll only take what belongs to me." Logan retrieved a saddlebag from below one of the rope beds. He strode to the door but looked back at Grady. "Stay out of the way of stray bullets."

Beau nodded. "Same to you."

Logan shifted his gaze to Liberty. "You can thank me for sparing your life. I have a soft spot for preachers. I never knew my father, God rest his soul, but he happened to be one." He took down his hat from a peg on the wall and adjusted it on his head. "If you'd said yes, I'd have shot you. I can't abide people who refuse to stand by their principles."

CHAPTER TWENTY-FOUR

Liberty was grateful for a roof over her head and the chance to lie down, even if only on a scraggly mattress over the loft floor. Finding a comfortable position with her hands tied to a post left something to be desired, however. After she'd exposed his lie, Beau had been none too gentle when hauling her into the loft. She ached from the bruises she'd collected due to his mishandling and also from the long journey on horseback.

Besides suffering physical discomfort, Liberty was too keyed up to sleep. Images plagued her. The mountain lion leaped in the moonlight once more. Chief ran away with his tail streaming, an empty saddle perched on his back. Pa's boots protruded from his horse's stall.

Please God, let Pa be all right.

Liberty had a lot to say to him—and to Ma as well. Being deprived of her home and family made them all the more precious. She wouldn't take her family or home for granted again, if only she could return to them.

She had to think of a way to escape. Straining at her bonds did no good. Pain from her chafed wrists kept her awake, which robbed her of strength. Liberty wracked her brain for a solution until her spinning thoughts made her dizzy. She rolled over with a sigh and gave up the struggle.

"Wake up!" Beau's command wrenched Liberty from sleep.

She tried to sit up, but her bonds held her back.

Beau untied her wrists. "Go down and cook breakfast."

"I need to—" Liberty turned away from his gaze. "I need to

visit the outhouse."

"All right, but I'll wait nearby, in case you get any ideas about running."

Liberty had been considering that very thing but chose to speak the truth. "I'm too tired to run. Wait at a distance, please."

A little later, as Liberty emerged from the outhouse, she spotted an outbuilding with a backward-sloped roof through the trees. A neigh rang out, making the other building's purpose clear.

Beau allowed Liberty to wash her hands in the spring before going inside. While Beau paced nearby, she lingered by the flowing water, loath to return to the confinement of the cabin.

"Stop dallying," Beau halted long enough to snap at her.

"I'm coming." Liberty jumped to her feet.

Inside the cabin, lumps in two of the rope beds indicated that Slade and Kid still slept. She eyed the rough counter and pot-bellied stove that served as a kitchen. "What am I to cook?"

"How do I know?" He shrugged. "I'd have to ask Jared, and he's gone. Come up with something."

She scanned the shelves above the counter and caught sight of a sack of flour. "I can bake bread, if you have the ingredients."

Beau carried a chair for her to stand on and held it while she searched. He was back to acting civil, which made life easier while it lasted. Liberty lifted down the supplies for biscuits and bacon gravy. She could guess that Beau and his friends would want food that stuck to their ribs.

Slade rolled out of bed first, followed by Kid. Both had slept in their clothes. From the state of their garments, that must be a regular occurrence. Liberty was sure she didn't look any better. One sleeve of her dress flapped around her elbow. It had ripped open when Chief tried to scrape her off on a clump of tall sagebrush. When she returned home, she would take a bath and change into clean clothes. Her dress was too tattered to be salvageable. Besides, she never wanted to see it again. It would go in the burn pile.

She'd doubted her ability to escape last night, but in the light of day it seemed possible. First, she had to figure out how.

Beau didn't trouble Liberty while she cooked, for which she was grateful. He contented himself instead with shaking Slade and Kid awake. Liberty made coffee while they grumbled. She hoped the hot brew would restore peace. After the outlaws took their places around the table with steaming mugs before them, their chatter became more amenable.

Liberty mixed and kneaded biscuit dough. She rolled it flat with a drinking glass, then cut circles with the rim. She let the biscuits rest in a cast-iron skillet while she fixed the bacon gravy in a second skillet.

As she reached for one of the blades in the knife box, an idea presented itself. Liberty almost cut herself on a sharp edge in her excitement. She finished cooking breakfast with renewed enthusiasm.

Rediscovering her appetite, Liberty wolfed down her own portion at the counter. She spent the day in kitchen duties. With her back to the outlaws while preparing supper, Liberty reached for the smallest knife in the box. Quick as she could, , she sliced a strip of fabric dangling from her sleeve. She folded the scrap over the blade as a makeshift sheath. The knife slipped into her good sleeve without mishap, and her cuff prevented it from falling out.

She restrained herself with difficulty from checking whether anyone had seen. Glancing at the men might make them suspicious. If someone had noticed, she would find out soon. Liberty selected another knife and began cutting up venison jerky for the stew.

The men continued their bantering throughout the day. Sometimes they went outside, but not together. Beau spent much of his time near her while watching the others. Liberty had a feeling he didn't trust any of them.

After supper, the whiskey came out, and the outlaws grew louder. Liberty took her time clearing up to avoid their company.

"Why are you hiding in the kitchen, darlin'" Beau, stinking of whiskey, draped himself over the counter. "Come sit with us."

Playing cards were strewn about the table, and a mess of bills and coins covered the center. She perched on a chair against the wall, keeping out of the way of the men. Beau glanced at her a couple of times at first, but then seemed to forget her. Liberty didn't understand the game they were playing and had nothing else to occupy her mind. She caught herself nodding and pushed herself more upright in her chair.

"I'm out." Beau threw down his hand and stood up. "All right Liberty, you've earned your sleep tonight."

"Aw! I was about to volunteer to put her to bed." Kid slurred.

"She's off limits, remember?" Beau's speech wasn't much clearer.

"You're just trying to keep her for yourself." Slade lurched to his feet.

"Sit down, Slade." Beau emphasized each word. "That's the liquor talking, or I'd take you to account."

Slade and Kid both subsided, much to Liberty's relief. For a moment, she'd wondered whether she would need to use the knife up her sleeve to defend herself. She wasn't certain she could stab someone, even to save her own life.

She held her breath as Beau tied her wrists to the post, but he didn't discover her secret. He left her in darkness except for the moonlight falling through the window. The stars were bright tonight. They called to mind a Bible passage Ma had taught her as a child.

"He healeth the broken in heart, and bindeth up their wounds." Liberty whispered the words of comfort from the Psalms. "He telleth the number of the stars. He calleth them all by their names." Surely the God who could name every star would remember her.

Unbuttoning her cuff proved harder than she'd imagined. She twisted her hand to reach the cord binding her wrists. It tightened, chafing her sore wrist. Liberty bit back her gasp. The rambunctious talk had turned to murmuring. The outlaws seemed to be winding down.

Liberty managed to unbutton her cuff at last, and the knife fell into her palm. Removing the makeshift sheath without dropping the knife proved tricky. After accomplishing it, she gave herself a moment's rest. Next came the hardest task of all— cutting through the cord without slicing her wrists.

Liberty took a deep breath and began.

The cabin grew quiet, and then snores lifted. Liberty stood, knife in hand. She tiptoed to the edge of the loft and looked down. The men were sprawled across the rope beds, quite clearly asleep. She turned and started down the ladder. Even though she knew the outlaws were unlikely to wake, the hair on the back of her neck prickled.

The bottom rung creaked beneath her weight.

Liberty froze. The knife slipped from her fingers and clattered to the floor. She sucked in a breath.

Beau snorted, rolled over, and lay still.

Still shaking, Liberty searched for the knife. She couldn't find it in the dark.

Kid muttered something she didn't catch.

Heart racing, she waited for him to sit up. Time ticked by, but Kid didn't stir. He must have been talking in his sleep.

Abandoning the knife, Liberty crept to the kitchen counter. She snatched up a small corked jug and the handful of leftover biscuits she'd earlier wrapped in a cloth. Liberty tucked the packet of biscuits into her bodice. She grabbed a cotton dishtowel to knot around the handle of the jug to serve as a sling. Her nerves screamed at the delay, but escaping would do her no good if she died of hunger or thirst. At the cabin door, Liberty shot the bolt and reached for the handle with every nerve jumping. If the outlaws were going to wake, it would be when she opened the door.

The wooden panel squeaked on its hinges. She eased herself through the narrow gap she'd opened and pulled the door to with a soft click.

Liberty kept to the shadows on her way to the stable. The meadow, so pleasant by day, was a different proposition at night. The rock walls gleamed in places but otherwise dissolved into blackness. The trees hunched over shadows where all manner of beasts might lurk. The moonlight silvering the path waited to expose her to the gaze of predators, including those who might peer through the cabin windows.

Moonbeams followed her into the stable and lit the wall in the tack room. Liberty took a bridle down from its peg with trembling hands.

Most of the horses were sleeping, but Beau's sorrel greeted her with a nicker. Liberty slipped the bridle over the horse's head and fastened it into place. It seemed fitting to free Beau's mistreated horse also. She must have chosen the correct bridle, for it needed little adjustment. On the way to the tack room for the sorrel's saddle, she paused to listen at the doorway. The spring gurgled, the night wind rustled the trees, and an owl hooted. No sounds intruded from the cabin.

Liberty thanked Phoebe silently for teaching her to saddle a horse. Her hands shook so badly that she almost gave up the effort in favor of riding bareback. She'd never tried it however, and the present didn't seem a good time to start.

The sorrel's hooves clopped on the path. With freedom within reach, Liberty could barely bring herself to stop at the spring. She bent over the moon-washed rocks and captured the bright outflow from one of its streams. Shivers ran up her spine. With her head low and the splash of water loud in her ears, she couldn't see or hear anyone approaching.

Liberty corked the bottle at last and tied the sling crosswise at her neck. She stepped back while the sorrel drank, and then climbed a little awkwardly into the saddle.

The canyon, little more than a fissure in the granite, reposed in deepest darkness. Liberty hesitated, remembering the mountain lion.

He shall call upon me, and I will answer him. I will be with him in trouble. I will deliver him, and honor him.

Liberty could only trust in the horse's night vision and the Lord's protection. She urged the sorrel forward.

Jake reined in. The tracks he and Shane followed led into a canyon, but fresher hoofprints came out again and headed westward. "What do you think?"

Shane lifted his hat and mopped his forehead with his bandana. "I think they went in but came out again."

"That's how it looks to me, too."

"It wouldn't hurt to check that direction before heading after the newer tracks. We don't really know whether Liberty, Beau, or both of them rode away."

Jake frowned at the delay. Shane's thoroughness grated on him no less for being wise. Each hour that passed without reaching Liberty thinned his patience a little more. They'd pushed for two days and still hadn't caught up to her.

Finding Liberty without Beau was unlikely unless she'd by some miracle commandeered his horse. He couldn't picture her doing something so assertive. The other possibility—that Beau might have left her behind for some reason—had him agreeing with Shane.

The morning sun penetrated the mist, but the night's coolness emanated from the granite walls rising on either side of them. Shane, in the lead, halted at the canyon's end. Glancing back, he held a finger to his lips.

Jake craned to see beyond Shane. His heartbeats quickened at the sight of the log cabin staring out at them. This must be Beau's hideout.

Shane emerged from the canyon and kept close to the cliff. Jake trailed behind him.

They dismounted and left their horses in a stand of pines which wouldn't be visible from the cabin. Jake followed Shane as he traveled a circuitous course through brush and behind trees to the log building. Pressed against the walls beside Shane, Jake edged toward the nearest window. As he reached it, the door burst open. Jake dove for the side of the house. Shane hunkered down beside him. Breathless minutes passed.

Footsteps started toward them. Jake pulled Shane with him into the shade beneath the firs.

"She cut herself loose with a kitchen knife." One of the men spoke in a high-pitched voice.

"She won't have gotten far." Although Beau spoke with confidence, he sounded thoroughly put out. Jake smiled, and Shane's countenance lightened. Liberty had escaped on her own.

"You sure you want her back?" a man with a lower voice asked. "That woman seems like a lot of trouble."

Beau said something that Jake couldn't make out as he sauntered past them. He strode down a path toward what might be a stable. Two men followed behind him. "They're going for their horses," Jake whispered. "We need to stop them."

Shane shook his head. "We're no match for three trained gunmen with quick reflexes. We'd be better off following and watching for a chance to tackle them, one at a time."

Jake nodded, although he didn't like the possibility that the outlaws might reach Liberty first.

Liberty sobbed with relief. Since leaving the cabin, she had traveled in circles. The lonely road she'd stumbled upon stretched a long way into the distance, but that didn't matter. It would carry her eastward, the direction she needed to go. She might even fall in with others going the same way—decent folk who would protect her. That seemed unlikely at the moment, but she could hope.

The hope of home pulled her onward. She could picture Ma kneading bread in the kitchen, the boys tending the garden, and her sisters hanging laundry. Memories of Pa poring over the Bible and writing notes for a sermon made her smile. She'd seen him doing that all her life. His service to others seemed a far cry from Doc Woburn's trickery. Phoebe had told her that folks who bought Doc Woburn's Natural Herbal Remedy were complaining that it didn't work as he'd claimed. It hardly seemed surprising. People like Doc Woburn and Beau made a game of using others.

Never again would she make herself vulnerable to such men. God did not require it, even for the sake of compassion. He alone had paid the price for the redemption of everyone in the world. Even those who seemed beyond deliverance to her—like Beau and Doc Woburn—might receive salvation, if they would only accept it. Until they acknowledged their sad state and turned away from wrongdoing, she could add nothing to their lives. Each of them had proven they would use what she meant as kindness against her. All she could truly give them was her forgiveness and prayers.

Weariness dragged at her, and the road blurred. Liberty jerked upright in the saddle. She needed to rest, and so did the horse. While traveling with Beau, she'd rested when he'd pulled into the shade during the worst heat of the day. He'd preferred riding in the cooler temperatures of night. This habit probably helped him elude pursuers, but it had also kept her skin from burning in the sun. Maybe she should adopt the same tactic. She shuddered. Being about while fearsome creatures hunted in the dark did not appeal to her. However, lying down in the midday shade certainly did.

Liberty pulled off the road at a stream. She refilled her jug, and the horse waded into the water to drink. Liberty stretched out beneath a tree while the sorrel cropped the grass. She wouldn't stay long. Beau must be trying to find her. He might find that difficult. She'd ridden in circles to scramble her tracks. Hopefully, she could count on being free of him.

Liberty sighed and closed her eyes for a moment. The burbling of the stream mingled with the homey sound of the horse's chewing. A bee bumbled nearby before speeding off. She slipped into uneasy slumber and dreamed of finding Jake waiting in the barn when she arrived home. He lifted her in his arms and swung her about, and then lowered his mouth to hers.

The click of a gun bolt intruded.

Liberty gasped awake. She sat up, staring, hardly able to credit what her eyes reported. One moment, Jake was holding her in his arms while she rejoiced in their love. The next, Beau was standing over her, his pistol aimed at her forehead.

"Thought you could escape me, did you?" He shook his head. "You should know me better than that by now."

Liberty pulled air into her constricted chest with difficulty. Why had she doubted that Beau would find her? No matter how many times she'd denied his attempts to 'court' her, he'd turned up again.

She wet her lips, thinking fast. "If you shoot me, my grandfather won't pay you for my return."

The gun shook in Beau's hand, but then steadied. "It might be worth the sacrifice. You've been nothing but trouble since I took you."

"Is killing me worth going to jail?" Liberty asked with the little breath she could summon.

"Anyone who charged me with your killing would have to stand in line." He smirked.

"Having a price on your head frees a man to do whatever he wants."

Liberty shuddered at the coldness in his eyes. "What if you could start anew, assured of forgiveness?"

He narrowed his eyes. "Don't start with me. I'm not interested in your religious talk. It was all I could do to sit through your pa's sermons."

Liberty bit back the remark that if he'd paid better attention, they might not be in this situation. Knowing better than to bang at a door that had been shut in her face, she fell silent.

His face contorted. "I ought to shoot you, reward be hanged."

Liberty met his glare without flinching. Beau might think he held her fate in his hands, but it belonged to God.

CHAPTER TWENTY-FIVE

"We must have missed something." Jake wished he'd paid better attention when his pa taught him how to track.

Shane nodded. "Since we haven't met Liberty while going around and around in circles, that's a fair observation."

Jake scanned the confusing hoofprints of the horses ridden by Liberty and the outlaws. "We haven't met Beau and his cohorts either."

"They were here before us. Let's hope they haven't already located the place Liberty's marks leave the loop she created."

Jake sighed in frustration. "We can't let Beau capture Liberty all over again."

"We'd better pray." Shane took off his hat and held it to his chest. He bowed his head.

Jake tensed his jaw. "We need to keep moving."

Shane glanced up. "Which direction would you suggest?"

Jake cast an uneasy glance about him. "You have a point. All right, but let's pray fast."

"That's fine. The Almighty doesn't require slow prayers."

Jake removed his own hat and bowed his head with the preacher.

"Dear Lord, thank you that you watch over Liberty and that you guide us," Shane said simply. "We don't know which way to go. Please show us where to turn. We'll trust you to keep us safe. Amen."

Jake lifted his head, feeling better. "Maybe it's finally occurred to Beau to hide his traces."

"I had the same thought. Following Liberty's tracks might have reminded him to hide his own."

"That would explain our difficulty. Liberty would head west, right?"

"She probably knew her general location, so yes. I taught her how to find the points on the compass with two sticks and a bit of time. I wanted her to know how to find her way if she ever got lost in the woods."

"I think we know which direction to search."

They rode eastward out of the loop, then split up to comb the area. After searching the immediate vicinity, they met up at a lone oak.

"I found marks made by Liberty's horse along the banks of the creek." Jake pointed to the willow-lined waterway. "But I also noticed the hoofprints of the outlaws' horses. We'll have to take our chances."

Shane gave a brief nod. "And trust in God's providence."

"Your reliance on God has a way of growing on a person."

"I'm glad to hear it. Before the day is out, unless I miss my guess, we're going to need a little divine intervention."

They set off together but reined in after a short while. Shane dismounted and surveyed the ground. "Beau and his companions overtook Liberty by this stream. I don't see signs of a struggle."

"That's just as well." Jake's spirits plummeted. The odds of rescuing Liberty weren't in their favor. There were two of them but three outlaws, and they'd lost the element of surprise. Concern for Liberty's safety would hamper them, but he doubted Beau would give that much consideration.

Shane studied him. "Don't quit before we start."

Jake blew out a breath. "Maybe I need some of your faith to rub off on me."

"Faith doesn't work that way. You'll need to find your own."

"How?"

Shane met his gaze. "Faith is choosing to trust God."

"That's easy to say."

"Being hard-headed is a good start." Shane smiled. "'It's a quality we share."

Jake quirked his lips in a wry smile. "I can't say that it's helped me much."

"Turn it the right way and it will. You don't want to fight with God like your Biblical namesake."

"That Jacob lost, as I recall." Jake pulled out of his doldrums with an effort. "I think Beau will have started back to the cabin."

"That makes sense. Liberty surprised them by escaping, so they wouldn't be packed and ready to go anywhere." Shane nodded toward a clump of sagebrush. "Their marks lead that direction."

"You can see them?" Jake gazed at the preacher with new respect. "I'm having trouble."

"I learned how to track during my circuit preacher days. Without the ability to hunt, I'd have starved. If it makes you feel any better, Beau is doing a sloppy job of concealing them."

"It doesn't, but thanks."

"The effort costs Beau time. We might be able to catch them before they reach the cabin."

"That's best. They will be harder to challenge after they reach it. I wonder—" Jake sat straighter in his eagerness. "What if we went back the way we came instead of following Beau west from here?"

"I don't know." Shane pushed back his hat. "That would take us by a longer route."

"But Beau is traveling slower. If we push, we might reach

the canyon before he does."

"What are you suggesting?" The preacher raked him with a glance that made him feel like he'd been sleeping in church.

"It's a good spot for an ambush."

"You've decided to fight after all, I see." Shane squinted into the distance. "It could work, if we're right about where they're headed. If not, we'd risk losing them."

"It's worth a try."

"All right, but tell me about this ambush of yours. I'd rather not dispatch any lost souls to their judgment today, but I wouldn't mind delivering them to the sheriff."

Liberty winced and turned her head. Beau, ahead of her as they crossed the bench, was venting his foul mood on his horse. He'd taken the sorrel for himself and put Liberty on a skittish black horse that shied at every bush. Tears blurred Liberty's vision. Trying to spare the sorrel from suffering had only made it worse. What a fool she'd been to pretend she could help the horse when she couldn't save herself. She'd failed them both. Knowing Beau might be on her trail, Liberty had allowed the heady taste of freedom to deceive her into resting when she should have kept going. She shouldn't have let down her guard for a single minute. The future would hold a long journey of captivity, followed by Beau's wrath when he discovered she wouldn't bring in money after all.

Long shadows from the ponderosa pines stretched over the dry grass as they crossed the bench. A deer lifted its head, and then broke and ran. Beau brought his rifle up fired off a shot, but thankfully, it had vanished into the trees. Liberty might have cheered the doe's escape, but her horse reared. She gritted her teeth and hung on. After enduring Chief's mischief, she ought to have withstood the horse's reaction but started shaking nonetheless.

Beau dismounted and caught her rearing horse's bridle. "We'll have none of that." He glared at Liberty as if she'd caused the horse to panic. The other outlaws snickered.

Liberty's horse followed Beau into the canyon that let out into the meadow where the cabin waited. As the walls rose about her, Liberty's spirits sank further. She would soon be hidden away where no one would find her.

The canyon lay mostly in shadow this late in the day. Lingering warmth radiated from the granite, and a strip of sunlight lingered on the path.

Riding in the lead, Beau reached the end of the canyon first. Entering the meadow behind him, Liberty barely restrained her gasp of surprise as Jake sprang from the shadows behind Beau.

Jake launched himself at Beau and pulled him from the saddle. They fell together into the grass, locked in battle. The sorrel whinnied and moved away, carrying off Beau's rifle in its saddle scabbard. The two men grappled, breathing hard. Beau brought the heel of his hand down on Jake's throat and pressed hard. Jake's face went red.

Jake managed to throw him off and heaved to his feet, coughing.

Beau's hand dropped to his hip as reached for his pistol.

Liberty bit back a warning. Crying out would warn the other outlaws.

Jake reached for Beau's hand and twisted it behind his back.

Pa rode out of the trees on Archibald, his rifle aimed at Beau. "Stand up."

Beau struggled to his feet with Jake's assistance.

Jake relieved Beau of his weapons while Pa leveled his rifle at the other outlaws emerging from the canyon. Jake stepped behind them, blocking any escape, his gun in his hand. "Hands up." Disarming them, he threw their weapons in a pile.

"Good day to you." Pa sounded, for all the world, as if he was greeting his congregation on a Sunday morning. "Come down from your horses, nice and slow, and line up against the cliff."

Beau dismounted first. "Hello, preacher. How are you going to square it with God if you shoot me?"

"I have no stomach for killing, to be honest. However, if you lay another hand on my daughter, I'd be inclined to shoot it off."

Beau's face went white. Losing his usual swagger, he slouched toward the cliff. The other two outlaws joined him in short order.

"Turn around and put your hands on the rock wall." Jake waited until the men obeyed, then checked each one for hidden weapons. He threw out a couple of knives and backed away. "Stay like that."

Pa flicked a glance sideways to Jake. "Care to find something to tie up our guests with?"

"I saw some cord in the stable." Liberty rode out from beside the wall.

"Are you all right, Liberty?" Pa never took his eyes off the outlaws.

"If Beau hurt you—" Jake's jaw tensed.

"I'm unharmed." Liberty hastened to assure them. It wasn't quite true. She had aches and pains and bruises, but this wasn't a good time to mention them. "There are more horses in the stalls too. I heard one of the outlaws say they were stolen. They shouldn't be left to starve."

"We'll take them with us." Pa spoke without turning his head. "The sheriff in Missoula might want a look at them."

"Good thinking." Jake mounted his horse. "After I fetch the cord, I'll go back for the horses.

Pa gave a quick nod. "I must admit that I'll feel better with this bunch of ne'er-do-wells tied up. Speaking of horses, we'd better water this lot. Liberty, would you do the honors?"

The spring wasn't all that far away, but Liberty hesitated.

"Pa, that would leave you guarding three men alone."

"That's perfectly fine." Her father beamed. "We'll pass the time by singing hymns."

"You're that crazy preacher from Liberty, aren't you?" Kid spat out. "I've heard about you."

"Have you? I'm honored."

"I'm not singing." Anger shook Beau's voice.

"Me neither," Slade's tones couldn't have been more disgusted.

"No?" Pa arched his eyebrows. "Since you don't want to sing, we'll go straight to the sermon then."

"Wait a minute, reverend." Kid piped up. "I didn't say I wouldn't sing."

Her father clearly had things in order. Liberty gathered the horses' reins and rode toward the spring with "Holy, Holy, Holy" ringing out behind her. Kid had a good voice and seemed to enter into the choruses with enthusiasm. After a few minutes, Slade joined in. Beau remained silent.

Liberty dismounted and led the horses toward the spring. They broke into a run and jostled for a position at the spring. Liberty stood back while they drank.

"Holy, Holy, Holy" yielded to "All Creatures of Our God and King." Abandoning their reluctance, Slade and Kid belted the alleluias with more gusto than tunefulness. "And all ye men of tender heart, forgiving others, take your part. Oh sing ye, alleluia! Ye who long pain and sorrow bear, praise God and on him cast your care. Oh praise him, Oh praise him."

Liberty didn't want to get back on the skittish horse Beau had made her ride, so she led the small herd on foot toward her pa. She'd almost reached him when Jake passed her on his horse, a coil of sturdy cord across his shoulder.

Liberty rejoined her father while the horses lowered their muzzles to graze. The men had finished singing, but Pa didn't make good on his threat to preach to them. Instead, he engaged Kid in quiet conversation, listening as often as he spoke. The conversation seemed personal, so Liberty tried not to listen. She caught the gist of it though. Kid was explaining how he'd become an outlaw, and Pa was helping him see the error of his ways. Pending arrest, Kid seemed more receptive than earlier.

Jake dismounted, cut a length of cord with his knife, and approached Beau. "Put your hands behind your back."

Beau spun about and clasped Jake around the throat with one arm. He brought a knife up. "You made a mistake, thinking I'd carry only one knife. Throw down your gun or I'll slice you like a gutted fish."

Liberty pressed her hand to her mouth. She'd sensed Beau wasn't all he seemed but could never have guessed his wickedness.

Jake's gun thudded to the grass.

"Stop this!" Pa pointed his rife at Beau.

"Shoot me, preacher, and he dies with me. Liberty, bring my gun belt."

She looked to her father. Pa nodded. Liberty picked out Beau's gun belt from the pile of discarded weapons. Holding it like a dead fish, she handed it to Beau at arm's length.

"I'm a little occupied." Beau chuckled. "You'll have to put it on me."

Pa shook his head. "I'll do it."

"Stay there!" Beau's hand shook, and the tip of his blade pricked Jake's flesh. "Put it on me, Liberty."

She stepped behind Beau and slid the belt around his waist. Liberty slipped her arms around him to fasten the buckle and secure the belt.

Beau shoved Jake to the ground and caught Liberty around the waist. Beau hauled her in front of him like a shield.

Jake lay face down on the ground without moving.

Liberty's scream cut off as Beau squeezed her middle. She fought to pull in air.

Jake sat up, touching a wound on his neck that trickled blood.

The world tilted, but Beau kept her upright. Cold steel pressed her throat.

"I want two horses." Beau's voice reached her from far away.

"What about us, Grady?" Slade whined.

"You just going to leave us?" Kid's voice shook.

"What do I care what happens to you?" Beau tilted his head with supreme arrogance. "You're nothing but a couple of misfits."

"We should have gone with Logan." Slade roared. He plowed into Beau.

The force of the impact shoved Liberty off-balance. She caught the glint of steel as the knife flew past. The ground rose up to smite her. Liberty didn't get up right away. When she pushed to her knees, the world spun.

Beau and Slade rolled toward her, locked in battle.

Kid jumped into the fray.

Liberty flung herself sideways, narrowly avoiding a collision with the brawling men. Gentle hands turned her over, and Liberty gazed up at Jake. He pulled her up by the arms and thrust her behind him. Her knees shook, but she managed to remain standing. Jake turned his head. "Stay back, Liberty."

Jake's gun flashed into his hand. He hurried toward the fighting men.

"A fight is no place for you." Pa's voice sounded near her ear. He pulled her backward, out of harm's way.

Jake leveled his gun. "Break it up."

The men continued flailing at one another as if he hadn't spoken.

Pa stepped away from Liberty and raised the rifle. Three gunshots blasted the air.

The outlaws froze in a deadly embrace.

Pa stood with his barrel pointed toward the sky. "You fellows seem hard of hearing. Jake told you to stop."

Another rifle clacked as it cocked.

Liberty started and turned her head.

Deputy Manchen, rifle at his shoulder, sat on his horse near the canyon entrance. The men were making so much noise, she hadn't heard him coming. He kept the outlaws in his sights. "I don't much care if I shoot any one of you. You're all varmints in my book."

The outlaws broke apart.

"This here's Grady Bradshaw." Slade, worse for wear with a bleeding lip and his hair standing on end, pointed to Beau.

The deputy smirked. "I figured that out for myself."

Beau stood with feet apart and head high. "How'd you find me?"

"You got sloppy, Bradshaw." Deputy Manchen dismounted in a fluid movement. "I reckon you were tired of running and wanted to get caught." He released a pair of handcuffs from his belt. "Your wish is about to come true."

After dealing with Beau, the deputy turned his attention to the other outlaws. It wasn't long before he had them all handcuffed and lined up. He paced before them. "You are under arrest, all of you, by the power vested in me as a Deputy Sheriff of Montana Territory. I'll start with you, Bradshaw. I'm bringing you in for holding up a bank robbery, numerous stagecoach robberies, tampering with the mail, horse theft, kidnap, several counts of assault, and twelve suspicions of murder, including the killing of Martha Riddler and her mother, Dorothea."

Jake lifted his head. "I'm sorry to learn of their fate."

"I was, too." The deputy nodded.

Jake stepped closer to him. "What happened?"

"They didn't run far enough. If I'd been an hour earlier—" He shook his head. "Martha lived long enough to confess she lied about you."

"Did she say why she did?"

"Apparently, Bradshaw paid her and her ma to put you in jail. You were getting in his way with Liberty and casting doubts about him in the community. Martha and her mother started having second thoughts about what they'd done. I don't think Bradshaw paid them enough for the privilege of perjuring themselves in a court of law. They had a falling out with him, which is why they left town."

"Poor woman. Neither she nor her mother deserved what they received. I'm glad, for Martha's sake, that she developed a conscience about what she did to me.'

"She didn't, more's the pity. Martha confessed because she wanted to make Bradshaw pay. Now, if you'll excuse me—" Deputy Manchen lowered a stern gaze on Jake. "I'd appreciate a little quiet while I'm arresting these men."

CHAPTER TWENTY-SIX

Liberty reined in with tears filling her eyes. "It's good to be home."

"That it is." Jake smiled. "Get some rest, Liberty. You deserve it."

Pa pulled Archibald up beside her in the barnyard. "Thanks for everything, Jake."

"I was more than glad to help." Jake's gaze wandered back to Liberty. "More than glad."

Liberty couldn't seem to look away from him. She'd known they would part when they reached home. How ridiculous to yearn for him not to leave her.

He turned down the road toward the Buckthorn driveway.

Pa dismounted and opened the barn door before leading Archibald inside. Liberty followed her father, blinking in the sudden dimness. Being in the barn felt so normal, except that she was riding the sorrel mare. The branding mark on her horse's haunch matched the one on the stolen horses. Deputy Manchen had allowed her to ride the sorrel home, since she had no other recourse. He would collect the horse later. Liberty hoped that the rightful owner would treat the mare kindly.

A horse whinnied inside the barn, and Archibald returned the greeting. The sorrel quivered and pricked her ears.

"What have we here?" Pa laughed. "I can't believe it."

Liberty's eyes were still adjusting, but she could make out the black horse in Chief's stall. "It can't be—"

"Chief!" Pa stroked the stallion's neck. "How did you get here?"

"He showed up one day, still wearing his saddle." Ma appeared in the doorway. She was breathing deeply. Ma must have come running after seeing Jake through the kitchen window. "He went into his stall, meek as a lamb. It gave me quite a turn, I must say. I've wondered ever since how his saddle came to be empty."

"I fell off." Liberty dismounted and embraced her mother.

"I feared as much." Ma held onto her for a long time.

Liberty blinked away fresh tears. "It's all over, Ma. Beau is in jail."

"I'm glad everyone is safe." Ma studied her at arm's length. "You'll want buttermilk for your face. It's seen too much sun. We'll heat water for a bath too. Would you like some tea? And I suppose you're hungry."

"Yes, Ma."

Pa smiled. "Go with your mother. I'll take care of the horses."

Liberty ran to her father and threw her arms around him. "Thank you."

He kissed her forehead. "I'd like to know how you managed to stay on Chief so long."

"Phoebe gave me riding lessons. Beyond that, I really don't know."

"Some people have a knack for horses. You must be one of them." He eyed Chief. "I don't seem to be."

She grinned. "Would you like me to give you some pointers?"

"Don't think I'll say no. I'm not above learning from someone younger than me. Maybe after a day or two though. You seem to have acquired a second wind, but I could use a little rest."

Ma joined them. "I've missed you, Shane."

Pa embraced her. "We have a lot of catching up to do, Mrs. Hayes. I'll be in shortly."

Ma put an arm around Liberty. "What kind of tea would you like?"

"Earl Grey—it's my favorite." Liberty walked along the path beside her mother. Birds trilled in the cottonwoods beyond the house, and the heady fragrance of roses greeted her at the arbor gate.

She was home.

A light tap came at Liberty's bedroom door. Ma stood in the hallway wearing her nightgown, her hair falling in a braid over one shoulder and a candlestick in her hand. Light from her candle picked out silver threads in her red-gold hair, but she otherwise appeared little older than Liberty. "I saw light under your door, so I thought I'd check on you."

"I'm a little restless." Liberty stepped back for her mother to enter.

Ma sat in the side chair next to the bed and placed her candlestick on the bedside table. "You've been through a hard time. I'm sure it will take a while for you to feel safe again."

Liberty perched on the edge of her bed. "I keep thinking about Martha. I didn't know her well, but it's hard to believe that she's dead at so young an age."

"None of us knows the number of our days. The best we can do is trust God to keep us in His care."

"I don't expect Martha did that, and I'm sure Beau hasn't. If he's guilty of all the crimes Deputy Manchen arrested him for, they'll hang him."

"It's not any wonder you're having trouble sleeping with all that on your mind." Ma left the chair and came to sit beside her on the bed. She took Liberty's hands. "Don't let it fret you so."

"But it does. It burdens me when lost people die without a

hope of redemption. Sometimes it feels as if the whole weight of the world rests on me."

"Don't make the mistake of trying to carry a load you were never meant to bear, Liberty. Our Savior is the only one strong enough to shoulder it. What you feel is a call to prayer and service."

"Thank you." Liberty sighed. "That helps put it in perspective."

"Try to sleep." Ma squeezed her hands and stood up.

"Ma?"

Her mother paused while reaching for her candlestick. "Yes?"

Liberty searched for words. "I've decided I can live with a secret."

Ma sank into the chair again and folded her hands in her lap. "I assume you mean the one pertaining to your birth."

Liberty nodded. "I've had time to ponder it. There's nothing wrong with keeping a matter private, especially when revealing it does no good and has the power to harm those I love."

The tears in Ma's eyes shimmered in the candlelight. "I'm sorry that my actions put you in this position. Pa told me what Kyle said. I hope you can forgive me for the choices I made that caused you pain."

"Oh, Ma. I love you." Liberty rushed to embrace her mother. "Of course, I do."

"Thank you." Ma stroked her hair. "I've reached out to my own father. Maybe we can salvage something of our family."

"You'll need to write that letter again. I happen to know that it went astray. Beau read it after robbing the stagecoach that carried it. That's why he decided to kidnap me. He wanted to collect a ransom from my grandfather."

"It's too bad he didn't turn his ambitions to a worthier

cause." She sighed. "I'll write the letter to my father again."

"Don't be too crushed if he doesn't want it." Liberty took her mother's hands. "I've learned that God has a way of giving us back, differently, what we miss in life."

Phoebe wasn't sure which Wilhelmina smiled the largest when the wrappings came off the carefully painted portrait. Phoebe had watched the younger Wilhelmina painting on a canvas at her easel, tongue poking from the side of her mouth as she frowned in concentration. The resulting masterpiece was a miracle of form, even if the substance seemed a bit blurred.

"I will cherish it, liebling." Oma Wilhelmina held up her likeness for the birthday guests to see. The whole family was gathered around the large oak table in Oma Wilhelmina's house. In Germany, as Fiona had explained to Phoebe, the person having a birthday threw the party.

"It's perfect." Aunt Elsa gazed with shining eyes at her mother and young daughter.

With the presents unwrapped and duly admired, Fiona brought out the *marmorkuchen,* a delicious pound cake with vanilla and almond flavoring. Phoebe jumped up to help Fiona carry around the slices Aunt Elsa cut. She sat down beside Liberty with her own piece.

Ma had told her what Liberty went through with Beau, but Phoebe refrained from bringing it up. She could guess the bullying tactics Beau had used to intimidate Liberty, and the cruelty with which he had treated her. Unless Liberty wanted to discuss it, there was nothing Phoebe needed to know.

"I rode Chief." Liberty broke her silence with the startling revelation.

Phoebe stared at her. "You did what?"

"I rode Chief. It was when—did you hear what happened?"

"Yes."

"It was then. Chief reared and ran away, but I stayed on him. Pa is amazed."

"He isn't the only one." Phoebe took a bite of cake and noticed Will watching her from across the table. She glanced back to Liberty. "You must have been terrified."

"I was, but I'm a lot less scared of horses now."

"I'm glad you weren't hurt and that something good came of the experience." Phoebe found her gaze straying to Will, who was talking with Seth beside him. Will turned his head and caught her staring. Her face heated, and she averted her gaze.

Liberty had fallen silent, as she'd done off and on throughout the party. Phoebe frowned. Liberty was not the most garrulous person, but she could usually hold her own at a party. Maybe she needed to be drawn out. "The party is going well, don't you think?"

Liberty smiled. "Oma Wilhelmina looks happy."

"She always is, when she has her family around her."

"Can I ask you something personal?" Liberty sounded hesitant.

"Go ahead."

"Do you ever feel like an outsider, since you're adopted?" Liberty glanced across the room at her father.

Phoebe stared at her in surprise. "Why would I ever? Pa chose Ma and me to be part of this family. That's an honor."

"I'm glad you feel that way."

"I remember your pa teaching that God adopts those who trust in Him." Phoebe smiled. "I figured that made me twice adopted and doubly special."

Liberty laughed. "I'm sure you're right."

"Do you want to go riding in the morning?"

"We're leaving early. Pa needs to work on his next sermon.

He's fallen behind." Liberty's forehead puckered. "We're all feeling a little—thin after what happened, but we wanted to come for Oma Wilhelmina's sake."

"I'm glad you did." Phoebe gave her a quick hug. "It wouldn't be the same without you."

Phoebe wasn't surprised when Liberty and her family left the party a little early. She would see her friend later in the room they shared in the ranch house.

Everyone was having a wonderful time, Phoebe could tell from the noise level. Phoebe thrived on gatherings, but even she needed a break now and again. She slipped through the door that gave onto the covered porch. Phoebe stepped to the railing and breathed in air that tasted of pine. The stars were out tonight. Beyond the Big Dipper, she couldn't remember what the constellations were called. Quinn and Murphy could name them all. Her brothers seemed to delight in her ignorance, for it highlighted their knowledge.

A wolf howled not very far away. The unnerving sound served as a reminder. She could stand on a platform with a porch rail to guard her and a lot of people within call, but she was alone at the edge of a wilderness. The forest stretched in darkness for a long way, unbroken by any light but the ones God had placed in the sky.

Phoebe's thoughts were making her uneasy. She turned to go inside.

The door opened, and Will stood on the threshold. He was attractive in a leather vest, blue striped shirt, and dress trousers. Will grimaced. "It's rambunctious in there."

Phoebe laughed. "That's why I stepped outside."

"Would you care for company, I hope?"

"I'd appreciate it, actually. A wolf howled over there." Phoebe pointed in the direction of the river. "I've been making myself nervous ever since."

His laughter warmed her. "You're not the first person who ever did that. The woods feel a lot different at night than they do by day."

"I've been meaning to talk with you." Phoebe curled her fingers around the porch railing. "I don't think I made it clear how badly I felt about taking advantage of your kindness when I invited you to town with Liberty and me."

"Oh, that." Will joined her at the rail. "It hurt a little, I can't deny it. I'd persuaded myself that all you and Liberty wanted from me was me to escort you so that your parents wouldn't worry about you."

"When you put it like that, I feel even worse." Phoebe looked him in the eye. "It will never happen again, I promise you."

"I reckon I can be big about it." Will sighed. "I can't make you want to be with me."

"Oh, but I did. It was—well, complicated." She glanced sideways at his outline in the dark. "Please, forgive me."

He turned to her. "Don't take it to heart so."

She wasn't sure how it happened, but suddenly she was in his arms. Phoebe looked up at him, startled. Will's lips came down to tease hers. She responded without thought, her lips answering his soft caresses.

Will moaned and broke away. "I guess I'd better apologize too."

Phoebe touched her lips and smiled. "I'm not certain that's necessary."

"I am quite sure. You're the niece of my employer. More than that, I'm not the kind of man who kisses a woman lightly."

"Is that what you did?"

He glanced away. "More or less."

Phoebe told herself not to be hurt, but she couldn't help it. "Well, I'll just remove myself so you won't be tempted to trespass again."

"Phoebe—"

She sighed. "We keep rubbing each other the wrong way. You're probably right that we shouldn't consider anything serious."

"I didn't say that, exactly."

Why did he sound miffed when she was agreeing with him? It was too confusing to sort out. "Let's call a truce, shall we?"

"All right, but we'd better not shake on it. Touching might land us in trouble."

"Liberty, are you still awake?" Phoebe whispered into the darkness of the bedchamber they would share.

"No." Liberty's sleepy voice came back.

"Because if you were, I'd want to talk."

"That's why I'm not." The sound of covers rustling reached Phoebe.

"Sweet dreams." Phoebe felt her way to her own bed and climbed beneath the sheets.

"All right, you." The blankets rustled again. "What is it?"

"Will." Phoebe let the name suffice.

"Oh. What happened?"

"He kissed me." Phoebe let out her breath on a sigh.

"And?" Liberty sounded much more awake.

She considered the question. "He wasn't happy about it."

"Were you?"

"I wasn't adverse." That was an understatement. She had, in fact, wanted it to go on.

"Oh. I'm sorry. I can tell that you like Will. I know you haven't enjoyed any of your other suitors."

"No, of course not. That would have been too easy." Phoebe settled beneath her covers. "Instead, I have to want someone who isn't interested in courting me."

"Are you sure he doesn't?"

"He said as much." Phoebe snapped out the words.

"Really? That surprises me, from what I observed."

So, Liberty had noticed her and Will. She didn't sound jealous at all. "Well, not in so many words, but that was the gist of what he said."

"Do you want my advice?"

"Maybe." Phoebe didn't know if advice could help, but it would be better than relying on her own muddled wits. "What would you do?"

Liberty laughed. "It occurs to me that I'm the last person qualified to give this kind of advice. I will anyway, but take it for what it's worth."

"I can hardly wait, you've sold your advice so well."

"Give it time. I believe you said something similar to me about Jake once. I wish I'd listened to you then. If I had, Jake and I would be together."

Phoebe sat up in bed. "You're admitting that you want to be with Jake?"

"Why do you sound so disbelieving?"

"Forgive me, but last time we talked, you swore up and down it wouldn't work between you."

"I was wrong." Liberty's voice shook. "I spoke to Jake too soon and rather thoroughly convinced him of my opinion."

Phoebe thought for a minute. "Have you considered telling him you've experienced a change of heart?"

"I doubt he'd believe me, I've led him such a dance."

Liberty sounded so sad that Phoebe's heart went out to her. "Don't give up. You'll never know until you try."

"You said that before too."

"Did I?" Phoebe smiled. "Maybe you should listen this time."

CHAPTER TWENTY-SEVEN

Outside the side door of the church, Jake paused for a moment to collect himself. He'd dressed in fine clothes for the occasion. However, his reflection in the door window revealed his failed attempt to tame his unruly hair. He'd have been better off leaving it springing from his head in its usual unruly state. Jake made a face at his image and turned the knob. The door swung inward on well-oiled hinges. Jake's boots clunked down the short hall leading to the office. The floorboards neither sagged nor squeaked, something he took pride in. He'd helped install them when the congregation built the church.

Jake knocked on the closed office door. He knew that Shane, from long habit, would be inside. Jake usually woke early and had noticed the preacher walking the pathway to the church with the constancy of the sun rising each morning. That was one of the reasons he was here. Jake stood waiting as the door opened.

"Jake." Shane blinked. "You're out and about early."

"May I have a word with you?" He cleared his throat to relieve a certain huskiness.

"Certainly." Shane stepped backward. "Take a seat."

Jake occupied one of the cushioned ladderback chairs.

Shane folded his hands on his desk top and fixed his piercing gaze on Jake. "What can I do for you this morning?"

"I've decided to become a preacher like you." Jake felt much better after spewing the news. "Don't try to talk me out of it."

Shane's smile held a bemused quality. "Why would I?

You'd make a fine preacher."

Jake couldn't hide his surprise. "I'm a lot of trouble."

"Nothing the Lord can't handle." Shane's eyes gleamed. "I've given him plenty of that myself. May I ask what prompted this decision?"

"I guess it's been coming over me slowly, but I didn't understand it. I thought my restlessness meant I should go mine for gold somewhere. Only, I could never decide where to go or when to leave."

"God has a way of arresting the plans we make in favor of his own." Shane smiled. "Go on."

"While the outlaws were fighting, I tried to break it up by threatening them with my gun."

"Ah, yes. I recall that it didn't work."

Jake nodded. "It might have if I'd fired a warning."

"Why didn't you?"

"The bullet might have ricocheted and hit one of them." Jake blew out a breath. "I couldn't bring myself to take such a risk."

"You're beginning to sound like me."

"You've had an impact. I've noticed your commitment to duty. When we were tracking Liberty, I envied your faith." Jake's voice wavered despite his efforts, and he glanced away with tears shimmering before his eyes.

"None of your words convinces me of your calling, but your tears do. During the Sermon on the Mount, Jesus said 'blessed are they which do hunger and thirst after righteousness—for they shall be filled.' I see that yearning in you."

"Then you'll help me?"

Shane walked to the window and looked out. "Have you taken the matter to prayer?"

"I've done little else since we returned."

Shane turned toward him. "That hasn't been very long."

"Does it need to be? I've never been more certain of anything in my life."

"You'd need to attend a theological school."

Ma wouldn't stand in the way, and Jake would find a way to earn the necessary money. "I'm prepared for that."

Shane's gaze searched his face. "I'll make inquiries on your behalf."

"Thank you." Jake smiled. "There's something more I need to ask. It's about Liberty."

"Go ahead."

"Would it be fair to ask her to wait for me to come home and court her?"

"I have nothing against it, if she wants to. Have you asked her?"

Jake shook his head. "I wanted your blessing first. Do I have it?"

"Yes, of course. I'd be proud to have you as a son-in-law, if it came to that."

"I'm honored to know it, whether or not she says yes."

Shane smiled. "You won't find out unless you ask her."

"Liberty, would you mind getting the door?" Ma called from the girl's room, where she was braiding Elizabeth's hair.

Liberty's heart pounded, but she reminded herself that Beau was behind bars. He wouldn't be waiting on the step. She leaned the broom in her hands against the kitchen wall and went to get the door.

Deputy Manchen stood on the stoop, appearing more in need of grooming than before. "I thought I'd better come by about that mare."

Liberty's heart sank. She'd known this day would arrive, but it still would be a wrench to part with the sorrel horse. She couldn't deny that taking care of the mare had increased her attachment. The horse whickered in greeting whenever Liberty entered the barn, which made her suspect that her sentiment was returned. Liberty stepped onto the porch. "She's out to pasture with the other horses. I'll get her for you." She started down the steps.

"One moment."

The deputy's voice arrested her. Turning, she waited for him to speak.

"Let's not be hasty." He cleared his throat. "I explained to the owners the circumstances by which the horse came into your possession. Of course, I kept your identity private. I hope you don't mind that I mentioned your fondness for the horse."

"Was it that apparent?"

"I could tell. The owners felt badly about what you went through. They asked me to give you the sorrel, assuming you'd like to keep her."

"I would." Liberty beamed. "Please tell them thank you for me. Let them know I'll take good care of her."

"I'll do that." Deputy Manchen peered into the distance, a certain brightness in his eyes. "I remember my first horse. Mustard died too soon."

"I'm sorry." Liberty looked away to give him a chance to recover. "Did they mention the sorrel's name?" Beau never had. The horse had been his possession, nothing more.

He shook his head. "I forgot to ask. You might want to rename her, anyway."

Liberty frowned. "I have no idea what to call her."

"Surely something will come to mind."

An idea struck. "I know. I'll call her Prudence."

"Prudence?" Jake laughed as he sat beside Liberty on their tree branch. "Why would you give your horse the middle name you hate?"

Liberty frowned. "You weren't supposed to know my middle name."

He grinned. "Blame Phoebe."

Liberty mustered a sense of outrage. "Phoebe told you?"

"Not directly. She let it slip. I was of course fascinated, since you'd only given me your middle initial before. Why do you hate the name?"

"It seemed out of date, but I've revised my opinion. If I'd exercised a little caution with Beau, it would have saved a lot of suffering."

"I'm glad you can see that." Jake smiled. "But I hope you can forgive yourself."

She glanced at him in suspicion. "You sound like Pa."

"Thank you." A beatific smile lit his face. "I'll take that as a compliment."

"I don't know what's gotten into you, but you're somehow—different."

"I'm glad to hear it."

Liberty didn't know what to make of such a statement, but she liked the confidence in his voice. "I can't thank you enough for riding after me. I don't know what I'd have done without you and Pa."

The bough swayed as he turned to her. "I'd do it again a thousand times to keep you safe."

Liberty had seen that gleam in his eyes before. This time she didn't want to withdraw from him.

Jake caught her hands. "I love you, Liberty. I have for a long time. I hope you feel the same about me, but I'll understand if you don't."

A sob choked her. "I thought I'd ruined everything—that it was too late."

His gaze softened. "That couldn't happen, darling. My heart has belonged to you since we were twelve."

She brushed away tears. "I love you, Jake."

He closed his eyes and drew a long breath. "I've waited a long time to hear you say that."

"I'm so sorry—"

Jake's lips cut off the rest of Liberty's words. His mouth slid over hers in an intimate embrace that made speech unnecessary. Jake kissed her with pent-up passion overlaid by restraint. The combination proved a heady elixir that exhilarated her even as it made her feel safe. Liberty clung to him with every ounce of her being and returned each caress of his mouth.

Jake set her gently from him but kept hold of her hands. His lips feathered kisses over her palms. "Liberty Prudence Hayes, I intend to love you with every fiber of my being all of my days."

Liberty caught her breath, recognizing the promise he'd made once long ago beneath this very tree. She lifted her gaze to his. "Jacob Graydon Buckthorn, I'll love you always, and one day I'll marry you."

He pulled her into his arms and rained kisses on her upturned face. "That day will come, I promise. Meanwhile, I need to ask you to wait."

"What do you mean?"

"I've figured out where I fit, Liberty." Enthusiasm throbbed in his voice. "I'm going to be a preacher."

She gazed at him with every doubt vanished. She no longer

cared what people thought about the match she made. Jake wasn't perfect, but neither was she. All that mattered was that Jake was a good man who loved her, and that she loved him back with all of her heart.

Author's Note

The Montana Gold series began the story of an Irish American family surviving in the Wild West. The Promise Tree opens the Montana Treasure series twelve years later. The Montana Gold Rush, which started in 1852 with the discovery of gold in Bannack, brought wealth to many. By the late 1880s, the city of Helena boasted more millionaires per capita than anywhere in the world. This was partly due to the rise of copper barons, but those who made their fortunes in gold also built prestigious homes in the city's Mansion District.

Reverend Shane Hayes and his cousin, Connor Walsh, chose to settle elsewhere for a simple reason. While driving home from a research trip that we took to Virginia City and Bannack ghost towns, my husband and I cut through the Bitterroot Valley. My cell phone lost service as our car rolled through a riparian paradise broken by idyllic farmland and small towns reminiscent of a past era. I caught my breath as rays penetrated the billowing clouds and sent light to gild the trees and tip the grasses. The Bitterroot River glinted in the sun. The ever-present mountains stood like sentinels against the wide sky. Tears sprang to my eyes at the beauty of the place, and I made up my mind to celebrate it in my books.

Setting the story in the Bitterroot Valley provided the opportunity to feature the cattle ranching for which Montana became famous. The luxuriant grasses that once sustained large herds of buffalo now fatten cattle. I based Con's Ranch on the Grant Kohrs Ranch, Montana's first cattle ranch, which still stands in the Deer Lodge Valley.

Both the Montana Gold and Montana Treasure series feature the struggles of the Bitterroot Salish tribe. A misunderstanding led to the tribe signing away the vast majority of its land in the Hellgate Treaty of 1855. The tribe retained the right to hunt and fish their ceded land. However, increased settlement in the Bitterroot Valley led to conflicts. In 1871, President Grant signed an Executive Order requiring the Salish tribe to remove to the Jocko reservation. An agreement specified that in exchange for going to the reservation, the Salish would receive $55,000, plots of dedicated land, new log houses, and a side of beef for each family.

Two Salish sub-chiefs signed the contract, but Chief Charlo's refusal rendered the agreement invalid. An 'x' nevertheless appeared under Charlo's name on the document, and the Senate approved it for ratification in 1872. Many Salish families refused to move to the reservation, but those who did were not safe from encroachment. In 1883, the tribe lost 1,430 acres of land when the Bitterroot Railroad went through the reservation. That was only the beginning. In 1891, Chief Charlo and the Salish were forcibly removed to the reservation. The Montana Treasure stories take place during this timeline.

Book Club Questions

1. What was Jake trying to accomplish by kissing Liberty in the first scene? Were his motives pure? How else might he have handled the situation?

2. Liberty's strong desire to please others works against her when she encounters Beau. It takes a lot for her to stand up for herself, but she finally learns to do it. What are the boundaries she should have observed from the beginning? How might events have changed if she had? Have you had a hard time drawing boundaries, and how did you overcome that difficulty?

3. Why didn't Jake defend himself when he received the blame for his friend's misdeeds? Should he have spoken up instead of remaining silent? How would you have suggested he handle it?

4. Phoebe inserted herself between Liberty and Beau to protect her friend when she wouldn't defend herself. Did she do the right thing, or should she have stayed out of Liberty's business? Why?

5. Why did Liberty's apology for encouraging Beau wound Jake? Do you believe there are times an apology is more harmful than staying silent?

6. Liberty believes that marrying Jake would hurt her father's reputation. How does this connect with her desire to please others?

7. Were Liberty's parents correct in shielding her from the circumstances of her birth? Have you had to keep a secret from someone you loved to keep from hurting them? Did it end up turning out well, or would the truth have been better?

8. What inspired Jake to walk Martha home? How did this action lead to trouble? How might matters have turned out if he'd resisted the urge?

9 Why did Liberty want to meet her natural father when staying away from him would have been easier? Are there times that doing the hard thing is better than taking the easy path? When have you had to deal with this in your own life?

10. Liberty's concern over the fate of the lost marks her calling to prayer and service but also becomes a burden for her. What does her mother tell her to do about it? Have you struggled with what your calling might be and how to understand or implement it in your life?

9 781953 957108